THE LANGUAGES OF LOVE

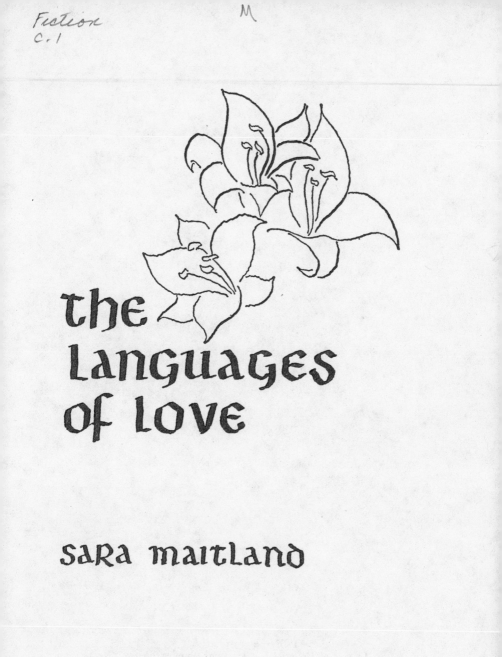

the languages of love

sara maitland

Doubleday & Company, Inc., Garden City, New York, 1980

ISBN: 0-385-17203-6
Library of Congress Catalog Card Number 80-943
Copyright © 1980 by Sara Maitland
All Rights Reserved
Printed in the United States of America
First Edition

For Donald and Mildred Lee

1.

APRIL

She pushed the balls of her thumbs into her eye-sockets, hard. Yellow streaks and whorls shot across the blue film. She pushed almost hard enough to hurt herself. She thought she might scream or faint or kill someone. After a small moment she found she had done none of these things and she leaned forward, elbows on her knees, exhausted, trying to relax. When she opened her eyes nothing had changed: the bus was still stopped at the red lights and below her a pretty girl in long skirts and a long scarf was trying to tuck both up so she could start her bike when the lights changed.

She was not going to go to work anyway. She was still afraid she might cry; and she refused to cry at work. If she went home the flat would be empty, and would stay empty for over six more hours. If she went to Nancy's, the baby, clumsy but determined, would struggle into her lap, would flop his heavy head against her and bring her his latest activity to admire. But that might be good. She could cry at Nancy's safely enough, they were well used to one another's tears now. Going to Nancy would certainly induce tears—of habit, relief and security, but that might be good. If she were going to cry there would be the best place, with Nancy tough and firm, but immensely generous.

But she did not understand, she could not understand. Another wave of misery threatened to engulf her; not just misery, but fear and a sense of shame. Which was silly. Perhaps she had deserved it anyway; perhaps she had asked for it. She looked down at her jeans rolled up to the knees, the green and yellow football socks, the fluorescent green sneakers.

"Are you wearing that lot to the clinic?" Ian had asked that morning. The bright red T-shirt with "I am a humourless feminist" stamped black across the bosom was hidden now by her donkey-jacket, but had been part of the view that both Ian and Dr. Marshall had enjoyed.

"Yes."

"Don't let him get to you, darling."

"I wear this lot pretty often."

"You know what I mean."

"Yes. I can't help it, Ian. He makes such assumptions. I see the other women there in their best coats, with their hair fresh done, as though it was a treat to get to see Mr. Mighty, giver of children, the rewarder of the virtuous . . . I want him, and them, to know I'm not taken in; that I refuse to feel like that."

"You're still dressing up for him."

"Don't be so clever."

He rocked her in his arms, half teasing, really tender. "Will you ring me?"

"If there's anything to say."

"No. Anyway . . ."

"No promises. I thought I might go over to Nancy's afterwards. Tony won't expect me back at work."

"Look, shall I come with you? I can easily get myself covered for the morning."

"Oh Ian, you don't have to do that. I'm a big girl now. I'm just sorry I make such a fuss every time. He is such a shit you know."

"It's not him, it's your relationship. His position. You wouldn't like him whatever. He seemed okay the times I've met him. Considerate and pretty sensitive, you know."

It was useless to tell Ian that it was precisely the doctor's sensitivity to *him* that made her dislike him so much. If he could be so tender of Ian's feelings, why was he so brutal to her? Or was he? What were her expectations anyway? She'd only been going to his clinic for ten months; it was not his fault if she did not get pregnant. Especially if his new line was correct. She disciplined herself against the new spasm of grief and made herself look at what the consultant had said: that she should see a psychiatrist; that the suppression of ovulation without apparent physical cause could have its roots in the rejection of the patient's own femininity.

"Look," Dr. Marshall had said, "this is not an easy thing to face up to, and if I had not found you so forthright, so willing to cooperate in everything we have suggested so far, I might beat about the proverbial bush a little more. But I have thought a good deal about all this, especially in relation to everything you have told me about your past, your, mm, sexual connections, your, shall I say, interests. Now even you would have to admit that the overall picture presenting, your politics, your unashamed promiscuity—past, I acknowledge—is hardly one of the standard, well-integrated woman."

She wanted to say, "I haven't the least idea what you are talking about." But she had a very good idea, and she sat dumbly listening.

"I wonder, professionally speaking I can't help but wonder, if you have consented consciously to having a child because your husband so very much wants one, in order to . . . well obviously this is putting it very crudely, but perhaps, in order to keep or earn his love . . . but your rejection of motherhood and the expectations that he and others have of you, have gone underground."

"That's not true."

"My dear Elizabeth, I don't for one moment suggest you have done this knowingly. The subconscious is a tricky customer of course. The fact that you have come so faithfully to the clinic and have been so unusually, admirably, consistent in following our recommendations may—and I repeat only may, which is why I want you to see a specialist, an expert in these sneaky hidden responses, who will work along with me on all this—it may all suggest precisely the power, the strength of will, with which you have suppressed these doubts. You are hardly what we would normally call a conformative type, after all, but we have seen you conforming impeccably for months. You have undergone all our nasty little procedures without a blush and have been extremely patient with our questions and intrusions. All this gives credence to my opinion. It's quite a common phenomenon you know, nothing to be ashamed of. Lots of women suppress their confusions about their gender rôle and it comes out here: you women are much more subtle than us, aren't you? Now surely, if you can conquer the initial barriers of embarrassment and actually come and seek help here, you can also face up to what I'm telling you."

A pause. He wanted her to say yes of course she was sure he was right, her feelings were of course not hurt by his frankness and she was willing to do whatever he told her. She said nothing.

"Mmm. Yes. Well, I'm sure all this is a bit of a shock. But think it through for yourself and see whether there is a chance that you will trust me for one more round. In the meantime keep going with your temperature chart, make sure you don't lose any more weight and relax and keep hoping. Come back in a month or so and we'll talk about this some more and perhaps I can introduce you to our friendly neighbourhood shrink."

He liked that, and smiled at her encouragingly, thinking he was clever and funny. She did not think he was remotely amusing, but hypnotically smiled back.

What the hell did the rejection of femininity mean anyway? Beyond a biological arrangement of facts. Of course she accepted her femininity: her own self as woman. "Rôle Model Confusion," the doctor called it. "Unresolved Conflicts in the Libido," but of course there were unresolved conflicts there. There had to be spaces unfilled, fears unexplored. Surely struggle there was normal not pathological?

What was she meant to say to Ian? I can't have your baby because I don't want to. Apparently I only married you because I did not want to have to cope with a Real Man (like James of course, Dr. Marshall's Real Man no doubt, who drove against her will, as he drove against her flesh—every encounter a battle that he would win. Damn him. Damn femininity, damn the Real Woman she could not risk becoming if she wanted to survive). Why had they told that bloody doctor so much about their pasts? Information they could so easily have suppressed. They thought they had found a friend. And a scientist, not a moralist, a safe repository for all their own doubts and guilts. He had taken it all in to use against them when his time came: flies for his web of self-importance.

That was childish. He was trying to help. If she rejected his ideas so inflexibly, perhaps there really was something that she was afraid to look at. She did not trust him. She did not believe that he had any concept of femininity that was of any use to her. But it was his job. If he had clinical reasons for believing in the suppression of ovulation through psychiatric causes perhaps he was right about her. Her whole life had been an escape from whom she was: her sexual adventures, her joining the Women's Movement, her love for Ian. Why should she think, though, that she wanted a child? To make Ian love her. That was rubbish. Really it was rubbish. Of course it was rubbish. It had to be rubbish. The more she insisted the less certain she became.

The bus lurched at the corner. If she were going to Nancy's she would have to get off here. She came to a decision: she would walk across Kensington Gardens to Nancy's home and stay there until Ian was back from work. She stood up, walked to the back of the bus, swung down the steps and jumped off as the bus came to a halt, suddenly jaunty. There were reasons beyond the rejection of femininity for wearing jeans and sneakers. She watched a young girl in a pencil skirt and high, high heels trying to hop on to the bus. But her difficulties were as nothing compared to those of a woman with two small children and a very obvious pregnancy. If ease in getting off buses was a symbol of anything it was that she came off best staying as she was: blue-jeaned, young, liberated.

Not the thoughts she wanted. She crossed back over the road and went into the park.

It was warm for the end of March; the sun was bright on the remains of the winter, and there were a lot of children. Their beauty dazzled her—alluring, heartbreaking, she almost wished she had not come this way. She was afraid she might try to talk to some of them. Nancy's baby Hugh sometimes seemed to glow with a warmth of his own making—an interior physical love that one could not help responding to. But these park children, unconnected to her, she felt stranger about. Running and wandering in the sun they reminded her of her own childhood: an unworried country childhood where she had been given a great deal of space and physical freedom. Surrounded by love and admiration, the only blight was that she was alone and not the boy her parents would have chosen for themselves. But lots of women she knew had spent their infancy wanting to be boys; there was nothing there, it was not surprising. Normal, normal, normal. Where did it come from then, the desire to have children? Why did she have it and other women, so like her in so many ways, emphatically not have it? It was a lust: sometimes her hands would go out on to her flat stomach in an agony. She repeated the lessons she gave herself over and over again: children are demanding, solipsistic and shitty. They tie you completely; soul and body. There is no proper pre-school provision available. The desire to have children is imposed on women, externally, by a sexist society. She could not believe one word of it.

It was not the life-style of a mummy that she wanted anyway: she had never thought of giving up her job, of wanting only to talk with other mothers in the park: those awful half-conversations she had overheard, where both participants are really watching like hawks wherever their own offspring is escaping to.

And the conversations, however leisurely and pleasant, are punctuated with completely needless calls of "Where are you, Don't do that, Be careful, Come here." That was not what she desired. But when Nancy had been breastfeeding Harriet or Hugh and had picked up the furious scarlet baby and bared her darkened nipple for its matching mouth and a sudden silence of total delight filled the room . . . when she saw women in cotton pinafores, with stretched jerseys underneath, who walked the unmistakable walk of pregnant women, who shifted themselves with their hands laid tenderly either side of the swelling . . . she felt jealous, a stabbing anger and pain that she had never felt for a man.

She tried to laugh at herself. A golden dream childhood wasted wishing she was a boy; and now a happy, fulfilling adulthood wasted trying to prove she was a real woman. Nutty. Perhaps the doctor was right after all, chasing impossible fantasies. Examine your life, he had instructed her; but she was too educated not to be self-conscious under her own gaze. Suppose her childhood desires had stayed with her at some level; that she still wanted to please her now dead daddy by not revealing that she was really a woman? Did she think that Ian would somehow prefer her not to be too much a woman, that his fear of what was female and other would be more than he could cope with? Perhaps she consented to his desire for a baby in order to keep his love, while secretly denying him because she was jealous of him for being a boy.

Her laughter started to choke her into tears. No. No. No.

She began to run. The children in the park were suddenly monstrous to her, their innocence a fraud, beneath which lurked a thousand nightmares, biding their patient time. Children were the tough ones—impervious to evil, burying everything they did not like to punish their waiting adult selves with. The destruction waited until society had warped and weakened the emerging adult. That was why she wanted a child: wanted that tough indifference around her to teach how to fight off the forces of darkness with the simple weapons of ignorance and blindness;

she wanted that egotistic anarchy; that simple security in her life.

Her overwhelming sense of relief at seeing the red-and-white striped pushchair—the absolute sign that Nancy was at home—brought her to her senses. There was no need for hysteria. This was Nancy's house: a sunny basement flat belonging to Nancy's aunt. Nancy and Edward lived here with their two children. Her friends. That was simple, safe. Safer still was the mockery, because Nancy, ardent socialist and feminist activist, lived in a beautiful, if decaying house, five minutes' walk from the park, with its own big garden, courtesy of her bourgeois family connections. But only a gentle mockery because who would not do likewise? The flat, the garden, the nominal rent. Fortune favours the brave. Nancy had probably earned her luck.

She rang the bell; a pause, scuffling noises and the door opened.

"Liz. What a nice thing. Come in. Do you want some lunch? How come you're not working?"

"Clinic day."

"Yeah. I forgot. I'm sorry. I gather from the general look of dejection that not this month, huh? You don't know your blessings, you really don't."

"Don't."

"All right. Want some lunch? Sausages and mash only, with the kids. But they're quite sweet today."

The strange pain when Hughie, knees sagging outwards, nappy dragging, totters across the floor. When Harriet wearing only her underpants hangs down over the back of the chair, spluttering, performing. And so self-conscious. Even as she tries not to, she watches her own gestures. Does she look like someone who is "good with children"? She knows she does not, though these two she actually knows and likes and they are glad to see her. Sometimes with these two she can even forget they are children and relax; not this morning though. She rubs her hands against her forehead, pushing the short hair upwards and looking for a moment frightened.

"Was it very bad then?"

"Later."

"Okay. Look, I've got another job, really nice and someone I can reasonably fleece."

"Yes? What is it."

"Some new restaurant up Chalk Farm way. Sign board, logo, menu cards and so on. Harri, don't flop on poor Liz like that."

"How do you find the time?"

"I have to. I'd go mad without, nothing but kid talk; and Edward comes in from teaching and I get more about kids. I never gave that adequate thought when I bullied him into infant teaching you know; that there would be nothing but unremitting infants day in and day out. A little sophisticated design work for trendies is just right. Did Tony give you the day off?"

"Not exactly, I took it. He won't mind."

"Do you want a drink?"

"Please. Yes. I'll get it."

The pale sunshine pours through the window, the plants that Nancy grows in such quantities dapple and glow, the scrubbed pine table, the children's art work hung on the wall with garlic crusher, photographs and sketches. Her tight-fitting rolled-up jeans, Nancy's pretty print smock and bare feet. It looks very good indeed. The chasm between the fact and her perception of it opens, she stares into it amazed. Once she was a teenager on the verge of sophistication and this was what she saw when she gazed into a golden future. Not the nappies and sleeplessness she craves now. Mad.

"The consultant says I ought to see a shrink."

"What?"

"He says I'm confused about my feminine identification and am suppressing ovulation."

"Come again. No, don't—just hang on one minute. Harri, will you lay the table for me, darling? Hughie, come on up and sit beside Liz. Chop up this sausage for him, will you? Hughie, come on, lovey. Harri, here's yours. After he's eaten we'll put Hughie down for a nap and then we may get some talk time."

"Can I ring Ian? I said I would."

"Sure, help yourself."

In the hallway she dialled his office and waited. Ian was out and they thought he would be out most of the afternoon. She was annoyed; he had asked her to ring him and the people in his office would think of her as an intruding wife. The people who worked with Ian were so radical and "right-on" she hated them. It did not matter. She did not know what she was going to say to him anyway. It hung over her parallel almost with the content of what she had to tell him. That wasn't fair. If only he did not care so much, if only her sadness did not make him so painfully sad.

She went back and helped give the children their lunch. She could not eat herself, just drank the wine that Nancy poured liberally into her glass.

"I thought you were meant to be putting on weight?"

"Well, the wine should do it. The amount I drink."

"You really are out on a limb aren't you? Here is everyone else I know trying to lose weight and not get pregnant; while you won't eat and can't . . . my love, I am sorry, it was meant for a joke."

"Why is Liz crying, Mummy?"

"Because she's unhappy."

Unhappy and neurotic, and totally isolated from even the closest of her friends. Nancy put Hugh to bed, settled Harri down with pens and paper and returned to Liz.

"Why a shrink then?"

"No physical cause for Ian and me not getting it on. Lively little sperms, welcoming environment, nice wide open tubes, apparently healthy ovaries; but the only time I seem to have ovulated in the last ten months was when Ian was in bloody Glasgow on a conference. You might think this was an unfortunate coincidence, but not my Dr. Marshall: he adds it up to Profound Gender Identity Repulsion. Rôle Expectation Confusion.

Penis Envy." (He had not actually said that, she was exaggerating, mocking him for her own protection, and she knew it.) She tried to be honest. "That's what he thinks anyway."

"Can that suppress ovulation?"

"I don't know. Presumably the good man didn't just make it up."

"Well I suppose not, but what about all those people who don't want babies and have them all over the place. Why doesn't suppression work for them? The new contraceptive: willpower."

They laughed. Liz said, encouraged now, "I expect he'd say that although they said they didn't want babies, obviously at a subconscious level they did, or else they wouldn't have conceived them . . . It's very crafty to judge desire by performance. Comforting too: if everyone wants what they get, then they've got what they want."

"If you can think like that about him, why are you bothered by anything he may say?"

"Shit, Nancy, you're not meant to ask that. Rejection of femininity. I don't even know what that means; it might be true. Look at my fucked-up past: those coils of emotional entanglements that never threatened me. I thought I was a liberated woman. Maybe I was just running. Why do I choose to marry a faggot?"

"Don't."

"Suppose he's right? Suppose he is bloody well right? It makes a nonsense of anything I do. It makes the choices impossible. I do reject a femininity of passivity and all that crap. Of course we do, which is why we toddle off Thursday nights and put our little heads together to foster the revolution. But no one told us that was the price. I don't know if I can pay that price. Nancy, try and imagine it. We think this is some sort of simple choice—I will have a child, I won't have a child. A Woman's Right to Choose. Great. Good slogan, simple implications that we can all understand. I choose; and the consequences don't follow the way they ought to. If you went and had an abortion and ended up still pregnant, you'd have a right to feel pissed off: that's how I feel, and I've felt that way for three years, but when he said that it was my own fault it was the last straw. I can't bear it. I just can't cope with it."

"My dear . . . oh dear . . . Liz, with the best will in the world I just don't know what to say. I feel paralysed; there doesn't seem to be a nice feminist answer. I just can't help. Really I can't help."

But it did help. It helped to have told Nancy, and know that she had a claim on her sympathy and attention, despite two pre-school children, a husband, half a job, and a thousand other concerns. It was help precisely because of those things. Nancy enjoyed being confidante; she would find it interesting material to mull over and gossip about; Liz's grief was not going to hurt Nancy. But Ian, she did not know what she could say to him. She was becoming so damned considerate of his feelings. And he of hers. He hadn't told her for four days that his sister was pregnant again. They were careful. Polite.

She did not want to hear the memories of their earlier security. In the first golden year of their marriage, polite was the one thing they were not.

"Ian, don't take those bloody Valium."

"Why not?"

"You know as well as I do. You're treating symptoms, and anyway you don't need them. You like to think you do, but it's a cop-out. You don't need them anymore."

"Is the love of a good woman going to do more for me than medical science?"

"I am not a good woman, sod you."

"I think you are a good woman, I think you're a lovely woman."

And despite the glow of knowing that it was true, that he did find her good, she would not be deflected. "Don't change the subject, you coward."

"It's not me that's the coward Liz, it's you. You can't bear to think that you alone can't make me happy and well. You don't mind tranquillisers for any of those sophisticated reasons you dream up; you just don't like me to take them, because you think they might prove you a failure."

But now that anger was carefully damped down, disguised. Everything was calculated by reference to the non-existent baby. As she walked around the flat waiting for him to come home she was bitterly aware of it. The flat was too small: two rooms ought to be enough for two people, but in their case it was not. The bedroom was too small even to put a chair in. If either wanted to entertain or have a meeting in the house alone, the other one had to go out. When they first took the flat it was meant to be temporary; they were just waiting until she was pregnant. Easier to look for a flat that you know would accept children. In the meantime the flat, though not perfectly located, would do; it was cheap, they could save, decide exactly where they wanted to live, and when she was pregnant they would move. Very sensible. And now two years later they were stuck with it. Because for either of them to suggest a move before the magical pregnancy was real would imply despair, or the other might think it implied despair and that might induce despair in the other. With each month that passed it was harder to say, with any innocence, "Look this flat is too small for us to live in. Let's move."

Strange that wanting anything as normal as a baby when you were married should lead to these emotional deadlocks, these traps from which she could see no escape. They had been so clear about what they were doing; that had charged the incidents of their life together with such a weight of formal meaning. Both of them escaping from chaotic lives of their own had found this clarity and sense of direction, had built on it with such attentiveness.

Suddenly it struck her as profoundly unfair: that actual events from the past should change even when they were done with. You thought they were past, solid as the history books, and then they would not lie still.

When she was thirteen she had staged a personal strike

against conditions of work. She had refused to go to school, because girls in her school were not allowed to do woodwork. She had announced that so long as such an unjust situation was allowed to continue she would not go to school. They could threaten and punish and do what they would: she would stay in her room until something was done about it. After about a fortnight she had won: triumphantly she had entered the woodwork class. And moreover with the secret, but ill-concealed admiration of both her father and the headmaster; and with the less concealed defeat of her mother and the woodwork master—the two people who were the villains of her imagination.

This was a story in which she had starred as the teenage heroine. She had related it at feminist gatherings, reflecting credit on herself, she who had stood out against conditioning and expectations: an isolated instance of victory in the fight they had all fought and lost as children. But now the memory clouded and went sour on her: she had not really sat in her room reading Brontë novels—she had lain on the bed and wept because Mummy was furious with her. The whole thing had not been a fight of principle, but an infantile desire to humiliate the grown-ups. And the woodwork master had, in reality won: he made his classes into a two-year humiliation of her. The more academically inclined boys had soon left the class anyway, but she had been obliged to continue with the tedium to the bitter end, and all for a risible, useless, "O" level in woodwork.

The fight had been against her mother and for the love of her father. Not a blow for women, but a use of the most despicable female wiles to score off another woman. It had been an attention-getting gambit, a crude weapon in the war to gain her father's love.

She lay down on her bed, flat out, and accepted the tiredness in her body, although she had done nothing all day. The dingy green walls and yellow ceiling disgusted her. She had to make some sense of what he had said. Dr. Marshall. She knew she wanted a child. She knew because it had surprised her that she

should. Why should the doctor imply that it was a response to
Ian? Because he was a sexist pig, who assumed that all women's
desires were part of a desire to please men. Because Men were
the fount of all desires. It was not true. But there was a gap between the sort of person she seemed to be and the idea of wanting a child. Not just being a feminist: lots of feminists had children now. No one wondered at Nancy, with her two. She
would not allow it to come back to physical type: Nancy, so soft
and rounded, little and warm-bosomed looked like a mother,
while she was skinny, breastless, and now, with her shorn hair,
did not . . . She must bring this up at her women's group sometime . . . But it was not just an external thing, because she had
been surprised by her own gut desire, whereas she had always
assumed that Nancy would have children. But Nancy had been
with Edward since before she had known her. Did that make a
difference? Promiscuous women don't have children. Or rather,
promiscuous women don't become mothers. Was she a promiscuous woman? Did one remain promiscuous all the days of one's
life, branded for ever, a threat, a social danger for ever and ever?

She wanted Ian. She wanted Ian to come home now and be
with her. The one man who believed in her as virtuous, who
had found her good and kept her good, and did not care about
her past.

There had been mornings when she had woken in a bed and
looked at the sleeper beside her and thought, "Who is this?" But
sex was good that way, no danger, no need to have regard for the
feelings of the other. There was no safety in love. And she
would clamber out of the bed, leave a cheerful kiss or witty note
and wander off into the dawn. In early summer mornings North
Oxford had a blessedly bourgeois calm about it; the big houses
turned discreetly in on themselves. Wet winter mornings had a
different charm; the rain showing as haloes round the lights, silver in the colleges and gold round the neon street lamps. She
must have seen more dawns than any other student of her year.
If you sleep with Liz she'll give you a good time, witty and
clever as well as sexy, fun to be with, and she won't lay anything

on you: no tears, no demands, not even an abortion, because she'll be somewhere else tomorrow. No sweat. And fun.

So was she to be punished now, like St. Augustine, for what she had not known to be wrong, assuming that she hadn't known, assuming that it had been wrong? Was she being punished for not being a good woman, for cutting her hair to inch-long stubble and for having nothing to abandon a bra for? If only Ian would come.

But when he did it was no help. He was in a tearing hurry, late as usual and getting later. She had forgotten he was going out, to some community group meeting he had promised to help. He had forgotten she had been to the clinic.

"What time will you be back?" she asked, trying to delay him.

"Not sure. We'll probably have a pint afterwards. Don't expect me till after closing time."

If she had asked him to stay she knew that he would. She was sure enough not to need to find out. But she did not want to make an issue of it. He was so vulnerable: if he knew how raw she felt, he would feel distanced from her, would try to fill the gap with his own empathy, would receive her pain naked, and hurt himself. If she asked him to stay in he would know how badly she felt. He would feel guilty that he had forgotten to ask. There was no need to expose him to the pain that she knew he would feel. She loved him so much.

And. She wanted to kill him, she hated him. Underneath all her calm rationalising, her assertions that he loved her, below the list of his responsibilities, his pressures, and important political commitments; underneath all this crap about his tender empathy and nobility of soul she was furious with him for forgetting what was so central and unforgettable in her life. She hated him because his marriage and childlessness did not dominate his mind; because it was not fair that she should be the one with the obsessions, the psychic illnesses, the one in need of loving ministrations, and psychiatrists and understanding, while he could toddle off to a meeting and a drink in the pub without even noticing.

She hated him for not asking.

If he had asked she would have told him not to fuss about her so.

Nothing was simple any more.

Thursday evenings were her women's group meetings. They had started as a reading group, and had become a satisfactory support network for each other. The reading subsided, occupying less and less of their time: occasionally they would berate themselves for their self-indulgence, for their middle-class ease and idleness. But mostly they enjoyed the sense of virtue they could get by giving their gossip a direction, a political framework which allowed them to give a high priority to their personal friendship.

Liz usually went to the meeting straight from work. Although in theory the meetings circulated from house to house, this high-mindedness was overlaid with practical considerations. The determining factor was the children, and in the long run this meant they nearly always met either at Paula's house or sometimes at Nancy's. When she had joined the group Liz had still been believing that by next month she would be pregnant: she loved being around children and their mothers gaining the inside knowledge she was about to need. Now, with the children no longer a joy but a subtle pain, she felt a moral pressure to prove that her original offers to "help" had not been an egotistical luxury.

They were at Paula's house again this week. Paula was divorced, her three children left over from an earlier life that she had grown out of. The children were less integrated with her than Nancy's were: the baby-sitting and administration more of a chore. She was more possessive too than Nancy was: filled with guilt about not feeling much enthusiasm for them, Paula was suspicious of anyone who too obviously did. They were older than Nancy's children, less in need of care and unwilling to be mauled over by childless feminists on the loose. Despite the tensions, it was less emotionally demanding to be at Paula's

than at Nancy's where the children swamped her with their love
and demands.

She cooked supper for them all and chatted with Paula for
the hour before the others started to arrive. An effortless way to
make yourself feel good, she mocked at herself, but she knew
that both Paula and the kids enjoyed the evenings. It was not
necessary to be so strict.

Mary-Ann arrived, then Nancy and Alice together. They
made more cups of coffee. Jane was always late; her energies
constantly directed in too many directions, involved in crucial
and diverse activities, never allowing time for transit, finding it
difficult to shift her sense of commitment on to the next project.
Once she had arrived she would give her total concentration to
where she was, but she would always be late. The rest of them
were both sympathetic and annoyed.

Liz looks at them as they chat, decide not to wait for Jane,
and then wait anyway. She loves Nancy, wishes she would find
a better use for her brains than designing mediocre signs for mediocre restaurants, knows her difficulties, hopes it will be better
when Harriet goes to school in the autumn. She feels warm towards Paula, though baffled by her bitterness about the loss of a
husband who she did not even like. She is curious too—Paula
has not slept with a man for eight years, not since her husband
left. Liz, who has hardly passed a single night alone in bed since
she went to university, finds it impossible to imagine; wonders if
having children absolves you from the binding need for intimacy she knows in herself; would a child be a way out of the ex-
cessive sexuality she fears in herself—would that redirect her
energies? She likes Alice and respects her; the determined inde-
pendence, the serious consideration she will give to any idea.
When they have talked about having children Alice is the most
ambivalent, she would like to, she says carefully, she is over
thirty, she must make her mind up soon; but she is equally engaged in Jane's declaration of gay-ness, giving that her imagina-
tive attention. Liz does not like Mary-Ann: she knows it is
because Mary-Ann had her second abortion a couple of months

ago. Since then Liz hates to listen to her high American voice pontificating on women's rights and the oppression of the nuclear family. She says Mary-Ann is narrow-minded and does not recognise other people's choices, but she knows that the murderous heart of her dislike is the casual way she can speak of scraping out of herself the one thing that Liz wants. It was Mary-Ann's first abortion, or the first that Liz knows of, that drove her to the infertility clinic ten months ago. Now Mary-Ann talks of sterilisation and tube-chopping, and Liz secretly plans methods of torture deliberately absurd enough to laugh at. And it is no good for Nancy to say, as she does, complacently, from time to time, "Liz we all have our insecurities." Mary-Ann is only twenty-four and she wants to be sterilised because she does not like the rich fruit that grows inside her. Unjust, unjust.

When Jane arrives and they finally settle down Nancy, inevitably, introduces the subject. "Liz and I have a discussion topic for tonight. Something we can't put together."

"Oh Nancy, don't. I don't want to talk about it. It's not that interesting."

She never did want to talk about it. In the beginning of their relationship, she and Ian had slept together for ten months without making love, and she had never told anyone about it. She had lain awake some nights grinding her teeth and her pelvis in an agony of frustration. They had gone about together, been acknowledged everywhere as a couple—she had even had to endure the good-humoured jokes about the superior virility of younger men—but even in the intimacy of women's groups she had never told anyone that he loved her and she loved him and he could not make love to her. There was no way out: the love and the desire were there, but his conflicts grew to match them. She did not leave him because she loved him and had led him into this impossible place of loving women and not being able to do anything about it. She did not leave him because it was him that she wanted, things were bound to work out, had to work out somehow. But the frustration and the fear did not go away.

She loved a man who was impotent with her. Who would not, could not make love to her. And for ten months she had not told anyone. Her one desire was not to have to talk about it.

When she had begun to worry about not getting pregnant: counting the days till her next period and wondering if perhaps there might be something wrong with her, with Ian, with them: it had been almost impossible for her to mention it. She needed people like Ian and Nancy in her life who were not afraid to pick at her scabs. But still, compulsively, she said, "Nancy I really don't want to talk about it." She hated the popular idea that everything was better out than in. There were private places that did not have to be shared; there were arrangements and editing of truths that made them more manageable. And at the time she knew that Nancy was right, and the group could help her make those editings, but only if she showed them the raw wound of rejection and fear.

So when she said that she did not want to talk about it, there was also a sense of relief in knowing that there was not a hope in hell that Nancy would pay any attention to such a protest. Nancy never perceived any need for secrecy or even privacy, and never, never locked loo doors: she would want to and would insist on talking about it.

She said, "Come on, Liz," in almost the same tone as she would say "Come on, Hughie" when he was dragging his heels walking home from the shop. "It's really interesting."

"Thank you."

"No seriously. It is and you know it is."

Paula said, "Well this isn't. It's boring. Tell or don't, but stop messing round."

Nancy put her hand out and let it rest on Liz's shoulder, warm and firm. But she said, "Liz's gynaecologist is of the professional opinion that Liz should see a shrink, because she's not properly adjusted to being a woman."

"What?" shrieked Alice, then perceiving the pain on Liz's face said, "I'm sorry. I mean, what criteria is he using?"

Nancy said, "I can't imagine. It sounds quite bizarre to me. She doesn't get pregnant so he says she isn't a real woman."

Liz felt angry. "Nancy, that's just silly. That's the sort of exaggerated simplification that leads us all into trouble. I could think of more rude things to say about him than you can imagine; but it is a little more involved than that. Or from my point of view it is. It's like this: Ian and I have both been tested up and down and round and round, as I have relayed to you month by boring month. And there is nothing wrong except that I don't ovulate when Ian is around. Only when he isn't."

Alice said, "Oh."

But Paula said,

"Basically then, you go to this doctor whose job is to get you pregnant and when he fails he turns round and says it's all your fault."

"Well . . ."

"Well?"

"Well, yes. I mean yes. I hadn't looked at it that way. It certainly acquits him. But Paula he, I mean, he must *know*. What sort of response can we have if he's right?"

"It doesn't seem to me a question of rightness, just a way of judging. Moralistic and simplistic. Unscientific if you like."

Alice said, "Come to think of it, it really is a classic of male so-called logic. First you take a whole group of women whose physical problem together with the way society leans on married women to have children, is bound to make them doubt their effectiveness and meaning as women. Then you take these perfectly normal, predictable doubts and confusions, shift them to the beginning and call them causes. It's quite impressive."

"And self-protective." That was Nancy.

"And foolproof"—Jane, amused almost—"because if we should try and argue, contest this with the doctor, that can be manipulated into proof that we aren't well adjusted to submissiveness and yer good old women's rôle. Then they can say, 'There you and then,' and threaten you with the punishment of not getting your baby."

Paula said, "Did you ask him what evidence he had, because I don't see what evidence there could possibly be? It's just more myth-making. Any evidence would have to be based on an *a priori* assumption that the act of pregnancy was somehow the nadir, the proof point of 'femininity,' of how we were adequate as women. I mean, how would he describe someone who had had a hysterectomy?"

Mary-Ann said, "Isn't that a reasonable biological basis actually? At an evolutionary level. I mean, of course I'm not saying that we all ought to have children or anything, as you can easily guess. More I'm saying that we really *are* in conflict with biology. That the women's struggle is based on a negation, rather than a denial of biological determinism. It actually is a struggle to assert the dominance of technology over biology."

"Most impressive, when did you practise that?" Nancy acknowledged, grinning.

"Don't be led astray, my child," Jane said thoughtfully. "It's too simple, and I must say from my own point of view as your token gay lady, dangerously defeatist, and narrow. Seriously, of course, I'm prepared to challenge biology as needed, but I don't see the need here. It's back to very crude assumptions. I mean 'getting her pregnant' isn't seen as the proof of masculinity, so much as ease of arousal and ejaculation. Right? What about ease of arousal and orgasm for women? On that basis I must be about the most 'feminine' woman in the world."

They all like that and grin in appreciation, but Jane goes on, "What about menopause? It's unique to the human species: perhaps that post-fertile period presents something crucial about womanhood. Even lactation, when ovulation is suppressed anyway, is a reasonable candidate for the 'most feminine state.' In primitive societies women must spend as much time doing it as they do getting pregnant. Culturally, Mary breastfeeding gets a much better coverage than Mary pregnant. And so on. So why should this doctor of Liz's assume that pregnancy is proof of adjustment? Answer: he is a male chauvinist pig and the women whom he sees are women already worried about themselves, specifically because they aren't getting pregnant."

Liz felt renewed. "Really I don't understand why I can't think of these things at the time, when I'm actually there. I make the most pathetic misdirected protests, like the clothes I wear, but I never challenge him. The heavy paternalistic kindliness really works. Big Daddy will look after you. You consent to it. I mean, I consent to it."

"What about the other women there?" Mary-Ann asked.

"What about them?"

"Well, how do they feel about it?"

"How should I know? They sit there in their nice coats looking both prim and excited, waiting for Mr. Mighty to dispense his magic tricks."

"Jesus, Liz, what a rotten thing to say. So you're the one with problems, the rest of them are schmucks. Those are your sisters; it's them you should be working this through with."

"You don't know what it's like."

"I can't imagine it's any different from the waiting-room at the abortion clinic, except that your lot are likely to be together longer. When I had my abortion this time we got quite a good rap session going. All you have to do is start. And you should."

"Okay, so I'm a lousy feminist. Thank you for your criticism, comrade."

"Liz," Alice says, and she looks almost shocked, "there's no need to be so paranoid. It wasn't a personal attack."

Do you want to bet? thought Liz. Mary-Ann hated her anyway, it wasn't one-sided. She hated her because Liz made her feel guilty. And she could not say that because feminists do not feel guilty about having abortions, only about wanting to have babies. Her motives and social pressures are under the microscope of the group, but Mary-Ann's aren't. As soon as she said she was pregnant and wanting an abortion there had been that wave of support and succour and understanding from everyone in the group. No one even asked her why. No need for self-questioning there. But her own needs and wants and feelings of inadequacy were a different matter. It would be nice for them to find her maladjusted anyway. She was a threat to the whole concept of the free woman, a danger to their belief that once they had recognised the basis of women's oppression they were free to choose what they wanted and then do it. But she cannot say those things; instead she tried a rueful grin.

"Oh dear, I am sorry. Was that paranoid? Perhaps I *should* see a shrink."

A joke against yourself will nearly always buy back the group's approval. It is quite cheap.

But Nancy is protective, almost angry. "I've known Liz for ages and there may have been times when I might have classed her as all sorts of neurotic, but that was always to do with the so-called feminine things: submissive, masochistic. Can't any of you understand the sane and well-adjusted strain of making a choice about your life, and not being able to implement it? There is nothing paranoid about getting freaked out by that. I got lots of sisterly support when Harri's nursery closed down, because I couldn't implement my choices. It's the same thing. Liz is as together as any of us!"

"Thank you friend."

"No honestly."

Which was very nice, and filled her with anger against the doctor and a determination not to submit to his authority. But did it direct her to any solution of her problem? Did it even bear on the problem? The doctor could be the worst sexist in the world and still be right. Would she pay the price in terms of her principles, self-esteem, perhaps even identity and friendship, in order to have her baby? Any answer seemed frightening.

"Ian," she said softly into the dark. If he were asleep it would save her telling him, but he was not.

"Mmm."

"Make a place for me." He lifted his arm so that she could curl her head into the soft skin below his shoulder. They were both so skinny that there were not many places they could cuddle against each other.

"What is it, love?"

"Do you know what Dr. Marshall really said to me last Tuesday?" She could feel the tension run into his muscles, preparing himself if necessary to suppress his own grief and comfort hers. "He said I was a nut-case and ought to see a shrink."

He relaxed, lay there for a moment and said, "That's ridiculous." The best possible response he could have made, and she relaxed too.

"Yeah, he noticed the hair growing on the palms of my hands and the left-over globs of blood hanging from my teeth and asked me if I realised that it was impossible for vampires to breed as they were already dead." They smiled; she could feel his smile, in the tightening of his face against the top of her head. She was pleased with herself. "No, seriously: he's come up with a brand new theory to neutralise his sense of medical failure. Namely; I only want to have this child to earn your love, so my body is rejecting the baby, because subconsciously I don't want it. Subtle, eh?" Thank God she had talked this over with her friends first. How she had felt on Tuesday would have pained Ian beyond bearing. Even this.

"Jesus Christ."

He sat up and turned on the light and looked at her. "You don't believe that do you? That I'm pressuring you into something that you don't really want? Darling."

"No. No, Ian, no. Whatever is going on I don't think it's there. Really truly." This was why she had been unhappy about telling him, he was going to eat himself up now. "Look, sure I want you to be the father of my baby, and want to have your baby. But this was even before I knew you wanted it too, wasn't it?"

The night when finally, holding their breaths and with little physical pleasure, they had made love: forcing things as little as possible, leaving them both always the space to withdraw with-

out damaging each other, without a moment of rejection, she
had realised that this was a moment of triumph. It was hardly an
act of passion for either of them, paler, more fragile; from Ian it
was a gift of confidence in her, a movement towards her
achieved with so much doubt and confusion, but still a movement, part of a tide that would swell inwards from here, a beginning rather than an accomplishment. But a victorious beginning.
When he finally penetrated her, when she finally welcomed him
there, he lay, gentle almost contemplative, with no wish to go
further and he had smiled and said, "How strange, I do think
that here is where I have always wanted to be." Then after an
experimental moment or two, he added, "Now there's only one
thing more—I'd like to make a baby here, one day."

And it had been a moment of recognition. She had flowed
with a magical delight.

"Really, Ian?" Her tough, thin body felt soft and other to her,
curved and contoured in new ways, as though he had trans-
formed her. A body coming into her, not saying, "It is safe? Are
you careful?" but saying instead, "What can we do with this?
Where can we go from here?" She had known, startled, at once,
that she would never leave him, that they were bound together.
A triumphant sense of having travelled and arrived, that went
beyond questions.

But now he was saying, "I never thought, I never meant to
do that to you, but now I remember the first thing I ever said to
you, after messing you about for nearly a year, once we were
making love, I said I wanted to have your baby. I'm so clumsy to
you."

"Ian, darling, no. It was you wanting to have that baby with
me that made me yours. You must know that."

"Yes, yes, I know. But . . . listen, Liz, we both come out of
these separate hells, these shitty relationships or in my case non-
relationships, like shipwrecked mariners or something, and we
find each other and we don't believe our luck. Right. And immediately we put names on it, we get married and we start plan-

ning for this baby. Maybe it isn't a baby you want, just the assurance that I would love you and not leave you, but oh no, I have to start laying terms. I'm the one who wanted us to be married, I couldn't bear the thought of you going away or something. The baby isn't just a symbol of security for us, is it?"

They were silent. Lying on the bed she looked at his back, stretched and bony, as he leaned forward with his hands round his hunched-up knees. It was a good back for anguish, she thought irrelevantly, thin and flexible. He was a good deal fitter than he looked, and his back was muscled, beautiful. She put out her hand, flat, and spread her fingers, touching it with her whole palm.

She spoke carefully. "I don't think there's any need for that sort of honesty. Of course I wanted security, the knowledge that I was not just loved, but approved, and I dare say the baby was some part of that. But sweetheart, if there's any conflicting pressure, it's in me, myself. It needn't be in reaction to you, need it? It needn't be in reaction to you. Even Dr. Marshall's famous rôle injection theory can be self-contained. That I want a baby for security, or affirmation of my own femininity or lovability, and at the same time I can't or won't face that responsibility: that I don't want to be a grown-up, don't want to have to behave like a mummy. You don't have to go into much profound psychology to see some truth in that. You don't have to blame you."

There was another pause. She knew that at some level he wanted to be able to blame himself, that he enjoyed guilt, that he hated having no real part in their anguish and grief, that he wanted to participate, however painfully, rather than be cut off from the drama. She also knew that he would not answer her at all until he was ready; that he would not be trapped into an unconsidered response, that she might have to wait days before he was ready to bring the subject up again. When he was ready he would say what he thought, and at least she would not have to sit around working out what he had meant, or if he had meant what he'd said. She waited, and while she waited she went on running her hand up and down his back: from where she lay she could not reach all the way up to his neck, but down at the bottom of his spinal column was an open country, a rich new land as though she had never seen it before. Fun.

"Cut that out, I'm supposed to be trying to think."

She moved her hand still lower, turning her wrist and burrowing through the bed-clothes. Teasing him, and feeling the beginning of his excitement. Still, after nearly four years it seemed almost a miracle to her that he not only loved her but could be brought to desiring her. The old impotence now only a hesitation which gave her the ability to control things. An undeserved, beautiful piece of luck, an unearned bonus.

And afterwards, snuggled back into his arms relaxing, she thought he sounded perfectly cheerful when he said, "Come to think about it, what is it that we expect from this baby? I mean, why do we want a baby?"

"I can't bear those monthly periods being for nothing, years of gross inconvenience all for nothing."

"You see, you connect it biologically back to your body. You do want a proof of femininity."

And although she knew he was joking she felt the same tremor of fear, shy to think that there was some part of her that she did not know, some strange, lurking "feminine" Liz whom she had never met.

He continued, "Whereas I want an heir to the family fortunes, a little son to carry on the noble name of Jones even unto the third and fourth generation. My own little lad to share my daily interests of fishing in the canal, dope-dealing and trolling gents' loos."

"And suppose she's a girl?"

"Impossible. A man of my obvious virility would not be likely to have a girl. Anyway, don't you remember when I did that sperm count, Dr. Marshall commented with pleasure on the masculine forces gathered therein."

They were laughing, easy. But she knew they had only begun trying to deal with the problem. It would take Ian a while to work it through for himself. It would take her a while to know what to do with the strength that she had gained from him and her friends. But it was better now she had told him, a little better.

"I'm sleepy," she said.

"Okay, sexy. I think I'll read for a bit."

She curled against him and slept.

So assent becomes the moment of conception. The assent with full knowledge, without even the hidden, subterranean doubt. With clarity and understanding. That purely conscious, unalienated woman who can so assent with the entirety of her person, needs no biological intrusion between her desire and its fulfilment. She needs no moment of enclosure—for such a woman's understanding of the act of penetration would be based on her own experience of it—no moment of enclosure, no lust, no lubrication, no semen racing and chasing, a gaggled mob over the tight lip of the cervix and through the dark cave, the genetic sorting-house, the crucible.

Here she is, a Semitic Arab adolescent, in the northern backwater of the minor Roman province of Palestine, some time after the annexation but before the destruction of the temple in A.D. 70. Probably vitamin and iron deficient; small, dark, devout Jew. Almost certainly illiterate, destined by custom of time and place to be given in marriage while still pubescent. In fact already engaged to a skilled manual labourer or small artisan, possibly considerably older than herself. Her day taken up with the small platitudinous tasks of drawing water, spinning, grinding and chasing scrawny chickens. But despite so dogging a destiny she is not, apparently, discouraged. An unconventional girl.

Holy Mary, Mother of God, pray for us sinners now and at the hour of our death.

Mary, Mother of God, bearer of the incarnate word, Theotokos, root and flower of womanhood. The ultimate Christopher, who carried him in the waters, through the storms and night places of foetal life. Who carried him in that darkness, and made it awash with light.

Her serene confidence shattering the peace of her upland village. Her unassailable self-assurance dominating her appalled family, and her patient, affectionate fiancé. A stumbling block to the Jews, with their guilt, and their legalism, and their very male God. A folly to the Greeks with their clever dualisms and unworldly spirituality. A slap in the face to anyone who wants to see the virgin birth as anti-sexuality. Her small tired face, weary with trying to explain the obvious, says sexuality goes beyond the moment of genital receptivity, goes inward and inward, along the path that men try to follow with their ejaculation, to where the children grow. Where the promised land of soft, white hills and warm, damp, flowering valleys, flowing with milk, is prepared for the traveller. The pilgrim who has pushed his way through oceans and deserts to the sunlit land where all wants are supplied.

Of course her assent is a sexual act, she tries to explain, pushing her hair back under her scarf, and grinding her bare toes into the coarse sand, because it was complete, it was made with the whole of her being. It was an assent to the totality of herself, to a womanhood so vital and empowered that it could break free of biology and submission, any dependence on or need for a masculine sexuality—that furrow in which the crop of women's sex has been held to be rooted.

She cannot explain. The neighbourhood is filled with delighted scandal: this might teach her not to walk about ignoring men and acting so high and free. But she is not afraid. Not her, in her moment of pure assent. She unrooted her desire and carried as far as it would go; carried it beyond mind and logic higher and higher to the throne of the living God, to the source of light, to the infinite word. She became her own messenger as well as her own sower. The gap between cause and effect is destroyed for ever; eternity penetrates time, without rape. She speaks her assent and Will takes on new meanings.

Assent becomes the moment of conception.

2.

MAY

She lay with her feet up in the stirrups and her chin tucked in, looking down towards the doctor. The nurse-receptionist at the clinic, whom she had been beginning to think of as some sort of ally, even friend, had given her this handy household hint: if, when lying on your back, you curve your neck down and lower your eyes your body is bound to relax; if you consciously look at a doctor doing an internal examination you are bound to assume this position. Amazingly it worked. The nurse had said too that she would find it very useful in labour, during troublesome delivery processes. She had said this quite casually: it was probably why Liz had started to like her. It might well be a cheap and conscious morale-boosting remark which she practised at home, but she managed it gracefully.

Looking at the doctor she had an odd view along her own body. The red and green striped jersey, heavy against the dull spring day, looked silly with nothing underneath it except the whiteness of her concave stomach, the rocky protrusion of her hip bones. She really was too thin. She could see, just below the navel, the minute scar from the laparoscopic examination.

She wished she could have seen that: the cold light, concentrated through tiny filaments of glass, lighting up the dark places inside her gut. The pear shape of the womb, the fallopian tubes waving, delicately inviting, at the ovaries. A strange knowledge gleaned of her while she was unconscious. The gas blowing up her stomach until she looked pregnant. The doctor had seen a vision of her, had a knowledge of her that she could never share. An intensely private knowing: suppose he had been her lover, what a delight to share with someone you loved the whole terrain of your inside. To know a woman like that.

She must not allow herself to make a biological mythology: it was dangerous, it was crude; body contains no knowledge. She had to believe that.

She said to the doctor, still amused by the contrast between thin white flesh, and thick woollen sweater, "It looks silly doesn't it?"

"Oh no," he said, concentrating on his own view, "you must not think that. It looks quite normal, very nice in fact. You must try to concentrate on positive images of yourself. Think how many people have found this desirable."

Damn him. That gave her value in his eyes. Although it made her an unfit mother, it sure as hell made her an interesting patient. If she had been a virgin, or better still a nice little wife sold off in the slave market at eighteen, he would have felt she deserved a baby, but he would not have found her so interesting.

As he probed he said, "That reminds me. What did you decide about what we talked about last time? What did your husband feel about it?"

Deep breath, chin tucked in to relax. "I decided that I ought to ask you whether you had any training in psychiatry. And if not, how you felt qualified to make any judgements like that about my mental health."

He jabbed quite deftly with the speculum: deliberate, or had she shaken him? Immediately the guilt and insecurity flowed back into her. She should at least have waited until she was the right way up with her knickers back on.

There was a long silence. He did not look up, continued instead his examination of her vagina. She could not make him re-

spond, apart from that sudden painful jag; he was strong enough
to wait her out. In the silence, she felt increasingly bad, the
compulsion to apologise gripped her. She would not, she would
not. It was a rational question, she had a right to ask it. But she
had not kept the aggression out of her voice, had not asked it as
a rational question, had turned it into an attack, a violation. She
had been rude.

"I'm sorry," she said, fighting to keep any tears out of her
eyes, out of her voice. "That was silly, I didn't mean it."

Still he did not answer. She composed herself, wishing more
and more that she was in a position of some dignity. She tried
again, schooling herself to subterfuge. "It's not easy you know,
what you said last month. I have thought about it, I have tried
to think about it, but it just makes me trust myself, and everything I do, less and less."

He was not going to be drawn, she would have to give him
something more than that. "I wondered"—meek now, trying to
placate him, ashamed—"I wondered how other women who
came here thought about this. I wondered if perhaps we could
have some sort of group discussion, group therapy if you like, so
we could get some sort of perspective."

He looked up at last. "Well that is quite an interesting idea."
He seemed prepared to give it about thirty seconds of consideration, then thoughtfully he said, "Don't you think that perhaps
it is rather a middle-class, or to use your vocabulary, rather an
élitist notion? For most of the women who come here, it is hard
enough for them to talk to me, or other members of my team. I
shouldn't really say this, but about five per cent of the women
who come to me haven't even been able to make normal love to
their husbands. They are not likely to be able to talk freely and
usefully with each other, you know. It is all right for you small
minority of articulate women, educated, practised in tearing up
your personal lives for the edification of your friends, but most
of the women here would be too embarrassed, too private, to
gain anything from such a conversation. I cannot, will not, risk
even one woman leaving this clinic because she is embarrassed

at having her privacy violated, for the sake of women like you, who find it an easy way out to discuss things in that sort of situation, instead of doing things through professional experts. You must see that."

When she had arrived that morning, stung by Mary-Ann and the criticism, encouraged by the rest of the group over the last couple of meetings, she had tried to speak to the woman sitting next to her in the waiting-room.

"Didn't I see you here last time?"

"Yes, that was my first time."

"How are you getting on?"

"Well, I thought he was lovely, he was so kind, but all those questions. And I've been reading a book, and I am frightened of all those things they may do to you. And I don't think my husband will like coming very much."

To her surprise the woman really was ready to talk, did want to reach out to her and share this thing. "We've been trying for a baby since we were married, you know, that's nearly five years. I didn't think of doing anything about it, but I had a friend and she went to someone, and she fell for her little girl in about three months. So I thought I'd give it a try. But now I'm a bit scared really."

"Oh, it's not bad. They haven't done anything to me that hurt much."

"What did you have to do?"

But then the receptionist came over and said, "Mrs. Jones it's time you went in," and to the other woman, "Is something worrying you? That's what I'm here for, you can ask me anything you want to know, come over and have a little chat. I haven't got to know you yet, have I?"

She grinned at Liz, but followed the uniformed woman over to her desk, with a slightly anxious smile.

Now, with all the control she could muster, she said to Dr. Marshall, "Other clinics have group therapy sessions."

"True," he said, "and other clinics do not have such a high

success rate as mine. If you want group therapy go to a different clinic. If you want a baby, stop fighting me, trust me."

That was so unfair, that was a direct bribe, and therefore inevitably a promise of punishment. He had her both ways, she did not know how to fight him. She was angry,

"You just want to keep your power, don't you? Your whole deal is set up, just to give you authority, to keep you in control. Women aren't even allowed to talk to each other in your waiting-room without having the most innocent conversations busted up by your well-trained snoop, with the fancy title of nurse-receptionist. You are afraid to risk any threat to your authority, aren't you? You like being the boss. You're an oppressive masculist pig."

She sounded like a child in a tantrum, and she knew she did. With her legs tied in the air she could not even sit up, she had as much dignity as a baby having its nappies changed, it was not surprising that she acted like one. And she was frightened. What would he do now? Would he refuse to treat her? Would he leave her high and dry and babyless? How would he punish her?

He left his end of her, walked up the examining table and stood just behind her head. Did he know and monitor the advice the nurse gave his patients? She was forced to turn her eyes upwards, awkwardly straining her neck to look at him.

"Look," he said, calm, dignified, in complete control. He would not need to punish her, she had not won anything, even his anger. "I do not mind that you take your aggression out on me. I can understand and accept that. I can take it. Week in and week out I have angry, baffled, hurt women here who know that they can trust me as a safe repository for all their self-doubts." Carried on the tide of his benevolence, she could not even formulate a protest. "But whether you know it or not, I am your friend. I want what you want, which is for you to have a child, as and when you are in physical and psychological shape to do so. You have sought me out because this clinic is one of the best in London, which means in the world. You chose this clinic

quite deliberately, and against the immediate advice of your
G.P.; you have fought well, bravely and with clarity for your
child. Please don't let yourself be tricked by yourself now. I have
seen more sub-fertile women than you have had hot dinners, if
you will excuse the vulgarism. You came to me because you
knew that. Diverting your energies into finding fault with me
may well relieve your feelings, but it is not going to obtain for
you your heart's desire. You must try to grow up with yourself,
be more honest with yourself, and trust those with knowledge in
this field. You trust a train driver to get you to your destination,
you don't have to drive the train yourself. You have been coming here for nearly a year. Because you are intelligent and in-
formed you know we have run the gamut of tests on you and
your husband, on Ian. What do you expect me to do?"

Stop making her feel guilty was one answer. Accept her word
that she was willing to risk the dangers of multiple births was
another.

"I'm sorry," she muttered. "It has been a bad month."

And now he took her bare feet tenderly down from the stirrups, raised her up, dressed her, ordered her some tea, and led
her off to his inner sanctum. She was restored in his affection,
forgiven. She had said sorry, so everything was all right again.
She wanted to go to the circus, she wanted a real satchel, she
wanted a baby. Crying for a baby just because she did not have
one. If she got one, within minutes she'd be running round London looking for someone else to look after it so that she could go
on reading the manuscripts and organising the lives of truly creative people, who could tell how life was and give birth to works
of art.

Uncreative. She read other people's books and played with
other people's children. She was cut off from the sources of other
women's experience: all engaged in avoiding or enduring children.

It was a private position, impossible to drag out into the arena
of politics where her friends all thrived and grew fat. This was
no blow from the State, no evil capitalist conspiracy they could

munch over and play with. This was not male exploitation or oppression, not something that she and Nancy and Alice and Jane and women all over the world could lean over kitchen tables, over pub tables, and whip each other into anger about. It was the random factor round which no campaign could be launched, no action taken. She had taken all the known actions, wrung from the National Health Service the very best they could offer. There was nothing she could ask them to do that they had not done. There was nothing wrong that anyone could put right. Just wait, they say. Leave it to time, they say, don't worry, try to relax, let things be. It will come out right, they say, just don't worry about it.

She had said that to Ian. Wait. Let it be. Don't worry. Try to relax. It will come out right in the end. She found it hard to take from him now. Had she driven him to the same pitch of frustration and anger that she felt now? Each evening they would move from having a good, easy time together, into the tension of whether he would be able to make love to her. They had both wanted to. They had lain in each other's arms and talked through the night. Played games, filled up the silences.

"I'll swap you a year." A favourite game.

"Okay. Which?"

She thought. "1956."

"Don't be stupid. I was only three."

"Sorry, I forgot. I was in school by then. You choose, Ian."

"'62."

In 1962 her father and she had gone to Spain together. A special holiday. A reward for being his daughter. It had been the climax of their love; her mother had stayed at home. Just the two of them, they had driven through the wild high country of central Spain. Together, holding hands, they had looked at Goyas and El Grecos and agreed in preferring the latter: more powerful, more spiritual. His words. They had looked at the great churches and her father had told her in almost magical language of how the *conquistadores* had gone to the new golden land across the sea and had built cathedrals there, every bit as large and splendid, in the rampant jungle. He had fed on the image of these nobly born men setting out to convert a new world, to exchange Christianity for gold and jewels. The British Empire was tarnished for him; but Southern America was how he would have liked the Empire to have been. In São Paulo was the only branch of Harrods. He always called Harrods the "small chain store" because of that.

By that autumn, under the influence of a new school teacher, she was becoming a socialist, no longer believed in God, no longer believed that He was made in the image of her father. The first great love affair of her life was coming to an end.

In 1962 Ian was ten, working for his Eleven Plus. His mother had refused to let him wear long trousers. He was scared, terribly, deeply scared that he would fail, that he would be condemned forever to the Secondary Mod. And although his fear was quite real, he had also known that he would not fail, that he was easily clever enough to pass, and that everyone assumed he would pass. He was unable to bring these two separate pieces of information together.

In 1962 she had "done the facts of life" in Health and Life Class in school. Her then best friend had started menstruating. She remembered being taken down to the bottom of the cloakroom to be told about it.

1962 was the year that Ian's oldest brother had had to get married. A quick do in the registry office.

Which stopped them in their playful wanderings. Which brought them back to where it all came back to. Sex. Ian would begin to shake. She would tighten her arms around him. "Darling, I love you. Darling, it will be all right. I won't leave you. Relax. Give it time. I understand. Don't worry." Rocking him in her arms like a baby.

Dr. Marshall, holding her arm tenderly, was walking her up and down. Gentle, concerned. "I do understand. Indeed I do. Just relax. If you relax, you will surprise yourself. Don't worry about anything. Let me do the worrying. I'm paid for it. There is nothing for you to be worried about. There is no need to eat yourself up with this guilt and bitterness. Just trust me and relax. I want to help you, and I will help you."

Yes. Yes. Yes. It was to him that she could cling. It was the others, her friends, her husband, her past, who were ambivalent, who did not want her to have a child. Dr. Marshall was the one who said Don't be afraid, I am with you always. Dr. Marshall who said I will make it all right. Relax, come with me, do not be afraid. When you are good I will reward you. I will be your father. You will be the Mother of the Child.

But ten mornings later she wakes up, Sunday. Ian always gets up before her at the weekend. She could sleep forever, wombed in softness. Lying in bed while her lover of the night before gets up and paddles round is one of the signs that she is safe. No getting up before dawn and sneaking home. And when she lived with James, he could not bear her to sleep once he was awake. He would be pouncing on her mind or her body, not willing to allow her even that secrecy. But now, warm and secure, she enjoys the vague consciousness of Ian getting up, washing and shaving as quietly as possible and making coffee in his special pot. She is quite content with instant coffee, but Ian, meticulous, loving, creates his coffee in a glass test-tube, adding water and ground beans with elaborate care.

The quiet before the storm, because he suddenly remembers what Sunday it is, comes back into the bedroom and looks at her. He thinks she is still asleep and the look is open, longing, optimistic. Immediately she is conscious, remembers too, feels the warmer stickiness between her warm legs, the matted pubic hair, the painless but distinct downward pull in her stomach. Not dissimilar from the morning sensations after making love, but it is not the colourless stickiness of old seminal fluid. It is the reddish-brown bloody stickiness of dead uterus.

She does not even need to speak about it. He looks at her and turns away so she will not have to see what is in his face, and she does not know, has never known, what he feels these Sunday mornings. She does not know what she feels either.

She says, "I'm sorry."

"For Christ's sake, don't be bloody sorry. It's not your fault."

Every fourth Sunday he says "Don't be sorry, it's not your fault." And she is never quite sure whether she believes him or not.

"I'll make you some coffee," he says and goes back across the landing and into the tiny kitchen.

But she has to get up and go to the bathroom and wash and stick a Tampax up herself; shoving it in angrily, right up high, right up to where she had once again been hoping that their baby might be resting.

Every fourth Sunday. An exemplary working model: one hundred and forty-four repeat performances, the envy of her friends, the admiration of her doctors. When she was a student she had been able to mark all twelve or thirteen occasions neatly in her diary at the beginning of the year. For twelve years. And for what? The precise machinery was exposed now, like Leonardo's aeroplanes; it was elegant, artistic and it did not work.

She disciplined herself to say, it has not worked this time.

As she rinsed the flannel through she tried to think of all the women all over the world for whom this monthly bleeding would be a joy, a source of relief, security, liberation. It did not change her hell. She is cursed. She watched the blood discolour the water and could not stop wondering what she was being punished for. She wiped the sink clean and wondered how she could be cleaned, how she could repent and prove her repentance. She could not repent, she had forgotten the formula, her hair was too short to wipe feet with. She was too busy being a feminist and claiming her rights to make a pious pilgrimage to the tomb of St. James of Compostela to cure her issue of blood and lift her curse.

In the privacy of the kitchen, Liz had once complained to her mother about having to endure this monthly seeping of blood. How totally unjust it seemed to her, that women should not only have to carry the children and suffer labour pains, and pregnancy and post-natal depression, but moreover they should have to put up with this monthly inconvenience, this insult.

Her mother said sharply, "Nonsense, it's the most natural thing in the world. There is nothing to make such a fuss about." All right for her mother who had had a hysterectomy before she was thirty. And anyway it was her mother who made the fuss. Her mother who taught her to creep down from her bedroom when everyone else was asleep, to burn the evidence on the fire in the dark, tip-toeing so she should not wake her father, would not have to invent a sudden thirst or hunger to explain her midnight wanderings about his house. It was imperative that he should not know. She had started wearing Tampax not for her own comfort, but for the sake of more perfect secrecy. So her father should not know that the blood curse was on his house and on his possessions.

At least with Ian the secrecy was gone. Ian replaced it with a curiosity. She remembered him fascinated, taking apart one of her Tampax, his long fingers exploring it with an innocent interest. But now they were back, trapped in the secrecy. It was different, it was not shameful, but for four or five days she struggled not to remind him, burying the cardboard tubes in the bottom of the kitchen garbage. He was equally careful not to remind her, not to ask, not to see. The fact was too painful, each felt, for the other to have to confront. They each confronted it alone.

But by Thursday she was feeling better again. She particularly enjoyed now the day the bleeding stopped. She felt as though her womb was somehow virgin again, that anything might happen, that matters were returned to her own hands. She knew that was a delusion: there is no stopping and starting, only a circle. Virgin or whore. Lesbian, mother, engine-driver, or all three: the process seeks no consent. Her womb will fill again with baby fodder, just as her mother used to keep the larder well-stocked "just in case." Her hormones will start doing their interior decorating in her uterus. The mucus in the cervix will soften. Nothing will change anything. But for a moment or two nothing happens; there is a resting time.

She gets a real pleasure from marking her temperature on her chart and seeing the line start moving forward into the future again, away from the failure of last month and into the possible.

So she sat at the women's meeting, pleased with herself and with the group. The discussion was gentle, not strongly directed; but in her sense of passivity she liked that. She was happy. She felt that the others were very warm to her tonight too, although she was not sure why. Nancy always kissed her when they met, but now she was sitting at her feet, and kept turning her face up to smile at Liz, and petting her knees. Even Mary-Ann seemed kindlier; perhaps she was sorry for the sharpness she had used when Liz tried to describe the débâcle of her attempts to make contact with the women at the clinic. They had fought about that last week; Paula agreeing with her that it was extremely difficult to challenge a medical authority who was actually treating you, describing her experience with the children's doctor. But Mary-Ann, and Jane too, insisting that the difficulty was easily overcome if you were strong-minded and clear about it. Nancy told them one more time about her battle, and success, in demanding a home delivery when Hugh was born. But today they let things go, gentle and warm towards her. She basked contentedly in the love and fondness that she felt but could not describe.

She enjoyed Jane's spiky humour and tactical exaggerations: Jane was trying to read to them from an article in some Trade Unionist magazine in which a stalwart miner explained that women's liberation is a middle-class, bourgeois phenomenon, that from the nineteenth century, and still today, the working-class movement has taken pride in its ability to protect women from the outrageous conditions of work. Keeping them out of the mines is, far from putting them down, a sign of their respect. Men are prepared to suffer to see women freed from that sort of gross and dangerous exploitation.

Liz could tell from the way that Jane read, that she liked the man, sensed him as friendly, though deluded. Jane laughs and proclaims that it is in the exceptions that the anti-discrimination laws allow, that society has confirmed its view of sex rôles. "Women can't be miners, men can't be midwives. You see, they are very important, they epitomise everything. The miner, alone and virile in his black shaft, challenges the ferocity of the unknown world of nature in his noble fight for energy. The work-stained, danger-hardened warrior who has made this nation great. And on the other hand we see the sweet, clean, uniformed girl whose high vocation it is to bring to fruition the rich harvest of seed sown in the fertile Mother Earth. The tender servant of the Real Woman who brings forth sons from her modest loins, in the calm chamber of love and joy."

Nancy said, "But I'd always want a woman midwife."

Liz is mainly impressed by Jane's verbal dexterity. She knew that she had not practised that in advance; it is an accomplishment to pull off a sentence like that. Professionally she speculated about whether Jane could write. Usually it annoyed her the way Jane could let style dominate content, when her exaggerations led away from any connection with truth, but now she enjoyed it.

The meeting meandered on. Paula was upset about something at her children's school, but the general mood of the evening mitigated against anger or confrontation. They comforted Paula with jokes and fondness. They consented to coffee, and humour and sympathy. The meeting began to break up.

Jane said, "Hang on a moment, I almost forgot. What's the matter with me?"

"Forgot what?"

"I was talking to the abortion demo organisers, and they are desperate for help with the last mailing."

Nancy said, "Well if there's anything I can do at home, let me know. I could squeeze the time."

"Actually I went a bit further than that, but you can all back off if you want to. I said we might give over a meeting to doing it for them. At the office. It will have to be next week if it's going to be any good for them."

Paula said, "Well I should think I could get a sitter if it's important."

Mary-Ann said, "I think it's a great idea. Good for us to do something other than talk our mouths off. And this is important."

Alice said, "Yeah, okay. It will be a big drag getting down there now. We West End trendies can't approve this mass exodus to the East you know. Where are they, Clerkenwell or somewhere impossible?"

"Hardly impossible."

"Well I know, but three years ago you never had to go East of Covent Garden, and now you practically have to trek to Kent to get anything done at all. I'm joking, of course we'll go. It's easy for me as a car owner anyway. Hey, Liz, do you want a lift?"

Liz felt paralysed. How could she go and rally women to the cause of abortion? How could these friends of hers forget her pain? "Look," she said, "count me out this time. I don't think I want to be involved."

"What do you mean? You don't want to be involved . . . in the biggest thing the Women's Movement has put on the streets for years? You can't not want to be involved. You have to be."

Trapped, she snapped, "Have to be. Have to be. Okay, Paula, you teach me the party line. Tell me, what do we do with dissidents?"

Jane chirped quickly, "Ninety-four years' minimum in the salt mines," but not quickly enough.

Paula turned round, stung. "Jesus, what was that for?"

And Mary-Ann weighed in. "Right. What is this aggression? Leaving that aside, are we allowed to ask for some rationale for not putting in three measly hours for the most important feminist platform that we've got?"

"I just don't want to, I can't, I . . . I've spent the last year telling you . . . Christ, I'm just not into abortion, right now, okay?" She did not want to blackmail them with tears, the easy access to sympathy and tenderness within the group, but she could feel the prickling behind her eyes. It was not fair, they could easily go without her, let her alone on this. She was alone. She deserved their support. They should not bend their collective will against her like this. She wanted them to love her.

"Look, you can easily do without me. It won't make any difference." She was beginning to apologise. "I'm sorry, I know I ought to, of course I ought to, but really I don't want to, I don't want to know anything about it, about the demo or anything."

She could not escape it. When she had carefully proposed to take their holiday in July, even Ian had said, "But that will include the weekend of the abortion demo." And although he had looked kindly at her, he would not let her off marching, not without heavy implications. And these women, who claimed that they loved her, would bring the same moral pressure to bear, be a good feminist, be a good sister.

It was an old, old pressure. Be a good child and Daddy will love you. Be a good woman, giving and giving and giving, having no needs of your own except making your man feel good and James will love you. Now, support this march and we will love you and listen to you. Don't, and we won't. Moral blackmail. Not meant like that. They just couldn't understand how the pictures of the anti-abortionists with the tiny perfect feet held in the huge cruel hand, made her feel sick with disgust, how Mary-Ann's gruesome descriptions of the abortion process made her consider cyanide as a reasonable weapon. Be good and we will love you. Be Liz, be yourself and we will withdraw that love, and you will be cold and naked and die, barren, cursed, unloved.

Alice said, quite gently, "Liz, love, you don't have to be into abortion, right here and now for yourself today, to realise why you have to support this demo, not just with a reluctant march, but with your time and energy. Right now I feel like you do, but politicise, woman, politicise. If I can go and address envelopes next week, so can you."

"What do you mean?" Even inside her frozen isolation she

could not miss the sudden mounting of tension from the others.

Jane, who was already halfway into her jacket, stopped and took it off, turning back into the group. Paula shrugged and started to collect the coffee mugs, while Mary-Ann backed away from the group. Alice stood there, slightly pink and Nancy reached up so that her hands were on Liz's shoulders, restraining or comforting.

"What is this?" Liz felt frightened, suddenly, under quite a different pressure from that of a few minutes before. Now pressure to join them again, to know what was happening and why this embarrassment and withdrawal.

Nancy said, "Liz, Alice is pregnant."

A sudden overwhelming surge of relief that it is not something that she has done wrong. Following that, the pain which they had all known she would feel. And a sense of exclusion because obviously they had all known and had been keeping the news from her.

"Really?" she said, looking for time, unable to stand the careful silence of the others.

"Really. About twelve or thirteen weeks. Liz, I'm sorry."

Alice began to cry. Jane put her arms round her, Nancy tightened the pressure on Liz's shoulders.

Liz said to Nancy, "How long have you known? How long have you all known and not told me?"

"Just this week, honestly. Just this week. We were planning to tell you tonight. We just didn't know how."

So that was why she had felt their love coming out to her, not an approval of her but an apology. She did not want their sodding sympathy. She had to deflect that.

She asked Alice, "What are you going to do?"

"Have it, of course." Alice looked up from her sniffles. "Now we're talking about it, I may as well say that I am utterly thrilled. I've been thinking about it, well, you all know I have, been thinking I'm over thirty and ought to soon if I was going to. I noticed I was getting slovenly about contraception. I reckon that's a good clue. So I stopped making an effort. I wasn't going to let it happen to me by mistake anyway."

"Who's the father?" It was a sexist question, but she had to keep talking, fill in the silences.

"No one that matters. I could say none of your business. I don't think it's much of my business either, certainly it's none of his."

"How brave." She meant how unfair, that Alice could just be pregnant, so casually. She had manoeuvred her whole life, made patterns, woven spells for this.

Alice said, "I wanted to tell you, I wanted you to know. I want everyone in the world to know. I don't even know if it's the right thing to do but I sure as hell know it is what I am going to do. Liz, I'm sorry."

"Christ, Alice, don't be sorry. I appreciate your concern, but I would hate to think that you were spoiling your happiness for me. I mean that. Just because I . . . I want something I can't get . . . I . . . it doesn't mean that other people should be prevented from exercising their choices. Really."

Mary-Ann said, "There you are, that's what the abortion demo is about then."

Alice, Jane and Nancy all said, almost simultaneously, "Shut up."

Liz just went on looking at Alice. There was nothing to look at, she looked just the same, there was no sign of the growing baby, no sign of a swelling. Perhaps they were making it up, perhaps they thought it was funny to test her reactions. She knew that was not true.

"What does it feel like?" She wanted to be close to the feelings, to learn the appropriate emotions so that she could share them, could know how to feel.

"Nauseous. Though that's going off now. But that's the main feeling. And pleasure, and worry that I won't be able to pull it off, that something will go wrong. But mostly nauseous."

"You don't have to make it sound bad so that I won't be hurt."

"Liz, that never occurred to me."

"Thank you." Now she wanted to get out, be alone, not have to talk about it anymore. That was enough. She said, "Congratulations. I mean that. About next Thursday, I'm not convinced. I'll think it through, okay? I've got to go now."

She could sense the relief of the group. A delicate situation worked through to the credit of all of them. No scenes, no grief. Free women who exercise free choices and love their friends.

She walked out alone, down the steps and on to the street. She thought about buses and tubes and what the time was and the fact that it was too far to walk home. Nancy caught up with her before she reached the corner.

"Liz."

"No."

"Come on, love."

"No."

"Don't be an ass. You did very well back in there."

"Thank you."

A pause. "You should have told me."

"If I had you wouldn't have come to the meeting. Anyway it wasn't my business to tell you."

"Have you all been cackling over the phone all week?"

"Yes. But only because we love you."

"Oh, fuck off, Nancy. I've had a shitty day and I just don't want to talk about it now."

"Well then, we'll talk about the abortion march thing."

"No. And No and No."

"Yes. Because you are wrong, and you know it."

"Look, I told you. I don't see why I should be morally blackmailed by your disapproval. I don't want to talk about it now."

"Well I do. Why is your wish more meaningful than mine?"

"Because. Because it is based on pain. How's that? Because I'm under enough pressure anyway without being pressured by your abundant love of chatter, into turning out and marching with a whole bunch of women who want . . ."

"Go on, say it. Who want to what?"

"You know what. Now look, I don't care how well you mean,

will you get off my back, I'll ring you tomorrow. You know how
I feel, stop trying to justify yourself."

"Okay then, I'll say it for you. A whole bunch of women who
want to control their own bodies and have the medical profession service their own decisions. Right?"

She could not help smiling. "Yes, right. And very clever. Yes
of course, for God's sake. But you know perfectly well that that
is just words, you can't catch me there. You bloody know that it
is not as simple as that."

"It is as simple as that. It's only your subjectivity that is putting the problems in. Can't you see that this is your personal particular fight? You can't expect us to listen and love for hours
about how the medicos fuck you around and try to impose their
interpretation of your life on to you, and how they make physical things into massive morality games, and then not support the
most active feminist lobby demanding the same thing. Everyone
ought to be at this demo: gays, mothers, childbirth specialists,
and you because abortion is just a tiny part of that whole right
to decide for yourself, to make choices about what uses you will
make of your own body. It's about the one thing that anyone has
a right to call their own. Mary-Ann's choice to abort, is the same
choice as Jane's to screw other women, or Paula's to screw no
one, or yours, mine and Alice's to have babies. That is all one. I
want to see this July thing come off, be the biggest thing that
women have put on the street, just because it is such a clear and
simple issue."

"And so to the barricades."

"Bitch. Yes it was a bit of oration, wasn't it? But I want to
separate it from your personal reaction to Alice having a baby."

"How do you feel about that anyway?" So easy to get Nancy
to talk about her own feelings.

"Well, honestly, a bit odd. I'm glad because it's what she
wants, but I think she's fantastically naive about what it is like
actually to have a baby, and on her own. I hate the thought of
her trapped on Social Security, and run into the ground by the
sheer mechanics of baby-care. I don't think she's really thought

it out. I know Paula thinks that too, and we're the ones who know. Then funnily, I'm actually jealous. I'm jealous, because I like being pregnant and don't realistically see my way to being so again. And I like being the Mummy expert, and I feel challenged. Also, and this is weird, I resent that she should get away with it so easily. You know, I'm married and I put up with a lot of hassles, and frustrations and say that they're necessary if you want to have a kid. And then Alice cuts through all that, and just gets pregnant. I hate the thought of her coming home free. Which is not very edifying."

"I think it's quite sweet actually. I'm glad you said it. It sort of legitimises my own feelings of spite and meanness. But surely you can see then, that it isn't a question of pure politics, abortion, right to choose, right to kill, right to life. Slogan, counter slogan. Blah, blah, blah. There is an emotional content. Not just this issue but all of them."

"I never said there wasn't an emotional content. The personal is the political and so on. I wouldn't want to deny that. All I'm saying is, of course I understand your ambivalence because I share it. Much easier, oddly, for me to support Mary-Ann's nth abortion than Alice's pregnancy, because that's no threat to me. I am saying, analyse that ambivalence, don't privatise it. God, I must get myself hired out as slogan maker to the movement. Analyse, don't privatise."

Liz laughs, eased now in herself. "Why do you think God made your eyes, to analyse."

"Very good, but don't dodge." They know each other's tricks too well. "Politicise rhymes in there too. That's the point. You mustn't let yourself make it only private, because that way you just fall into their hands. Let them split up issues and women, accepting their control. Conforming."

"Nance, listen, something you probably can't understand. Like tonight, if they laid down terms for this baby, I'd buy. You don't understand how badly . . . I know it's 'wrong,' 'bad feminism,' that stuff, but if I was persuaded that conforming to some doctor's feminine ideal would get me pregnant, I'd conform."

They had walked down to Notting Hill Gate, there were more people on the street, conversation was more difficult. Trying to keep the close contact they stopped walking and stood facing each other, trying to keep their eyes off the sight and movement all around them, but it was harder. Nancy touched the collar of Liz's jacket, and said, "I just don't believe that. It was good tonight at the meeting, I could feel you lapping it up. You couldn't do without that and you know it. You are here now. Next Thursday you'll be at that office. Come July you'll march. Okay?"

"Yes, ma'am."

Nancy stuck her tongue out at her playfully. Liz glanced at her watch, worrying about the late tubes. They were separating, easily but inevitably. But Liz was immensely glad and relieved that she had let Nancy bring the whole thing out.

On the tube she sang silently, "Don't privatise, analyse, politicise, collectivise, civilise." She felt warmed all through and looked forward to seeing Ian. Briefly she was genuinely glad for Alice, although she did not know how she would tell Ian without arousing his sympathy. She did not want their sympathy; not his, not Nancy's, not the others'. She wanted their strength. And their love.

Mary has achieved this conception of will and faith and love. Now she is frightened at herself, at the power she has found within herself, frightened by her own potency. She cannot bear to be alone. It is impossible for her to be alone. And miraculously, naturally, there is another woman to share this with her. At, once, with great haste, she goes rushing off to visit an elderly relative.

Poor Elizabeth. The family have been saying this for years, not without the usual modicum of relish. She is in her fifties now. Even her patient hormones which for forty-odd years have monthly prepared the perfect support system for her child—a warm red resting-place, a playground where gravity has been delightfully denied, a warm water swimming pool for the longed-for infant—even her hormones have abandoned hope and her, packed in the job, given up in despair. And menopause has not treated her kindly; her complexion has collapsed quickly and her breasts are withering, while round the hips she is putting on weight. Poor Elizabeth, she has the slight eccentricities of barren women. There is no firm link between her and her contemporaries; there is nothing to persuade her to conform to their standards; there are no children exercising that subtle criticism and softly named need that keeps so many mothers in line. Not only is poor Elizabeth really going a little mad, now her husband has suffered some sort of stroke—how embarrassing, and at work too—and he is struck with total aphasia: can't say a word and quite likely his brain is touched too. Poor Elizabeth. The beauty of the family once, the olive skin and strong features carried with a serenity and confidence it was difficult not to be convinced by. And now she is putting on weight at a ridiculous rate and even babbling about pregnancy. Her family know better than that; she need not hope to recapture attention; she is passed over. Poor Elizabeth.

It is Elizabeth whom Mary needs now. Mary knows that she must see her, now. Mary believes her. She knows. If she is pregnant then there is no reason why Elizabeth should not be. In fact she is. Mary knows that they must be together, these unconventional women, hold together, strengthen one another, explain to one another. Already they are having trouble with the family. The gossips have put their heads together. Elizabeth can easily be dismissed as insane, the moon madness from which childless women suffer when it is too late for hope and they know they will have to go down to their graves with the barely concealed mockery and scorn echoing across the barren desert of their flesh. And Mary: well, she had always held herself above them, so abstracted and silent and unattractively opinionated, so uninterested in the vital petty concerns of village life. There was real juice in her fall from virtue, real meat to feed on from the flesh of her disgrace. The fingers were out, pointing and poking. Even the most loving cannot be pleased by this behaviour, by these two women. Too young, too old. Husbandless, a husband who has passed all usefulness. Too fertile, too barren. Too much not exactly like everyone else. The terrain of their lives open to the ploughs, to the viciousness of the folk who claim to love them.

But there in one another's arms, and only there, they are affirmed, encouraged, borne up, freed. Elizabeth feels her baby drumming, drumming inside her, like a butterfly in a tantrum, and she knows he is real, not an evil growth of mind or gut, but her child. And in the arms of her friend, her sister, within the strength of another woman Mary conceives again: the flowering of the great song of praise and power and triumph, the love song that unites her not just to Elizabeth but to all the other difficult women everywhere and everywhen. The mighty are cast down, the humble exalted. The hungry are filled, the proud smashed and the slaves freed. The horse and the warrior are cast into the sea. The pilgrim people of Israel walk dryshod through the sea, and the women go out with tambourines, singing and dancing. Swords are melted down into ploughshares, and spears into pruning hooks. And still the strong women cling together. The children in their wombs are pressed closer to each other and whisper that the triumph of their mothers is not complete, that there is much more to come and most of it will be bad. But the women hold one another, empowered by one another they declare for the new order, together they feel and sing and love themselves towards the new Jerusalem.

3. JUNE

She made Ian come with her to the party. She thought about it for some time, but decided the horror for him would be less than the horror for her without him. Ian hated large parties, she knew his fear of them was genuine.

When she first knew him he would refuse point blank to go, and if forced would hide in corners, unable to talk to anyone, and drink or smoke dope until he was oblivious. He was not antisocial, he loved to be with other people in small groups, loved to talk through the night, spin webs of conversation, hated to be alone for long periods of time, but he did not like parties. She had made him go sometimes, and now he was much better. He did not like it but it would not hurt him.

This was a launch party for one of her authors. The reason why she wanted Ian there was because she was embarrassed and miserable about the whole thing, and knowing she had no professional need to be only made things worse. During her first flush of real enthusiasm for having a baby she had haunted circles where babies and mothers were likely to be found. Among other people she had met a young New Zealander who was engaged in the home delivery fight. Amanda had been energetic and clever and extremely well-informed, and everything she had said about childbirth, maternal bonding and non-interference by the medical profession had struck Liz with a surprising and welcome warmth. This was going to be *her* book, the book that she would be needing. Amanda had not wanted to write a book; Liz had been urgent, insistent, compulsive. She had nursed the book and Amanda in the face of Tony's indifference. She had forcibly extracted outlines and sample chapters, she had even engaged herself in research, she had pounded round publishers pouring out her eagerness. She had sold the book, she had kept Amanda working and now it was obviously going to be a success. She hated it. While even Tony was delighted and Amanda grateful, she thought it was a sentimentalised glorification of motherhood, slick, cheap, easy. And she thought Amanda was a crashing bore. She could not say so, Amanda was her baby, everyone congratulated her on her perception, her competence. There was no getting out of the party, but she made Ian come with her.

It was the very worst sort of party. No one there for pleasure or company, only for what they could get, judging their chances, planning how they would relate to the book. At least there was booze, she knew in advance she would get drunk.

Tony greeted her on arrival. "I was wrong, I apologise. Aren't I magnanimous?" He gave her a hug—quite unnecessary, he would never do so at the office. He was high on self-importance and pleasure. This was what he liked best, parties like this where people would notice him as a man who ran a good firm, small but not unimportant. The waves of excitement came off him physically, they made him very attractive. "Liz, we ought to do more of this stuff; I haven't used you and your connections enough to generate the right sort of feminist stuff, the market is still wide open for that, for the right people, the right books. You are waking me up." She loved him, loved working for him, his energy, his gossip, his blend of self-assertion and lack of self-confidence, but she did not like the evening, she wanted to be at home. She got a drink and looked round for Ian, she could not see him, if he had gone to hide in the loo she would kill him. She knew she had to talk to Amanda and wound her way through the crowd looking for her. Of course there was nothing personal in her dislike of the book—only that it was not as good as it could have been.

Amanda was looking excited, her long hair falling forward over her face and giving her a frail look, which, while out of character with the toughness of the book, did serve to emphasise the fact that she was pregnant. She had four children already, the older two were there—blond, well-behaved, charming. Like her husband, a well-known field biologist. They were too bloody perfect for words, it made her sick. He studied the mating habits of migratory birds—maybe they should get a popular book off him too.

In all honesty she knew it was the four children, the swelling in Amanda's belly that made her angry; the complacency of the book, the serene assumption of initiation into the sacred cult of motherhood. Already Alice, with her pregnancy hardly showing, carried that casual mystery, like a caste mark of superiority. It was easy for Jane, gay and uninterested, to tease Alice about the Real Womanly Woman, the bearer of the children. Liz believed it.

Resentment and jealousy filled her; she wanted to attack. She smiled. "Hi. How goes it?"

"Liz, how nice. Well this seems to be going okay."

"Sure. I promised you. What is the next book going to be?"

"Not yet, not yet. I've got to get this little horror out of the way first." She patted her bulge affectionately. "It's all right for you. Late pregnancy always makes me feel stupid, you know, cow-like and contented. I can't imagine ever writing another word. This winter perhaps. I feel so vast and wallowy at the moment."

Liz wanted to say, "You look it." She wanted to hit her. Apart from all else there was that ghastly, grating antipodean accent. She did not look vast and wallowy and she knew that she did not; it was the sort of remark she felt it appropriate to make in the face of Real Feminists. The kindly pretence that there was, of course, another acceptable way of life, although she herself did not believe it. God, Liz thought, I really am cracking up, and she reached for another drink from a passing tray.

Obsession. The eating away of rationality: nibble, nibble, nibble. Swelling up inside like a cancer, distorting her body.

Her father had had a number of friends who were nuns. Her mother had never liked them. "Women who don't have children, who repress that whole side of themselves are never normal, not really."

"Rubbish," said her father, "there are always compensations."

"That's because you're a man, Edward. Look at history. Look at Mary Tudor."

Mary Tudor had filled her belly with desire and envy. Had poured out blood to create the blood her child needed to live on. Her sister Elizabeth must have watched and decided there and then that she would never risk that loss and pain. Mary's will was stronger—she filled her belly with desire, enflamed the country with her desire, lit Latimer and Ridley's candle with the strength of her longing. Mistress Mary, they sung on the streets, how does your garden grow? And pilgrims carried their cockleshells all the way to Jerusalem, bells jingling in every church in the land, young women forced into childless but holy lives processed in neat rows to yet another mass, and still her garden did not grow with the rich fruit she wanted. She submitted herself to contempt and to ravages from a man as rapacious and far less charming than her own huge, jovial father, and still God did not forgive her. Until she no longer cared, until the hatred and bitterness were enough to fill her and round her out to what she knew was her proper shape. She loved the cancer like a child, when it kicked and gnawed at her she was contented. She would bring bitterness and fear and hatred to birth if she could not bear the child.

Liz was frightened. She would not forgive her mother for that remark. She would not forgive Amanda. She looked round, saw Ian at last and beckoned him over. At least Amanda should know that she too had a husband, more beautiful, more interesting than a biologist with a tan and a cheap smile.

"Ian, this is my author."

"Yes. How do you do. I liked your book."

"Did you really read it?"

Ian liked that and grinned. "Do you doubt me?"

"Well, I certainly doubt that all the men who have told me tonight that they like my book have really read it. Why should I make an exception for you?"

"Because I happen to be interested in the subject. Childbirth and parenthood aren't the exclusive prerogative of women, even if pregnancy is."

"Oh, I'm glad you think that. I try to draw on that in the book."

"I know, I've read it. I told you. I found that emphasis rather exciting, especially those pictures, the tenderness of that couple together, and some nice ones of a guy and his baby in the bath together. That seemed like something I could really get into, really want for myself."

Liz could not avoid Amanda's despising glance. A woman who would deprive her man of such a pleasure, just to further her career! She felt terribly threatened. Amanda said to Ian, "If you want it, you should have children, it's very simple." Liz knew that Amanda was trying to get Ian to side against her, luring Ian into a little tight knot against her: and this woman called herself a feminist.

Ian said, still smiling—how dare he? It went beyond the necessary bounds of politeness—"They can't always be had for the asking, you know."

"You must ask harder then." Amanda pushed back her pretty hair and looked up at Ian. The gesture lost some of its point because he was so small, it would work better with her hulking spouse.

She needed another drink. She didn't have to listen while Ian told this woman his wife was barren. Let them flirt, she would not care. She found a drink, and found Tony. She leaned against him affectionately, wondered vaguely how much he fancied her. Quite a lot probably in a restrained sort of way, she might be able to respond to that. She tried to focus on the party. Looked back at him and said, "A goodie."

"Yep. Of course it's good being guests at these things, let the publishers do the work and foot the bill. Much less effort."

"We could have a party ourselves. For our gang. Make them feel we love them all."

"Sure. Look, why don't you chat up Graham Forthwell. He's never cared much for me, but they have a pretty good list and we ought to know them better."

"How could anyone not care for you?"

"Fi on you, flattery will not get you a raise. Actually his wife is an ex-mistress of mine."

"Bloody literary in-scene. Really? Is she here?"

"Bloody literary fringe parasites who feed on our gossip. No, she's not here, she's just had a baby."

"Everybody in the bloody world seems to have just had a baby but me."

"Oh dear, I'm sorry."

"Forget it. How do you feel about your ex-mistress having someone else's baby?"

"Weird actually. I don't care about her, but I'm still jealous, as though it ought to be my baby. When we were living together she had an abortion. I mean, I encouraged that and wanted and indeed paid, but now I feel as though she killed my baby to have his. Unreasonable, you may well say, but true. But, to work, my friend, the good literary agent is never at rest."

Taking another drink she went over and congratulated Graham Forthwell on the birth of his child. Drew him into continuing chat.

She observes herself: a witty slip of a girl, just old enough to have authority, to be worth time. She is rather charming and very chic: tight trousers into long boots, embroidered jacket, short cute hairstyle, quick. She accepts this man's appraisal, knows she will do better with him than Tony, even without the unfortunate past. He finds her charming.

Her father had found her bouncy attentions charming as long as they were directed at him. When she was fifteen she started to read books he had not read, have friends he did not know, ideas he did not share. He withdrew his approval: she had betrayed him. They hated each other. "Just a phase," said her mother to both of them, "it will come out right in the end." It never had a chance to come out right. Now she still wanted the approval of fathers. She tried to beguile this man into approving her, briefly creating herself as a child with the admiration of an older man. Not much older, actually, but powerful, male, and finding her charming.

She takes another cigarette out of her bag, leans forward for him to light it. She must not be child only, not enough for a man whose first son is right now lying on his wife's breast. She must be the free woman who he lost nine months ago.

She pulled herself together. She must be drunker than she reckoned. She did not have to seduce him just in order to persuade him to buy manuscripts that were not even written. She was embarrassed, turned away from him slightly, looked for another drink.

Ian is still talking to Amanda. They are standing at the other side of the room talking to each other at a level of reality with which she cannot compete. She has only a brief glance as the other party guests shift, but in that glance, Liz sees Amanda take Ian's hand in her own pink one and place it flat on her stretched belly, and Ian's face lights up with a grin of simple pleasure, tender and amused. Amanda takes her hand away but Ian leaves his lingering there. The people move again, Graham Forthwell commands her attention, she cannot see them any more.

Ian had been shattered by years of public loos and brutality when she had met him. She was going to be his saviour. She had had a sense of romantic mission, which all her shame had not diminished. She was going to introduce him to health and normality and joy. And it was she who was abnormal. She who had promised him so much, was not able to come through with the goods. He wanted to push a pram in the park, he wanted to sprinkle baby powder on his warm and naked daughter, he wanted to sit in a delivery room and put his arms round her and say, "Come on, darling, of course you can do it." He wanted to be a father. A few months ago they had watched a television programme about natural childbirth. The father in the film played softly on a guitar during the early stages of the labour. Later the pace had hotted up, both of them had been sweating with excitement and hard work. The woman had worn glasses, she had wanted to keep them on so she could see what was happening, and the man had taken them off and wiped them and slid them gently back on again. At the end, the baby—born, washed, fed, wrapped—had been tucked away and the couple had sunk into each other's arms, giggling with relief, and pride and simple pleasure. Liz and Ian had watched in compulsive silence. The moment the film was over Liz had jumped up, turned the machine off sharply and said, "I expect it isn't really like that. That has got to be a sentimentalisation." Then she had looked at Ian and he was crying.

She abandoned her publisher as abruptly as she could without him noticing her sudden change of mood. She went back to the bar needing more drink. Tony was there talking to someone; she leaned against him and he put his arm round her shoulders; simple comfort and she knew he had sensed her distress. He held her as tightly as he could without anyone being able to notice.

"Hello sweetie, how are you doing?"

"Drunk," she said. It was near enough to being true.

"How very unprofessional. This is my drunk partner," he said to the woman he was talking to.

"Assistant," Liz said.

"I didn't know you were married, Tony," the woman said to him.

"No, no. Liz is married to someone quite different. Professional partner." Liz guessed he was trying to impress this woman as the bright liberal who promotes young women to partners in his firm. She was not going to let him get away with that. She said, "You can't be a partner without collateral. I'm saving up."

The woman smiled and asked her what she thought of Amanda's book, and introduced herself as the secretary of some childbirth group.

Tony said, "It's Liz's book, nearly as much as it's Amanda's. She created it, dragged it into the world."

"Do you have children yourself?" the woman asked.

"No."

She just wanted to go home. There did not seem to her much to add to this conversation, but the woman was determined.

"But you are married?"

"Yes."

"You should have children, you know. As soon as possible. Don't worry about the money side of it."

"I don't."

This had to be a nightmare. She looked carefully at the woman, expensively dressed, middle-aged, a goddam crusader. Her shoulder nudged at Tony, but he was already looking round for someone else to beguile, now Liz was engaged with this not-unimportant woman. The only possible good thing is that they were standing beside the bar. The woman was in full flood.

"Really, you know, you cannot imagine how fulfilling it is. Mine are older now, of course, but such a delight. You younger women seem to think that motherhood is a step down or something, such a mistake. I must say it is the one thing I have against women's libbers. You have such a chance to show the world the fullest glory of womanhood and you seem to be passing up the opportunity. For what, just to work for your charming Tony. When my husband and I were in Hong Kong I used to notice, those native women are so serene, you know, when they have children, such a richness of giving which I suppose can only come out of their simplicity, their freedom from materialism."

"Do you mean their poverty?" Liz interrupted. She meant it to sound aggressive, but her voice was drowned in the flood of this woman's enthusiasm.

Last time she had been to the clinic she had realised her mistake in asking Dr. Marshall about group therapy, now if she even talked to the women there, he would accuse her of disobedience. She felt Big Daddy watching her. But she looked at the women with curiosity, smiling every time she caught someone's eye, and getting back an assortment of expressions from fear to blandness. She thought they all looked strained. But on the bus coming home she had watched a woman, with a baby on her lap, slap quite savagely at the legs of her older son, only because he wanted to kneel up and look out the window. It was not fair to try and persuade herself that a child brought serenity and giving to London women anyway whatever they might do in the distant East. She refused to be duped by this woman, or by her own grief. She tried to listen again.

The woman had returned from the Orient and was back on the subject of Liz's job.

"But if you find it creative to be a midwife to other people's literary work, only think how much more creative to bring your own into the world. The parallel between childbirth and art is not a new one, but I think it is an image women should do more to claim for themselves: the creative artists, the real artists of our society. What is a Mona Lisa compared to a newborn baby?"

"I never cared much for the Mona Lisa myself," said Liz desperately. "When I first saw it in the Louvre I distinctly remember a real feeling of let-down. It had been built up into the great art experience of Western civilisation, and I just felt bitterly disappointed. Do you think that could be to do with the way that it's hung there? Or is the disappointment inevitable?"

"There you are, you see, but you would not feel that disappointment about your own child. Especially with a birth procedure which allows a real natural bonding between mother and child. You can notice how mothers with that real bonding never want to hand them over to some nursery at six months, to rush back to some boring job."

"I don't think that takes account of the economic and social realities, really."

"And of course that creative process goes on, right through infancy at the least. 'Give me a child till he's seven.' I really don't understand why you libbers have so demoted motherhood: it is the linking experience for women of every country, right through all human history. Properly understood, motherhood could be the great force for peace and liberty in the world. You see I'm not apolitical, but first and foremost it is the great fulfilling experience for any woman. All you skinny young things don't seem to realise that it is the pregnant woman who has the real shape of femininity as any anthropologist will tell you—look at those clay figurines." A little smile. "Compare yourself with, say Amanda. Who looks more womanly?"

The woman had to be drunk, or else she was so drunk she was hallucinating. No one could talk like this to someone they had never met before. She did not understand why she bothered to smile, why she said politely, "Well, it is not always so simple you know."

"Of course it's simple. If you think the difficulty is your husband, I'm sure you'll find he'll come round to the idea once you're pregnant. They always do, but men are so selfish. Although I support all their aims of course, it does worry me that women's lib seems to want to share precisely that selfishness which is the very worst thing about men." She gave Liz what Liz assumed was meant to be a conspiratorial wink, "Come now, admit it. It really is just selfishness and material greed that makes you unwilling to start on the greatest adventure of a woman's life."

All right then, you old cow. "Actually, no. In my case it seems to be more a matter of my hypothalmic glands."

"Sorry?"

She was too tired now to inflict embarrassment on this unspeakable woman, too tired even to be rude. She said, "Well, I shall have to think about all this. I will say though that I don't think you'll be able to persuade me that motherhood is the mystic be-all and end-all of any woman's life."

She would not need to be persuaded, she already believed it. Damn the bloody woman, damn her to hell. Damn herself as well. She had brought this on her own head—she had launched Amanda on the world as this week's Real Woman from the Women's Movement.

"I have to go," she said, and resisted a last-minute temptation to stick a handy sausage stick from the bar into the shored-up bosom. The corseting would probably have broken the stick anyway.

Selfish. She had heard it before. It was the easy, the cheap insult to throw at people who did not want to have children. Even wanting to she felt it as unfair. Her mother said it.

Last Christmas when they had been there, she had refused to leave the subject of children alone, had trapped Liz in the kitchen, her hands covered in pastry, escape impossible and lectured her.

"I don't understand you. You had such a happy, loving childhood, you know you did. I don't understand how you can be so selfish. I'm sure Ian wants a son. Please, Liz, do think about it. It gets harder as you get older you know. And you will regret it, I know you will. If I could I would have had more children. You just can't imagine the joy they give you, and how I felt deprived."

She did not remember the great joy she had given her mother; instead she had deprived her of her son. She had torn her way so violently into the world that her mother was never able to have any more children. She could not forgive her mother for throwing that in her face. She did not want her mother's pity, she wanted still to condemn her.

"Mummy, there are other things in life than children you know. Ian and I can decide for ourselves what we, as a couple, want. Honestly, it just is not your business." Her hands attacked the pastry with such ferocity that it would arrive on the table as heavy as lead, but her mother, pressing at the soil round the base of one of her pot-plants, and refusing to look at Liz, embarrassed, feeling morally obliged to speak openly, would not listen to her appeal.

"It is selfish. Ian says, to me if he dare not say to you, that he wants children." (Traitor, she thought, she would kill him for giving her mother one weapon in the struggle.) "Think of your father, Liz, if you won't think of Ian and me. He would have loved grandchildren." Liz muttered into the mixing bowl. "What did you say, Liz?"

"I said, 'He's dead, Mummy.' It doesn't matter any more what he would or would not have wanted."

Her mother left the kitchen in tears, but she would not be blackmailed by her dead father, she would no longer act just to gain his approval, just to supply him with the son she had failed to be.

Ian and she both left the party drunk.

"You fancied her." She tried to tease Ian about Amanda.

"Well, I certainly didn't fancy him."

"Who?"

"Her healthy husband."

"But you did fancy her."

"No. But I think I fancied the idea of fancying her."

"That's casuistry."

"You think? I don't. But I like the idea of myself being able to fancy earth mother types like that."

"You can't be an earth mother if you're only five foot two."

"That's definitely masculist thinking. We've colonised your mind. Your earth mother corresponds to some masculine ideal, six feet tall and Amazonian. My ideal earth mother is more quintessentially feminine."

"Be serious."

"I can't be serious if you're seriously asking me if I fancied her."

"I saw you, you did."

"How could I? You can't make love to someone that shape, can you? If I fancied her, which I do deny, it's my subconscious fear of women rearing their ugly heads again. I fancy a seven-months pregnant woman—very impractical. And I fancy a married woman."

"Who?"

"You."

"Oh, idiot child."

But she woke up in the night, and knew that he was awake beside her. "Ian, what is it?"

"Nothing." She could hear his voice trying to steady itself.

"It's not nothing."

"Liz, she took my hand and held it so I had to feel that baby kicking. You could feel it moving. She put my hand right down, I was almost scared I'd feel her pubic hair, and said, 'There, can you feel the head?' And then right up on top of the bulge, and she said, 'There, that's his feet, you can feel both of the feet' and I could. I could feel these two separate little feet kicking upwards. Liz"—he sounded as though he might cry—"that turned me on."

She could not breathe in the darkness. No part of them was touching the other. They both lay on their backs looking outwards.

"You have to understand. It was not her. I promise you. It was the baby. It was so real, standing on its head with its feet kicking. It turned me on." He made an effort to lighten the tone. "Can you imagine, in those tight cords, with a drink in one hand and the other clamped to this woman's belly, with a massive hard-on."

She could not say anything. She knew that he needed her to say something, to mitigate the pain, to join him in his dark place. She was frozen, she could not even think.

"Liz, what's wrong with me?"

He had said that once before. Once during the painful early months of their relationship he had got aroused. And at once she was filled with hope, reached for him tenderly, caressing, encouraging wordlessly. And suddenly he had lost his head, and shouted at her, "Turn over."

Taken by surprise she had not responded. He pushed her away from him, yelling, "Turn over, I said turn over. On your front." She had tried to look at him, to gauge his mood, but his anger was immense. "Turn over, you silly bitch."

He had not hit her but she knew he was ready to. She rolled over and lay there suspicious and frightened. She had never been frightened of him, but she was used to the feeling: James had frightened her all the time, emotionally with his threats to prove her inadequacy, and physically with his aggression, his refusal to take no for an answer. But not Ian, Ian was her gentle friend, her child, her playmate. Now he was pushing and shoving at her, violent, fierce, not seeking her consent, forcing her head down, his angry claws pulling at her buttocks, scrambling on to her. She lay there blankly, thought vaguely that she ought to have realised that he would find things easier this way up, but she wanted to see his face; she could sense the anger that gripped him and she needed to see what he was thinking.

"Lie still," he barked, and slapped at her bottom.

"Ian . . ." But she could not cry out against this holocaust of wrath. She knew then that he wanted to bugger her. "Ian, no." He slapped her again. "No. No." She started to fight him. "Ian."

"Shut up, you cow."

She pushed against him, struggling desperately now. "Ian, I won't."

Defeated he sat back on his heels, the anger still naked. "Well, who would ever have guessed that the whore of North Oxford had such delicate scruples?"

"Ian, don't, it's not that." She was fighting to contain her own distress, not to become involved in this emotional cyclone. "I'll be your whore if that will help, but I won't be your bum boy."

"Don't ever use that word to me! How dare you?"

"How dare you? Don't try laying anti-gay things on me just to justify yourself. You know there is nothing in there. If you want to screw blokes, go and bloody screw them, but you can't use me as a substitute. You can screw me however you want, you can even do it that way, but it has got to be me."

"And since when does our Liz demand these meaningful, personal relationships? It's not what they say round the boozers of this town, you know. Since when?"

"Since I met you." And she started to cry. There was no sound in the room except her tears. He knelt there stunned, she lay there crying. After a long time he got off the bed and went and crouched in the corner, facing the wall, covering his face. He always did that when the world got too tough for him. She did not say anything, even her tears stopped. He was muttering into his arms. She could not hear him. She could hear someone moving in the room above; detached suddenly, she hoped that they had not heard.

He muttered again, more audibly, "I've never fucked anyone, you know, only been fucked."

Then the silence continued. Still without looking round he said, "I love you." She knew it was a response to her last remark; that he was trying to absorb the pain of being that important to anyone, of meaning that much to her. But she still could not say anything.

"Liz, what's wrong with me?"

And then she was off the bed and in his corner. He was in her arms, her tears dried, his pouring. She cradled him, petted him, comforted him, minimised her own fear, and her lust for him. They had arrived some place together: she crushed her fears about where.

But now when he said, "Liz what's wrong with me?" in that same baffled and defeated tone, she could not respond to him. The wrong was not in him, but in her. She had betrayed him, brought him this far only to say that she did not know the way forward, that she could not carry his child.

The silence was solid between them. When his hand reached out and touched her hip it made her jump. He said, "Darling, I'm sorry." His fingers lay gently against her skin. She reached and held his hand, gripped it tight. He must not know, she must never let him know, how much his longing hurt her. The least she could do, since she could not do what he wanted, was to protect him from the enormity, the hideousness of her own pain.

She said, "Yes. I remember feeling Nancy's babies when she was carrying them. It is strange, isn't it? The skin is so hard and firm, not flabby at all. You do get a sense of the baby in there. And drumming gently, kick, kick kick, just to let you know that he's there. Nancy was at a meeting once with a cup of coffee resting on her lap and the baby kicked it right off, clear into the air."

He held her in his arms and they both pretended to drift off to sleep.

Three days later the silence still lay between them. She became desperate. He was going out to a tenants' meeting: the Voluntary Service Unit he worked for loaned him out as an expert to them. She knew he was excited by the group's possibilities. But she wanted to intrude; wanted to break into his professional world. She asked him, on an impulse, if he could pass Amanda's house and drop off a package for her: it was difficult to think of anything to put in the package. Ian seemed unsurprised.

"Sure, I'll do it on the way back if you like."

She did not like at all. She was frightened of what she was doing, wondering if she was insane. But she needed for him to see Amanda again, to sit in that warm, rich house with the evidence of the children around him and feel the magical baby throbbing in the pit of that woman.

"I'm tired. I think I'll go to bed early, so don't worry if you're late." Amanda would be bound to ask him in; Liz knew that prosperous hospitality well. Ian would not be able to resist the omnivorous welcome even if he wanted to. Would he want to?

What did she want to come of this? She did not like Amanda very much, found her serenity and assurance based only on the income her husband earned for her. She thought she was a shallow woman, an intellectual cheat. Amanda believed that the unborn child did not swim and bob in a secret world, she believed that it could hear music, loud and rhythmical sounds, that the stretched skin in later pregnancy was permeable to light: if you lay in the sun the child would be bathed in a rich red glow that would make it happy. But she did not have the nerve to take this belief to its logical conclusion. She carefully, discreetly, implied that the consciousness began only after the time permissible for abortion had ended. Amanda was not brave enough to offend the pro-abortion lobby. All Liz wanted was for Ian to see through her cow-like placidity, to realise that Liz, childless and skinny, had qualities that Amanda did not and would never have. Of course that was all she wanted.

She got up and made herself a cup of coffee and settled at the table to read a new manuscript. She did not even want that, she just wanted Ian to deliver a package for her. She knew it was not true. She would not be shamed into comparing herself with Amanda in Ian's eyes.

Her stretched skin might let in light, Liz did not care. Her own skin had let it out again. A magical experience.

She had lain on her back in the dark and watched the television screen in the clinic's radiography department. The doctor had turned on the equipment and she had seen the secrets of her bony pelvis, the amazingly round ball-like bones from the top of her hips that kept her legs moving. She had felt like a child waiting for the conjuring trick to begin: the fine cliffs of bone and the harbour between them where the baby could lie and wait, protected by the craggy pier of her spine. The radiographer —young, Indian and rather beautiful—had been patient and detailed. "See, here is the hip bone of you, here the pelvis, relax while I put this plastic tube here tight." She could not see that on the screen but she saw the bones move as she shifted for him.

"Now we pour in my liquid." And suddenly, appearing on the screen, the shape of that magic organ—the Garden of Eden and the seat of madness—it looked moonlike, so close to the moon in its moods and fluctuations. She was fascinated, she cried, "Oh I wish Ian could see." The insult that James had used with most power against her had been "hysterical": he had pounded at her personality, just as, riding the waves of desire, he had pounded at her body. With his mind and his body he had made her acquiescent, had reduced her to a simple heap of quivering need; any resistance, any holding back from him, any demand of her own and he had lashed at her with that particular insult, "Hysterical." And watching her womb bathed in inner light, the sting had fallen away from the word, it meant only that she was the possessor of this perfect thing, glowing in the dark: a firm little shape with slightly serrated edges. Beautiful. And the radiographer had been so pleased with his trick and with her. "Look," he said, "so nice. No polyps, no divisions. Nice firm cervix, with no spilling-outs; that would be showing below, you understand. Very nice." The womb soared out at the top, curved but with quite precise corners, and the light flowed into the corners, then out along the tubes: they were not rigid, but flexible cords of light. And at the end of the tubes there was a sudden burst into flower: delicate tendrils of light, like seaweed. Her radiographer said, "This is very nice. You see both tubes, no resistance. Also sometimes this of himself is a cure, I say not a cure, but a help, washing to bring them nearer to the ovaries. There you see their outline, not so clear because the fluid runs all ways to be soaking into the body. Absorbing." Gradually the show faded, the ovaries pale islands in the sea of light.

She wished Ian had come to see the thrilling journey that his sperm made night after night. If she had known what a performance her body was going to lay on she would have made him come.

Afterwards she had realised that the whole thing had been uncomfortable. It could so easily have seemed like an intrusion.

She thanked the man profusely. He had made a magic out of what could have been an insult.

She jerked herself back to her manuscript, wished people would learn to type better, insisted again that she would have no part in biological madness. She rejected insanity, rejected her own obsession. Amanda was a nice gentle woman, it was good for Ian to have women friends, he did not have enough, she was a woman who would not threaten him. He had liked her, had spent an evening talking to her and would enjoy another such. She was no jealous wife, she did not need to be. Only a few years ago he would have been scared out of his mind by her: scared of the warmth that exuded from Amanda's enthusiastic flesh. She had liberated him of those fears. But she could not forget the expression on his face when Ian had felt Amanda's baby kick against his hand, had felt the child say, This is me. In the beginning I am. I can communicate to you.

She had freed Ian from his fear of women. She had taught him that their bodies could be lovable and that their minds could return affection, undemanding, unthreatening. If Ian ever fell in love with another woman, if he left her and had his child by someone else, it would not matter, it would still be her child, because she had freed him to love women.

There was no possibility of Ian leaving her, Ian loved her. She was being silly, if not crazy. She did not like herself like this.

But he had fancied Amanda. He did. She was not deceived, although he might be. She wanted him to fancy her. She saw them, him, her, together on the Heal's sofa. She would show him the glossies, some of which they had used for the book— naked women breastfeeding; fathers bathing tiny children; women in labour smiling; newborn babies asleep. And Ian would tell her, softly, that his wife could not have a child, that his wife was barren, that his wife was keeping him from his child by the force of her wicked will. And Amanda would comfort him.

She pushed the typescript away from her; the top pages fell on to the floor and she swore. She got up, picked up the telephone and called Nancy. Do something ordinary, something safe, talk to her friends, gossip. She could even pull Amanda's book apart. She knew that Nancy was immensely critical about it. Knew that Nancy would be critical of any book on the subject, knew that Nancy liked to think of herself as the feminist mother *par excellence*. Probably Nancy was somewhere offended that Liz had not asked her to write the book. She could tell her about the party, making mock of the people there—presenting Tony as sycophantic, Graham Forthwell as paternalistic and everyone as bourgeois.

Edward answered the phone and said that Nancy was out for the evening. Could he take a message? No she had just wanted to chat, it was nothing important. The impulse to turn to her friends collapsed. They would not give her support. Even if she described the party it would only be a denunciation of herself and her rôle in the world.

She knew they despised her for being a literary agent. It was impossible for her to explain why she liked it, without bringing Jane and Mary-Ann and to a lesser extent the others crashing down on her with their analysis of how and why it made her nothing but a parasite of the establishment at the expense of real writers. She could not write, but she could nurture other people's writing.

She could not have a baby, but she could nurture other people's babies.

If Ian had a baby by another woman she would be the midwife of that birth.

Two years ago Ian had been seized with an enthusiasm to adopt a Cambodian war-orphan, which he was convinced were readily available. She had pressed down her revulsion, had rationalised her sudden horror. She had explained as calmly as she could that ex-gays with Marxist tendencies married to women four years older than they were who went on feminist rallies were exactly the people that adoption agencies would regard

about as favourably as the bubonic plague. She had been furious
with him for giving up hope in her, for expressing even by implication the idea that they would not have a child of their own,
for pretending that such a substitution could be the real thing,
for not understanding that the craving was in her gut and that
craving could only be alleviated there.

But now. If Ian had a baby by another woman . . . It was
better not to think about it. She thought about it only because
the house was empty and she was depressed. It was silly. If Ian
had a baby by another woman, it would be her baby in a particular way, because she had taught him to love women and to
want babies. If she could find a woman, a woman who did not
want the child, but would have the pregnancy. The child could
grow there in their lives. She could use the body of another
woman to satisfy her longings, to satisfy his longing. If she were
clever, clever enough, she would not even have to lose his love.

Damn. He did not love her only because she was going to
have his child. He loved her. Wasn't that enough? She tried to
laugh at herself, laugh at the silly games she was playing. If he
did not love her without the child, what was that to her? She
could live without his love. She was horrible; some sort of
scheming conniving witch. She had not time for those sorts of
silly games, fantasies of adolescence, self-dramatisations. . . .

Midwives. Childbirth was locked deep in women's ancient
knowledge. Knowledge was power. The local midwife might be
despised, pointed out for a witch, treated with suspicion and
calumny, but they needed her. In the springtime she made
white magic, when the nervous rangings in the hedgerows prepared the mood for her love-potions and binding spells. Spring
was her time, loosing the passions of the young women and giving them particular direction. The cuckoos encouraging the
foolish. The summertime was the priest's, putting the seal on
what she had already created, closing the mouths of the gossips
with a Latin Benediction which sounded little different from the
spells with which she had opened the thighs. But winter was
her time again, her blossom time. The prettiest women, married

now to the men she had chosen for them, were ready for her, needing her. Muttering over the huge bellies she could bring out what she chose, from that darkness: life or death, heaven or hell. Again the priest's garbled blessing, washing away with words and water the effects of her work. But it was too late; she had created the desire and brought forth the children. In the end they would have to torture and burn such power; they would have to steal away such knowledge. Men could not risk the strength, the skill, the magic, the mightiness of the witch.

And now she makes herself another cup of coffee, and works diligently at her typescript and looks amused at herself; she looks like what she is: a bright middle-class young feminist, with an interest in her work and a pleasurable, equal marriage. But she hates herself because she knows that she is the witch, the spell-spinner, the one who holds life and death in her hands, who will move the little toy-like people in the circles that she wants. They do not count any more; her desire and anger have taken over and she will minister to them only. She sees Ian at Amanda's house, where she has sent him, being taught, by her—not by Amanda who is only her tool—a new direction, a new solution to his desire.

She can feed that desire and fuel it and accomplish it. She will bring him to some bed, and watch, titillated, while he creates a baby at her behest. She has the power. She has Ian at her mercy.

A little after ten Ian came in. She heard him moving in the stairwell outside, and with a shock, realised that he was not alone.

The door opened and there was an avalanche of noise and warmth. "Poppet, how good to see you." And she was wrapped in arms that she knew were Tim's. Escaping, she saw that Lenny was there too, his arm round Ian's shoulder and screeching at her with enthusiasm. She stood up, hugged Tim again and said, "Darlings. How wonderful. I thought you were in the north."

"Could we stay away from you any longer? No, actually we are seeking sunnier climes. Holiday time."

She was glad to see them. Old friends from Oxford; she rested refreshed in Tim's arms, and gabbled her pleasure.

"Why didn't you phone? Do you want to crash here? Where are you going? Where did you find Ian? Do you want some food?"

Lenny laughed and said, "Hang on. One: no time, we came suddenly. Two: no, we're staying with Phil and Co at Evelyn Street. Three: I can't remember the question. Four: in the pub, what do you expect, and five: yes please."

"Okay. We do like Lenny you know, he's such a good listener. I expect there's some spaghetti or something. Hang on and I'll put a pan on."

"We do like Liz you know, she's so quiet and restful."

"Bugger off."

"Hey. It is good to see you again."

"Oh my dears; well you ought to live in London."

"No, no. We like those tough sailor types you get in Liverpool."

"I know, I know. They're so good those boys, they do the most marvellous work. Why, if the poor homeless sailors don't come they even go out and scour the streets for them."

"You stole that from Hinge and Bracket."

"I confess. You should hear Ian do their cat song."

"I'd as soon not."

She went into the tiny kitchen and bent down for the big saucepan. She stood up again so sharply that she had to pause to regain her balance.

"Ian love, did you take that parcel to Amanda's?"

"Yes, of course I did."

"What did she say?"

"I didn't go in, just shoved it through the letter-box. Was there some answer? You didn't say so. Here, do you want me to cook?"

"I'll put the pan on then you can come and work some magic with a can of tomatoes and three bits of elderly bacon."

"Eggs? Cheese?"

"Yes, both."

He came into the kitchen behind her. It was so small that she would have difficulty getting out again. He grabbed her round the neck and blew in her ear. She could sense his happiness. He whispered, "You don't mind my bringing them?"

"Ian, of course not, don't be silly."

"You said you were tired."

"Not now."

Our lies will find us out. How could she have worried, wasted an evening like that? If he was going to leave her it would never be for some curvaceous mother figure, it would be for this easy comradeship. For people like Tim, and Lenny. God, she loved him.

Tim called, "Break it up in there, you two. It's revolting. You may be consenting adults but you're not in private."

"Don't be like that," Ian yelled back. "We straights are an oppressed minority."

"Like hell."

"But we're all right really. It's probably just a phase we're going through."

"You might corrupt us, mightn't they Lenny?"

"Tim dear, you must get over your prejudices. There's nothing wrong with it. Some of my best friends are straight."

"Well poor things, if they're born like that, we ought to feel sorry for them."

"That's all very well in a few isolated cases, Tim. Take Liz, for example. But Ian has definitely been corrupted. I mean he was a nice little boy once, just like us. And look at him now. Heavily into marriage, which as you probably know can be seriously addictive and often leads on to much worse things."

"I surely do hate to see a young gay go to the bad like this."

Liz disentangled herself from Ian and came out of the kitchen. She went and lay on the floor with her head on Tim's lap. He ran his beringed fingers across her face and petted her hair.

"You've cut it even shorter. How are you then?"

"Pretty good. And you?"

"Mmmm. Contented."

Tim had introduced her to Ian. Ian and she had been two of the bits of flotsam that had floated round his room on the Iffley Road sucking in his cheerful love. She always meant to ask him what his intentions had been, if any.

Tim had hated James. Unlike most of her friends who had been impressed by him, Ian had been clear. "I can't think what you see in that piggie. Just don't bring him round here." James had retaliated; more discreetly or less honestly: "Of course I don't dislike him because he's queer. That is nothing to me; it's none of my business and I don't want it to be. But all that gay rights stuff is just wanking and you know it." She had laughed at him and said they didn't just wank they sodomised each other as well, but she had mistimed it. James's easy anger was turned on her. "Look woman, I can't make you take important things seriously. If you want to run about with types like that Tim, that's your own business. I think fag-hagging is pretty bloody low myself, but if you feel that that is the sort of relationship where you can measure up, well all I can say is, I see your point. Now hush up, sweetie, because I've got some work to do."

She had lain on Tim's floor, for hours she would lie about afterwards, and wept. "He hates me. He hates me to be anything that I want. He hates me even to want."

"Why stay with him then?"

"Tim, I think he's right about me. I'm not serious. I don't face up to myself. Everything I do is geared to an audience; it's a performance to escape my own silence. He is willing to take me seriously, to take a gamble on me as a human being."

"You just said that was what he was not prepared to do."

"Yes. No. I don't know. He can be such a shit, but he is putting out for me. He's on my side. And Tim . . ."

"Yes?"

"I really fancy him."

"Well, there is that. I don't think you fancy him though; I think you like the idea of him fancying you. I know he's a big shot, an important student politico, but he's not making you happy and he's not making you good."

"If I leave him I'll be back where I started, in and out of beds, discounted by everyone, a cheap lay. I can't go back there. But James has taken a chance on me. He took me as I was, with my god-awful reputation and everything. He wants me to be his woman."

"Reputation. Jesus Christ, Liz, has he said that?"

"Well, not exactly."

"But he lays everything he can get his hands on, you know he did."

She tried a laugh. "He calls that 'organising.' Anyway, I don't mind that, but he has to put up with the fact that his friends don't approve of me, think I'm a step down—an inadequate Marxist, and a loose woman."

"Count your blessings. I won't have his smug opportunist voice overlaying my darling Liz's sturdy tones. You're lovable, I love you, you're lovely. You don't have to be grateful to that bastard. He's the one who ought . . . God I'm so angry. You ought to stop being sad, you ought to be angry. You ought to be in one of those women's groups learning how to be angry with him, with your father, probably with me, with all the men who put a price on a little respect and affection."

She began to cry, weeping into his tea-cup, sobbing and sobbing. His hands stroked and petted her, his heavy rings moving against her face, mechanically graceful, immensely kind. "It's so bad, so bad, so bad. You just don't know. Shitty. I can't cope. Can't cope with him, can't cope without him. He's so horrible. And suddenly he'll turn round, just the other way and it's so wonderful. But I have to dance to his tune, and he'll never tell me in advance what it is going to be. Good, bad. Up, down. He'll drown me, he'll drown me in my desire to please him."

"Liz, you don't need him. Don't let him tell you that you

need him. God, you're even keeping him. You are brighter, and better and more beautiful than he is, and you sure don't need a man like that to keep your conscience for you."

He fed her tea and cakes. He made her smile. A good friend. And now she lay looking up at his face and joking with him and Lenny while Ian made them supper. She thought how safe she was. How she was surrounded by love. How she had escaped from that hell too and was wrapped in good friendly love. She was not a witch, a midwife, a mere-wife. She would not mother the monsters in her head. She was happy.

And yet, when far too late, Tim and Lenny went and she and Ian settled into bed, she found it difficult to give up her fantasy. To give up the heady power she had found in the idea of Ian having a child by another woman. Warm, drowsy, contented she turned to the dream again, now without the nightmare qualities, and imagined him being the father of a baby. His delight, his joy which she would have given him—freed him from the pressure and longings. When she finally noticed that the face of the mother in the dream was her own, she laughed at herself and went to sleep.

Sarah's laugh, in the tent, by the oaks of Mamre, rings uncomfortably in the ear. Sarah the beautiful, whom kings have desired. Sarah the courageous, who had followed her adventurous husband about the whole world. Sarah the gracious, laughing in the curtain and trying to deny it so her guests will not be embarrassed. Sarah the old and barren.

She is laughing because it is too late: to be pregnant now will be a final twist of spite by a God who has ignored her too long. She used to pray to him, begging him for the child who would cement her crazy husband to her, and later praying for the child to fill the gap which seems enormous now she knows she cannot love the man she left home for. Once she prayed with the same zeal and faith as her husband. She learned that this God of his was not hers. Everything she knew of belonged to Abraham: the sheep, the servants, the tents, herself. And his God too. His God did not listen to a word Sarah said to him. After a while she stopped believing that her prayers would be answered; after a little longer she stopped praying.

Hagar is young and lovely. Sarah despises Abraham for desiring her. She is lovely, but she is neither wise nor beautiful as Sarah was. The Pharaoh of Egypt had desired Sarah. But Hagar is lovely, and young. Sarah loves her: she loves Sarah. She does not love Abraham who pesters her with his hot but old hands. With the slave's sensitivity to what is and is not permissible she tells Sarah that Abraham fancies her; she does not tell that the old man disgusts her.

Sarah is a woman of great dignity. She is not going to have her husband touching up slave girls behind the tents. She is not going to have Hagar, her maidservant and friend, made a by-word for sheep-boys. She loves Hagar: the energy that once went out to her husband is now redirected. Some evenings when Hagar is brushing her hair, tenderly back away from her face, brushing it admiringly up from the nape of the neck, sending shivers down Sarah's spine, Sarah reaches up a single hand and touches the younger woman's wrist, or she leans back so that her head rests on the pliant stomach of her friend. Hagar is young enough to be her daughter; she has won this lovely daughter for herself. From there on it is easy: she lures the two of them to bed, teasing and encouraging Hagar, driving Abraham by more subtle reins. So Hagar's baby is her baby; she created the mating that conceived Ishmael. Ishmael is her delight, her son: she had achieved him by the use of the power that she holds in her two hands.

"Ishmael, Ishmael," she calls, and he comes, crawling, staggering, then running from Hagar to Sarah. Sarah is not jealous of Hagar, she and Hagar remain good friends. They share the child, they share the relief that Abraham, now satisfied, bothers them less. They are both free to concentrate on their son. Sarah is happy; now she is a mother twice over. A mother to Hagar whose man she chose with truly maternal care, whose back she supported while the child was pushed laboriously into life. A mother to Ishmael, because she created him, not by lust but by intelligence. Moreover she no longer has to endure the embraces of the senile goat she used to love.

She stifles her laugh in the curtains of the tent because it is not a very nice laugh. She does not want Abraham's child: she already has her own children. It is a last trick by Abraham's God. Although she does not believe that Abraham's God listens to or cares about her, she has doubt that he exists and that her husband and his God plot together to get the best of all possible worlds for Abraham.

She thought she had outwitted them and her puny body is going to betray her.

"Why are you laughing?" say Abraham and God's messenger.

"Laughing? Me? I wasn't laughing."

"You were laughing. Don't you believe that you are going to have my son? Don't you believe that my God can do anything he wants?"

The laughter turns to racking sobs, but the men don't hear them. The sobs continue, painful, unending, for nine months. Isaac is born. She hates him. He is not her son, she did not consent to him. Isaac looks like his father from birth. He is not beautiful and spoiled like Ishmael: he is sturdy and clever and arrogant. She weeps and weeps. Hagar and Ishmael are sent away: they must not detract from the real son. Abraham says Sarah is jealous of Hagar and Ishmael, and that this will spoil her milk. Ishmael sucked at her empty breasts for the pleasure of it, but Isaac will not feed from her at all. Her breasts are huge, distended with milk, but he will not suck. The milk will not flow, her tears flow instead. She wishes she were dead. She does not want Isaac, she wants the children of her heart and mind, not this child of her gut.

When she hears the messenger speak, down by oaks of Mamre, she knows that she, who has plotted and schemed so carefully for so long, has been outwitted. The joke, subtle and tortuous, is—like all the best jokes—a matter of timing. She is a sophisticated, witty woman. Of course she laughs.

She laughs at herself and all her plotting. It is best to laugh at foolish women who think they can get their own way in a world where even God is a man and on the other side.

4.

JULY

"We saw your picture in the paper."

"Oh." The minute it had escaped from her mouth like a little, depressed sigh, she knew she should have made it at least interrogative, better still ferocious. She should have said, "Oh yeah?" or "Dr. Marshall, I'm so impressed to discover that you read a highbrow newspaper."

Her receptionist friend had been chilly when Liz had greeted her; had pointed out a seat the opposite end of the room from where most of the other women were sitting. And although Liz, in a gesture of rebellion, had moved almost immediately back to the more crowded section she had felt the weight of disapproval bearing down on her and had hardly dared even to look at the other women. She had schooled herself to believe that she was only imagining it, that she had nothing to feel guilty about and that in any case no one would know. But Dr. Marshall's "We saw . . ." made a lie out of her hopes. He could manage to say "we" for his whole team without ever giving up his prerogative to say "I." Head-of-a-team was a position of special power: he would know that and use it to the full.

She looked at his face surreptitiously. He was a very good-looking man, the sort for whom the word handsome had been patented. She and Ian had liked him so much when they had first come to him. It had not been an easy decision: Liz had begun to wonder what was wrong with her months before. The day that Ian heard he had got the job he wanted they had ritually flushed her pills down the loo. Giggling and groping each other they had taken them one by one out of the foil containers and dropped them neatly into the pan. The very act had turned them on; they had fallen giggling into bed and pretended that they could conceive their baby that very minute. They were more sensible than that really; they knew it might take a while for Liz's system to sort itself out after years of artificial-hormone-taking. They knew that they did not make love so often that it would be easy for them to conceive, they knew that they would have to wait a little while. But even with so much good logic Liz had felt a pang of grief even when she had quite expected withdrawal bleeding three days later.

That had only been the beginning. Nearly a year later Mary-Ann was cursing: "One sodding time without that jelly, and here I am. I can't believe it. Just once. Oh shit." Liz asked Nancy how long it had taken her to conceive her children and Nancy had laughed and said, "Oh, I don't think I'm one of those super-fertile types. Quite a long time, four or five months." That was the first time Liz was frightened. She did not tell Nancy why she had asked, and she did not tell Ian, but she went to see their G.P. He had been friendly but casual: "Don't start fretting, a year is nothing. You were on the pill for quite a while, weren't you? Takes Mother Nature time to assert herself, you know." Back with her women's group she tentatively began asking questions, but none of them knew the ranges of normal or the things to do. They did talk about reversing the safe period and rumours they had heard about different positions, but she hardly liked to raise this with Ian. One day Jane said, "Liz, you are getting quite morbid. Take your pill and don't worry, it can't be that easy to get pregnant." And, without any warning, she had burst into tears, appalled at herself, and she had been forced to confess to the dread truth, that she wanted a baby and was not conceiving.

That night she had told Ian that she thought they should go and see a specialist. To her surprise he agreed immediately. "I'd been wondering about that myself, but I just didn't know what to expect." Back to their doctor, who was still not inclined to take them seriously, who seemed almost embarrassed as he asked them elementary questions about their sex life, who told them not to worry, just be patient, just wait, they were young, there was plenty of time. Together they had got angry, started doing their homework, started leaning on the doctor. They picked out the clinic for themselves from periodicals on the subject, from investigations through friends. No one seemed very sympathetic, they did not know the people who wanted to have children, they only knew those who did not.

Then after several months of frustration and being fobbed off, the walls fell in, they got their appointment and appeared before the great Dr. Marshall. He had been sensible. After filling in innumerable forms and answering endless questions they were received into the presence. And this smiling personable man congratulated them on their good sense in coming. He made them welcome, said he was especially pleased to see Ian there, that not all couples were willing to take joint responsibility for what was very much a joint enterprise. "I'm not promising you any miracles. Some of the couples we see here turn out to have grave and uncorrectable abnormalities that we can do little about. But at least we can tell them, put them out of their misery, if you like, by being able to say that they will not be able to have the child they want. I believe that that is better, healthier and shows more respect for them as individuals. On the other hand, while, as I say, I cannot promise miracles, I can tell you that the majority of couples who come to us are pregnant within the year. This clinic has one of the highest success rates going. I am proud of that, frankly. We have a high reputation and with good cause. I believe in every one of my couples and will do everything that can be done." He went through their questionnaires with them, checking, rechecking, making jokes and encouraging noises. At the end he said, "Now have you told me everything?" Ian grinned and said, "No." "You will, you will," laughed the doctor. And they had. He had drawn their whole lives out of them, gently and carefully. Offering them his sanity, his good sense, and his technology in exchange for their confidences.

She looked at him now and wondered with dread where that open-minded amiability had gone. Perhaps he was still as sensible as he had been. Perhaps it was they, not her, who had deviated from good sense. It was all right for her women friends to say, secure in their own choices, that he was angry with her because his magic was not working, his spells and moral incantations were not having the desired effect and he hated her rather than acknowledge his failure. Nancy and Alice and even Paula had their own magic to set against his: the magic of their children, the magic of a belly that swelled with fruitfulness and breasts which filled with the sweet thin milk that made children glow golden and pulsate while they slept. She and Ian had no such magic: they had to seek out the mage to manipulate their moon signs and show them the way through the dark maze.

And now their master, the lord to whom they had given their allegiance looked coldly at her and said, "Well?"

"Well what?"

"Well, when I saw that picture I wondered what on earth you think you are doing. Are you here just to experiment, at someone else's expense, with your bodily functions? Are you planning to flush down some back-street john the products of my team's valuable experience?"

Jesus, he could not really have said that, she was hallucinating, she was going out of her mind. But she was intimidated. "No," she said sullenly, like a child. She might have guessed he was a bloody *Telegraph* reader.

Because, to her surprise, the demonstration had been terrific. Thoughout the week before she had felt her enthusiasm mounting. At the Thursday night meeting, once the others had been certain that she was coming their support and understanding wrapped her up. They were pleased with her, she could even feel that they admired her ability to politicise her private feelings. The overtones of moralism disappeared, she had proved a good girl after all. The feeling made her uneasy, but she was not going to destroy the pleasure of it by complaining.

On Friday evening she came home late from the office; riding high on the bus and looking at the sunshine streets filled with tourists and shoppers tired after a long day. She had arrived home to find Tim and Lenny, back from Italy, tanned and happy, sprawled across the living-room, and Ian in high delight. They had forgotten it was the weekend of the march, but now they were planning to stay south, and spent the evening on the phone encouraging and exhorting friends and groups that they knew to turn out. Between their calls a friend of hers from Oxford rang up to say that her group was in London and they looked forward to seeing her tomorrow. She had the sensation of being at the centre of where things happen; the whole invisible movement that it was easy to forget about most of the time seemed to be converging on London and there was a feeling of power, of pleasure, at belonging with these others, of being part of a whole.

The Saturday was high. The sun was bright, even the organisers were pleased with the turn-out. They marched and sang and waved banners; Liz felt the energy and colourfulness and solid unanimity of the women; the immense diversity of the women's movement coalesced for a while into a single long column which held up the traffic of the West End.

The newspaper picture had just been an incident, unimportant, in the golden day: there had inevitably been a counter-demonstration. The route had been marked periodically with anti-abortionist standard-bearers, in small but angry groups, shouting ugly insults at the marching snake, which hissed. But at one point there had been a hiatus, the march stopped by the police to let traffic through. It had happened at a point where there had been a strong group of anti-abortionists and as the march relaxed itself there had been time for a more detailed exchange of views and hatreds. The photographer had caught her apparently jeering, mouth wide in an unattractive gape, at a poster reading, "Abortion Murders Babies." The picture and its implication had shocked her when she had seen it a couple of days later: she had been jeering, jeering affectionately at Alice, not visible in the picture, pregnant and pushing Hugh's pushchair. Her long Indian cotton dress had become hopelessly entangled in the wheels of the pushchair, Hughie had been helpless with laughter, and Alice was having difficulty bending down enough to untangle herself. A moment later she had been on her knees helping her, still laughing, excited, friendly towards mother and child. The photographer's picture was a lie. And it was very ugly. Ugly because she had been so careful not to engage in the exchanges of abuse, ugly because she had felt a tolerance and understanding towards the opposition which she liked to believe must be nearly unique on the march. Ugly because the priests and nuns ranged against them had brought back, against her will, her memories and guilts about her father. Ugly because it was not true.

And she did not feel that she could say any of this to Dr. Marshall. She would not give him the weapon of her own divided feelings to use against her. He did not need the weapon anyway; he had had his own powerful battery to make her feel guilty.

"Are you really a pro-abortionist? I simply do not begin to understand how you can be. When you see and share with all the women here in this clinic, who want, who need children, who are crying out for them. If it was not for this wicked, murderous Act I hope you realise that you would probably have been able to adopt a child yourself by now; which, if my diagnosis has any validity, would probably also mean that you would be having one of your own. You would be a family. I really do not understand you. I admit that I am quite disturbed. What exactly do you want?"

"I want some choice in my life. I want a medical profession

which is responsive to the needs of women, whatever they are; responsive to women who want control over their own bodies." Thank God for Nancy, thank God for her friends, the connection she had been reluctant to make was clear now. She ought to stop, but now she had started she wanted to cut through a year of grovelling and offer him her clarity.

"Actually, no, I do not find it easy to be a pro-abortionist. Of course the idea sickens me, I'm not without feelings, you know. A friend of mine had an abortion a little while ago and I could hardly bear to speak to her; I still find it difficult, it has ruined the friendship probably. But that's my problem, isn't it? Not hers and certainly not yours. Emotionally it may be hard, but rationally I don't see why me not being able to do what I want should force her to do what she *doesn't* want. Look, abortion isn't the issue, or not the whole issue: the issue is the matter of choices—we want to implement our own choices, and we want a technology which is not too arrogant to let us. We want contraception that works, we want abortions. That's why I'm here, not to gratify you and your bloody team. Not to be the walking living proof that you can get 62 per cent of women who come to you pregnant in the first twelve months. . . . And you are proud of that statistic. It's not good enough, it's not good enough I tell you. We, *my* team, my women friends, want a lot better than that."

"Now, Elizabeth, now calm down. I am truly sorry if I spoke sharply. I have feelings too, but perhaps you are right and I should not allow myself the indulgence of them here. You know I really do understand the sort of depression that you poor women go through; this grieving without an object, for the baby that you want and who does not seem to want you. I do indeed understand. But my dear, rushing round in over-excited circles is not going to help. Believe me. A calmer life-style would probably be more conducive. . . . You know, really you *do* know, that we are doing everything we can, and doing it more speedily than usual in response to your pressure; no, you really cannot call us unresponsive bureaucrats. You are right, I was wrong to attack you for being driven by your friends into that silly escapade, but perhaps you should have other friends."

Other friends. Arm in arm with Nancy walking down the street, and between songs and slogan-chanting laughing at the changes in friends they had not seen for months. Laughing at each other for the people they had been before they were involved in feminism, laughing at themselves for their own backslidings. Seeing Jane with her gay women's group grin at her with appreciation; a mocking acknowledgment of the distance between them in terms of personal choice, but, equally, an unmocking recognition of their closeness in terms of recognition. Edward, carrying Harriet in his arms, the two of them wearing matching red T-shirts, and him talking to her incessantly so that she should not hear the hatred in the insults exchanged between Nancy and a sweet-looking old woman with an SPUC button. And Ian, his hands in his jeans pockets and his face lit up with excitement at the excellent organisation. Thank God Dr. Marshall had not been there to see him marching under a gay liberation banner with Lenny and Tim and others. There were no other friends for her: the solidarity, the sense of belonging to each other in the bright sunshine. If Dr. Marshall promised her a baby at their expense she did not think she would be able to accept.

Anyway, that was not the choice. She refused to accept that that was the choice. Children were conceived here, there and everywhere. All over the globe, couples locked in preposterous embraces, night after night. Starving, rich, bleak, pampered. And within those embraces children were conceived, grew in wombs, regardless of whether they were wanted there, disregarding chemicals and wire coils and fervent prayers and desperate counting; denials, withdrawals, thrombosis risks and simple inconvenience. She refused to believe that changing her life-style, finding new friends, was going to work the spell for her.

At Monserrat the Black Madonna smiled benignly on the faithful, pleased by the extravagance of their votive offerings. It was her special providence to bring fruitfulness to Catholic marriages. Liz remembered her father vividly: he had been delighted by the rich vulgarity of the place; he had bent his head in prayer. Had he been asking His Lady for the gift of a son? He was a believer; he knew that if She had transcended the problem of virginity She could easily have coped with the womb-lessness of his wife—if She wanted to. The magical exuberance of growth or the jagged mountain, rising from the Catalonian plain; the mysterious blackness of the image; the caves and wildness dusted over with violets and honeysuckle and roses. Promises, promises. The Black Madonna of the rocky mountain has absorbed the power of darkness, the older magic and has dominated it. She is the source of power, her secrecy and knowl-edge are mysterious and mighty. But her father's prayer is not answered. The magic does not work for him.

Henry, the Third, by the grace of God, King of France, and his barren wife Louise of Lorraine dressed themselves in sack-cloth every winter to walk the fifty miles barefoot to Chartres to intercede for an heir. At Chartres, encased with devotion, is the shift that the Queen of Heaven had worn at the moment of her conceiving, the very garment which had modestly draped the moment of her fiat, of her union with the Spirit. And the King and Queen of the ancient House of Valois knelt there, begging the shift to shift for them. What more could they have done? The magic had not worked for them either: they were murdered and their noble blood died with them.

Why should the magic work for them? She could make her bus-top pilgrimage every month and lie naked on Dr. Marshall's table. His magic was no more potent than the Virgin Mary's. Her faith was not strong enough; she was not a believer; she was not humble enough; she was not obedient enough; she was not loving enough. He had seen through her. He was asking for proof of her devotion, and she would refuse it. He would punish her. Her heart was not really here with him, she obeyed only the externals. Her heart was really out there with the wicked women who murdered babies in the womb and ate the flesh of their unborn children. She slept in the arms of a half-man because she did not dare to offer herself to the fullness and beauty and power of the man. Dr. Marshall was a man.

Once she had been perfectly honest with Dr. Marshall. She could not do that any more. There was no way of saying to him, "It was difficult for me to go on the march; it is difficult for me to accept my friends; it is difficult for me even to love my husband anymore. You have made me centre all my energies here, and now I wish that I had never started this. I even wish that you would declare me officially infertile so that I could abandon hope and decide what to do instead. So I could come to terms with my amputated self." He could not do anything for her any more. He had stopped being scientist and had become moralist. He had made her dependent on him and she could not trust him. She could not even give up and go back on the pill; just taking it every night would be an admission that she could not believe herself to be barren.

She went back to work when she left the clinic, because she did not want to have a chance to think. Tony emerged from his office as she arrived.

"Good morning, my love. Only four hours late."

"I told you—medical reasons."

"Sorry."

When she had first come to work for him she had told him she was hoping to have a child, but meant to go on working. They had discussed it, maternity leave, baby-care, joking, casual, adult. He was the one person with whom that casualness remained. Here at work her inadequacies were hidden. He would, privately, rather she did not have a child, did not disrupt his work schedules. He was a nice man; he knew her problems and was affectionately considerate, but there was no issue. He preferred her work and the fact that she made him laugh. She could trust him, and he now gave her far more scope than she had hoped for when she started working for him.

Now he said, "Do you want lunch?"

"I thought you were complaining that I was late." They grinned.

"A working lunch," he said swiftly.

"I'm not hungry, don't waste your money."

"Who said I was offering to pay? Well, forget it. Of course I feel deeply rejected. Come in my office and we'll do cash-flow sums."

"Bully."

"When you're a partner . . ."

"I'll never be a partner on what you pay me and you know it."

"Well perhaps your mum'll leave you a fortune."

"I wish."

She might though. She thought about her mother. She had not worked after her father had died; but she thought of her as well-off. She had never thought of asking—her mother would find that impertinent but she ought to find out if she was all right. Her relationship with her mother was so tied up in guilt: she had betrayed her from the start, gone over to the enemy, sold herself to the highest bidder. She had prevented her mother from having the son by the accidental ferocity with which she had torn her way into the world. She had killed her mother's husband.

Tony said, "Why are you twitching?"

"Twitching?"

"Wincing then?"

"The very thought of my mother induces such acute symptoms of guilt."

"Why? Are you planning to kill her so that you can buy into partnership with me?"

"Hmm. You're not worth it. Judging by these figures I would be out of my mind to invest my ill-gotten gains in so shaky an enterprise."

"Seriously, Liz, has something upset you?"

She was not going to tell him that seeing Dr. Marshall left her weak about the edges for days. He had had a chance to know that if he wanted to; but he did not have to want to.

"No, no," she protested.

"Come on, love, tell your Uncle Tony."

"It's nothing. I fight with my husband and my boss does not pay me enough."

"I shall have to speak to him. Your boss, I mean; I have very little influence with your husband. I did not think he looked like the fighting kind."

"He isn't."

"But you fight with him?"

"No. Well. He's okay. He's going through a rough patch at the moment. Not easy trying to be a radical social worker you know."

"*The Easy Life of a Radical Social Worker*—great title, that. Memoirs of an Easy Social Worker. Men you know, we're all intolerable really. Think how noble of me never to have gone in for marrying much."

They were not exactly fighting though: they were just very separate. He was apparently totally engrossed in training his new Job Creation Programme Community workers. She had thought him busy—had failed to notice. She felt stupid, blind about Ian. After the abortion march they had all gone to the pub: Jane and her new girlfriend whose name Liz had not yet discovered, and Alice and Mary-Ann and Ian, Lenny and Tim, some friends of theirs, some woman who worked with Ian. They were still high from the afternoon's sun and crowd. Noisy, close, happy. There were not enough seats and she had sat on Tim's lap, a comfortable place, unendangered. He told her about their holiday, about some mutual friends whom he saw in Liverpool, easy chatty things. Sometime, halfway down the second pint, Tim said, "Hey Liz, what's eating Ian?" She looked round for him, but he was standing at the bar with Mary-Ann.

"What, now? Nothing that I can see."

"I don't mean now this minute. I mean now in general."

"I'm not with you."

"He's . . . well he seems to me to be a bit depressed, and he doesn't seem easy with you, or with us if you're around."

"Tim! Well he's been fantastically busy. They're expanding their case loads not their workers. I mean the new people have to be trained and stuff."

"Oh, come on Liz. Look I've known him a long time. I don't want to interfere. You know I love you both."

"No. It's cool. Go on."

"Sure? I mean I've held his hand through his nervous breakdown, and taken the Oxford No. 1 bus out to Littlemore daily to see him, and poured him into bed drunk and held his hand at the clap clinic. Seen him . . . frightened if that's the right word, and I won't see him back there if I can do anything to stop it. Look, when he first told me that you and he were getting it together, were thinking of getting married, I thought you were both out of your minds, were trying to find some way into respectability. Especially him. But then suddenly it seemed right. You know, I don't have to tell you, it was really good. And now something has gone wrong; he's disappearing down his own backside again or something. He's cute and clever, but he isn't there. What's eating him?"

She looked away over to where he was standing. He seemed compact to her, an island entire unto himself. The first time she had met him she had walked into Tim's room meaning to describe to him the women's group that she was beginning to get involved with. Tim was there and with him a tiny, deadly pale boy. The two of them were setting out the board to play Monopoly—one of Tim's constant pastimes. Tim invited her to join them; he and she joked and rapped while the pale person sat quite still and silent, except for what was necessary to play. His eyes had bugged out at her in a fixed stare whenever he had thought she was not looking, and several times Tim had to remind him when it was his turn. And each time after he had thrown the dice Tim would lean forward and move his piece, the iron, for him. She enjoyed the game, the silly feeling of power that it gave you, but she had still been aware of the tension, had wondered if she ought to go. After about forty-five minutes Tim had got up to make coffee and said they should play on until his next turn. Liz played, moved and handed the dice to the boy. He had thrown them quickly and then, for the first time, reached out for his own counter. His hand was shaking so badly that he could hardly bring it into contact with the piece, and putting it down again he joggled the whole board so that three hotels and a number of houses crashed on to the floor. The boy began to cry, curling his arms across his chest. Liz simply bent down and put all the bits back on the table, arranging them with the greatest care. Tim came back across the room quickly, put his arms round the weeping figure and said quite fiercely, "Stop it. Now." And then almost in a whisper, "Ian, please, stop it. It doesn't matter." They stopped playing. Tim brought the coffee; he had put red children's straws in all three cups; she was touched at his care that this Ian should not have to pick up the cup.

Looking at Ian now, standing at the bar, it was impossible to believe that he had ever been like that. He had a self-sufficiency that she admired even though she battled against it, battled to be allowed in. He was tougher than she was, more certain of himself as a person. But she had seen him before, and knew that, unlike Tim, she had never seen him at his worst. She knew why Tim was careful with him, loved Tim for that. But she could not bear to think that he had retreated into his private fortress, and drawn up an impregnable drawbridge while she had not even noticed.

"Let's go for a walk," she said to Tim.

"Good."

They got up. Tim leaned forward and murmured in Lenny's ear. She caught Ian's eye. When he came over she told him she was going for a walk with Tim. Looking at him freshly she saw a nervous start, a moment of doubt. But all he said was, "Okay. Don't get cold. I expect some of us will go on home afterwards if you don't get back here." She was getting hypersensitive. Bloody Tim, she knew Ian better than he did, he just liked to be thought of as perceptive and caring, he just loved drama. Of course Ian was all right, he had to be.

The two of them went out into the summer night. He put his arm round her shoulders and they began to walk, rather fast as suited them both. She felt nostalgic: they had so often walked round Oxford like this.

"You are my security blanket," she said.

"No way."

"We want to have a baby."

"So?"

"We can't."

His arm tightened round her, and she tucked her head into his shoulder. She could not walk that way with Ian, because he was too small. After a little while he said, "But Liz . . . look . . . I mean I know at the beginning you and he had a lot of difficulty. I mean getting it on, he told me." She felt a stab of anger: so Ian had told, had he, had found sympathy, while she had kept her lips sealed to protect him. She knew that she was dishonest, that it had not just been for his sake that she had refused to talk about his impotence, that it had been for her own, because of her own shame and lack of confidence. But the anger remained.

Tim said hesitantly, "But when you actually got married, well, I just assumed that you had worked it out . . . I mean I knew Ian, that he wasn't, well I knew he could." (She knew that Ian and he had slept together, it did not matter to her, she did not want Tim to think she was jealous of that.)

"God Tim, it's not that. I mean, Jesus why should this be embarrassing? It's not because Ian's not fucking that we can't have a baby. That is good for us now, in our own little way."

There was another silence, while Tim processed what she was saying, and finally shrugged, laughed and said, "I'm sorry, I'm an old faggot and you will have to elaborate."

(She felt a curiosity about Ian and Tim in bed together, but there was no way of exploring the details. She realised she had never seen Tim without his clothes on.) She said, "We get into bed and we make out and we enjoy it and we do it at the right times of the month and those things and we don't conceive a tiny embryo."

"Do you think that's Ian's fault?"

"Jesus, no. In fact I know it isn't. It's mine."

"How do you know?"

"I go to something called a sub-fertility clinic and there they tell me." She knew suddenly that he could not really understand, that he could not fully imagine what she was talking about. For a brief moment she understood her mother's embarrassment about teaching her the facts of life, but she had to try, she had to help him understand. She looked to him for comfort and now she had to help him.

"Look, it's a mechanical failure. If you want to have a baby you don't just have to screw, you have to have lots of healthy tail-wagging sperm—which Ian has. You have to have the right sort of bits and pieces inside—which I have. And you need some nice little eggs popping down the relevant tubes at the relevant moments."

"For God's sake, Liz, I'm not totally ignorant of female biology, you know. I do know all that."

"Well, there you are then. They don't pop."

"I see." There was another pause and he asked, "Ever?"

"Quick thinking, Timothy my boy; that is exactly the problem. The answer is occasionally, but apparently not while Ian's around. Or not yet. Or something. If they never do, or not regularly, they can give you drugs, that encourages them, sometimes. They've had a look you see, the equipment's all there and looks okay. But if they sometimes do and sometimes don't, the drug thing gets tricky, multiple births, quins and stuff, you know."

"Go on."

"This is the difficult bit." She pulled away from his arm although she still walked very close to him. "I think Ian and I are about ready to risk that problem now, but the doctor isn't."

"It's not his business."

"Okay. But he doesn't agree. And he is the prescribing machine."

"Change doctors."

"He's the best there is."

"Not in your case."

"It's not that simple. He, this doctor, has a theory that the reason why I don't ovulate isn't physical. He says I'm repressing it because I don't really want to have a baby."

"What?"

"Well, I'm a women's libber with a reputation for gross immorality, and I've married a gay guy, so obviously I'm not fit to be a mother. God, Tim, you know the State takes real live children away from their mothers for less than Dr. Marshall has got on me. He thinks I should see a shrink."

"And?"

"I don't know. Sometimes I think he may be right."

"Where does that fit into where Ian and you are?"

"Tim, listen, there's no way you can imagine. You have to fuck on certain nights and not on others; you're supposed to do it in certain positions; you have to write on little charts whether you came or not and if not they ask you why not. It's hard enough for Ian to do it at all; that pressure really dries him up. Then I find I only want to fuck when the times are right, I can't stifle the feeling of 'wasting sperm' or something like that; and he wants to opt out of the responsibility and only do it when the time is conspicuously wrong. And quite apart from sex: Ian really wants that baby. I've failed him, that's all. If it hadn't been for that dream baby he would probably still be gay. I believe that, actually. I've failed him. It's not surprising he's withdrawing from me, and it scares me to hell."

A few minutes before she had been hotly denying his withdrawal, now she was explaining it. She noticed that, wondered about the honesty of her own motives; how much was she manipulating Tim's sympathy? How much was she freed to speak the truth because of his sympathy?

"You can't understand, Tim. Even Ian can't understand. Everything I put my hand to I turn into a mess. Maybe the doctor's right, maybe I'm just fucked up."

"Well, go and see a shrink then."

"But the terms. He was quite specific; not adjusted to my womanly role. Would you go and see a shrink, for any reason, if you knew his main commitment was to 'curing' you of being gay? I won't buy a child at the price of some stereotype 'femininity.' Maybe if I was this mythic Real Woman, I would still be with James bloody Price. That is this doctor's standard."

"Does Ian feel responsible?"

"I don't know."

"Haven't you asked him?"

"I can't cope with having to be responsible for his sense of responsibility. Guilty about his guilt as well as my own. Don't try to lay that on me. He doesn't ask me if I feel responsible or guilty. He knows I do, and doesn't want to rub it in. Very kind of him. I feel shitty enough about the whole thing without having to take on feeling shitty about him feeling shitty. He should bloody well grow up. Just for a change I'm the one with needs." Her anger was suddenly enormous; towards Tim and towards Ian, and their closeness, their care for each other. "Did he set you up for this guru talk? Has he been saying I don't give his tender sensibilities enough wifely, motherly attention?"

"Liz."

"Oh Tim, I'm sorry." Her anger dissipated as suddenly as it had come. She felt exhausted. "Really, I'm sorry. I don't know what to think anymore. He gets so hurt, on my behalf. I can't bear him to be so hurt for me, so I don't tell him and then I suppose he knows that too."

Years ago it seemed, Liz had said to Tim, "I think I love him."

And Tim had looked up from where he was lying on the floor mending his stereo. "Rubbish, he's too young for you."

"Tim, what a maternal thing to say. Only four years, it's not much."

"It's a hell of a lot, and you know it. You want to mother him."

"Partly. Only partly. I want him to love me."

"He's sick and he's gay."

"He's getting better. About the latter, I know, it's one of the problems. But sometimes . . . the way he is with me . . . it might not be an insuperable problem, you know. People change."

"You're telling me," said Tim. There was a long pause; he left off fiddling with the machine and curled round so he was sitting beside her, legs crossed. "If you're serious, you should tell him. Oh bugger, it makes me laugh. If you promise not to tell him I told you, he was sitting here not two hours ago and he told me he thought he loved you. I said you were too old, too experienced, too wide. And he said 'Only four years, it's not much.' He asked me not to tell you, he didn't want you to laugh at him. He won't tell you himself, but you could tell him. He'll be here tomorrow at tea-time, I could go out if you wanted."

"Uncle Pandarus," she teased him.

"I will not run your love errands for you." He had been angry. But he had set the whole thing up, she ought to feel conspired against. And now his anger. Afterwards she guessed that Tim loved Ian, wanted to be his salvation, and it was difficult for him to bear that Ian should have chosen a woman.

"Tim," she said now, inserting her head back into his shoulder, "what shall I do?"

"My love, I am hardly qualified to tell you. But he won't leave you though. You'll make no headway with that solution to your problems. You may kill him first but he won't leave you."

"Everyone thinks I'm the tough guy, because of where we started from. I don't believe that any more. He has powers of survival that make mine look amateur. Look what he has coped with so far. If he wants the baby enough and I think he does, he could find himself a real woman now; not the pseudo bridging sort I may have been for him."

"God, Liz, that's sick. I don't think he wants your so-called Real Woman. I know what he wants is you. It's you, you're not playing fair with him. I don't understand how you can do this to him, betray him. Cheat him of yourself."

She hated the word. She hated it so much that she gave him credit for not knowing that. Betray. She was the traitor. Ten years ago she had fled her father's house and gone to Oxford, wanting to be quit of him. He had taught her to be clever and impudent; to use her wits against the adult world; he had wanted her to think for herself, to be original, not to conform; to believe in her own righteousness against the standard of this world. Why should he hate her for learning her lesson so well? They had fought with unparalleled viciousness for a year—she resorting at the worst to screaming abuse, he to nursery punishments, slapping her, sending her to her bedroom. They mocked each other in public, and scourged each other in private: each believing that the other was the Judas, theirself the Christ. She was clever enough to know what ailed him: he had become the authority that he had rewarded her for fighting; that he was jealous, eaten with jealousy. She had told him that too. All through her adolescence she never had a boyfriend: she knew now that she had not wanted to deflect his attention from her, to give him an object for his wrath which was not her.

Six months later, delighted with the freedom she had found, frustrated by her inability to get anyone to attend to her the way he had attended, she decided to sleep with her then boyfriend. She did not even desire him that much: it was a rational, cold-blooded decision. She had done her three preparatory weeks on the pill, had fixed the date and smuggled him into her college room. They had smoked some hash and drunk some cheap red wine. About where they were taking their clothes off she heard the telephone ring. After a while the girl from the next room had knocked on the door and said someone wanted to speak to her. "Say I'm out," she called through the door, giggling in the arms of her about-to-be lover. The footsteps padded away, disapproving, and returned to say it had been her mother and would she ring urgently as soon as she got in. The conspiratorial air between them encouraged them both, and they had succeeded in losing her virginity and, as it turned out, his as well quite effectively until the morning.

She forgot, she forgot about the telephone-call until lunch the next day when her neighbour asked her what her mother had wanted. Guiltily she had fled to the telephone box, had found she had the wrong change, and had let the whole thing go until after tea. Her father had had a massive heart attack the evening before; he was now in hospital more or less totally paralysed. Her mother berated her for being out, and she put such fervency into her protestation of innocence that it was not until some hours later that she realised that she had been lying. He lived another two weeks, but only semi-consciously, he had not recognised her when she went to visit him, strange and small in the hospital. Her mother urged her to stay but she would not, wanting only to get back to Oxford. She expected that her mother was glad really; at least she had her husband back for his dying. She had betrayed all that he stood for, betrayed his love and killed him. She never slept with the boy again; and instead started experimenting with increasing pleasure and release with the many beds and bodies of her most casual acquaintances. But she knew she had broken his heart and killed him.

Once in a consciousness-raising group she tried to talk about it, but found she had to bring it down to the level of farce: "It's too corny for words, my father died the night I lost my virginity. No one would believe it. Really cheap stuff." But she knew she had betrayed him and killed him. That their relationship was an unfinished business. She had betrayed him.

Stung with pain she yelled at Tim, "All right take sides. Before our marriage has even broken up start mauling over the bits. Choose your own half, choose your friend. I just don't want to discuss it with you. There is nothing to say."

She broke away from him and moved rapidly down the street.

The one thing she does not want to do is fight with her dear friend. The one thing she cannot do is respond to his concern for Ian. Away from him she feels the lateness of the evening; she is still wearing only a sleeveless T-shirt and she feels cold and alone. She wants to be back in the pub, back in the closeness they had generated that afternoon, back in that tolerant warmth. Their comradeship will last the evening out, if little longer; it will cuddle and embrace them. She does not want Tim to break into that, she does not want Tim to show her that they are not all one and united. She does not want Tim at all.

He runs after her down the street; catches her by the shoulder and pulls her round against him; she begins to cry. She does not want to cry on his breast, she does not totally trust him. Crying is safe only with her women friends. Nancy is on her side, regardless, she knows that and can cry there. But she cries. Tim says, "I'm sorry, love, I did not mean it like that." But she is no longer crying because of what he said; she is crying because she has discovered that she cannot trust him, cannot trust anyone. Even her body is not on her side. She cries because she loves Ian and had thought that she could share everything with him, thought that she knew him and could trust him. She cries because the failure in her body is spreading to her whole person. She has not given Ian enough of her love. She has betrayed him, has been tried and found wanting.

"Look," says Tim. There is a nervousness in his voice; he is used to being the strong pillar that people lean on, he is used to his own brand of loving admonition and camp humour, soothing the troubled breast of his friends. He is tense with the conflict between Ian and Liz. He wants to talk about Ian, where he feels he can talk with authority and affection. He feels trapped by the intensely female direction this conversation is taking, but he cannot surrender his role, cannot say that frankly he does not understand and is not at all sure that he wants to. "Look," he says, "I know I'm probably not the best person for this, but I'll try. Tell me why you and Ian want this baby so badly that you

will let it ruin the great romantic love of our later adolescence?"
He says it tenderly but mocking, his tone more reassured.

"Why? Why? I don't even know why anymore. It was one of
the things that brought me and Ian together in the first place:
someone else eager to share that wanting. It was the seal between us if you like, what distinguished ours from all those
other relationships. The baby was the magical reason why we
sold out and actually signed our names on the dotted line and
got married."

Their actual wedding had been a botched and confused affair.
They had imagined it as some powerful public statement of
their love; an occasion for celebration among their friends. It
had not worked out. Liz's mother had had strong preconceptions
about how her only daughter should be married, but these ideas
had been balanced by her cordial dislike of Ian. So she had not
been immediately resistant to the idea of the Oxford Registry
Office. Then, after agreeing, she had begun to feel guilty that
she was not doing well by her daughter, worried that her friends
might think she was ashamed of her son-in-law's social standing,
might think Liz was pregnant or that she and Liz had fought.
She had changed her mind and increased the pressure for a Real
Wedding at just about the time when it was too late for Liz and
Ian to change theirs. Liz and her mother spent the night before
the wedding in her mother's room in the Randolf Hotel, carefully not fighting. By the morning they were both tired and
cross. She could no longer please her father with a nuptial Mass,
because he was dead. Neither of his women would invoke his
name to the other, but his ghost stood between them all night.
They were both aware of the force with which he would have
bullied, manipulated and cajoled his wife, Ian, and through
them Liz too, into compliance. They did not name him, but
their inability to do so, their inability to tackle the layers of aggression and jealousy and freedom from him, tangled them and
made everything they said less than the truth. Her mother had
given Liz a lot of money to buy a dress for the occasion, and Liz

did not dare to tell her that Ian would certainly come in jeans, if
he came at all. The dress she had chosen her mother did not like
—because it was black and scarlet and weird, and because the
style would fail to convince anyone who thought they were getting married because Liz was pregnant.

At the Registry Office, in the cool dignity of St. Giles's her
mother had worn a smart Chanel suit, a new hat and white
gloves; Liz had worn her expensive but gaudy dress; Ian and
Tim were late, stoned, and slightly dirty. Nancy and Edward
came with their baby who screamed without ceasing throughout
the ceremony, even when Nancy tried to breastfeed her right
there in the office. Two of Ian's brothers attended, looking as
outraged as Liz's mother—their shiny vulgar suits even more of
an insult to her feelings than Ian's jeans. Ian's parents had made
it quite clear that they were not coming all that way for what
they did not consider to be a real wedding.

Tim had been there. He knew how hesitant and silly the
whole thing must have looked. So casual and painful and style-
less an occasion, and now she was claiming that it had been of
the greatest importance to her.

She can sense that Tim is about to laugh at the wedding, so
she rushes on: "But the wanting did not start there, the baby
was something we both shared from before we even met. I know
I feel I was badly mothered and wanted somehow to make
amends. I thought too, I think, that I wanted the responsibility,
that a baby would make me a grown-up, the way I used to think
that sex would, would free me from being always Daddy's little
girl for ever. And exactly the opposite: I do want that anarchy
that kids generate and distribute around them. I want to learn
from that untampered will. But, Tim, all those things are
blurred now: there is simply a desire that I have in my gut,
when I see pregnant women on the street, like fancying some
staggeringly beautiful bloke. A stab of passion for that new
shape taking you over, the way I never found sex did, something
in the body, not the head and the heart. With James, oddly, I

found that loss of control sometimes in bed, but I felt he took advantage, I felt afraid. Perhaps I just want a relationship where I can have the power, where I can do the loving. I feel that it just isn't fair. I feel I've failed, been cheated . . . and yes, I do blame Ian, sort of, because he wants that too and feels that I've failed, and that he has exposed me to that failure, because without him I probably would never have tried and found out. Been found out."

She trails off. She knows there is nothing for him there. They are not ideas that he can attach himself to. No calming advice that he can hand out. Her aggression drains away and she feels almost sorry for him, dragged in and lost among such curved labyrinthine ways. She tucks back into his armpit, trying to show that she loves and trusts him, so that he need not feel he has failed her.

"I'll tell you something," she says. "I was so glad that you and the other gay groups were there today. It was important to me. I felt it justified my being there. That you were widening things to include me. I went because I thought I ought, sisterly solidarity and things. But then I realised that we could widen the 'Right to Choose' thing out into a way of approaching all sorts of 'deviant sexuality.' I was so proud that you had all seen that. It made me feel that it was my own struggle too, that my fights with Mr. Mighty, the fertility and morality expert of Greater London were a real legitimate part of the Demo."

He smiled at her, hugged her tighter and said, "We're all together in there, you know." And they went back to the pub and had a last pint in the warmth of the others. And Tim and Ian shadow-boxed and cuffed at each other, the way men who love each other do and she laughed at them and felt eased.

But Tim and Lenny had gone back to Liverpool the next day. The excitement of the march and the power generated by their show of strength had worn off, burned away in three evenings too long of talking and feeling close to each other. She was left with the knowledge that Tim felt she had betrayed Ian. Left with the fact that she had exposed the weakness within her mar-

riage to Tony, something she had always been exquisitely careful not to do. Left with the knowledge that Dr. Marshall had
seen her ugly sneering grin on page three of his important newspaper: that he disliked her more than ever, that she had given
him one more weapon to turn on her, one more reason for with-
holding the magical drugs that would heal the bleeding between
her legs, would seal up that hole for nearly a year and give something a chance to grow there. Left with the pain and grief that
she and Ian were no longer as close as she had pretended, that
Ian was suffering because of it, and that she was so self-obsessed
that she had not even noticed.

That everything was her fault.

Delilah sat by the shore of the Great Sea, her legs folded
under her, her veil covering her red lips, her beautiful eyes staring blankly at the waves. She considered drowning herself in
their welcoming blue embrace, and was sick to discover that she
had neither the energy nor the courage for any such course. She
will not look behind her; across the fertile sea-plain she knows
that she would see in the distance the cloud of dust that still
hangs over Gaza, and now rising above that cloud will be the
smoke from the pyres of the Princes of the Philistines.

She cannot tell now why she did it. He was a lovely man, and
he had loved her. Samson, the hero of the Israelites, who had
killed his thousands with the ass's jaw-bone, who had tied the
foxes' tails and burned the standing corn and the olive groves of
her people. Samson the strong man, who had loved only pagan
women, who had sought out their softness and sweetness in contrast to the embattled secrecy of his own women. Samson, the
man who had loved her.

There had been his strength, which she had loved. With his
long hair plaited in the seven thick oiled plaits which hung
round his neck like the manes of the warhorses of Gaza and
Askelon when the army had gone out to fight. The pure
strength of his arms and back, so that he could have snapped her
in half if he had wanted, anytime. When she lay in his arms, her

head thrown back to show him the lithe beauty of her neck, and she had known that he could kill her if he wanted, she had been more excited than she had known was possible. There had been the wisdom of him that she loved. For ten years, although he still seemed young, he had been a high judge of his people. She did not understand what that meant, for the Israelites had strange ways and she did not like him to talk of them because it made her feel outside and apart from him, but it was important. His people sought him out, heard his opinions and obeyed them, although he had no way of making them do so. With her, that wisdom came in soft, witty jokes, and kindliness towards the follies and prides of other men that made her feel silly and young—though she must be older than he was.

There was a softness in him which she did not love, which she despised, which made her want to destroy him. They would say that she had sold him for the silver, that she had tricked and trapped him and betrayed him for money, that she was a whore. But it was not true. She pestered him for the secret of his strength, because she could not bear the knowledge that he would tell her. He was meant to be a man, and yet she a puny woman had got round him. It made her sick. When he lied to her, told her untruths, tricked her, she had been delighted. Each time she had bound him according to his instructions and he had broken free with such ease she had been happy. When she had taken, at last, his strong sleeping head on her lap and set the knife to each of the plaits in turn she had hated him, hated him for giving her the power over him.

She had been brought up among real men, who killed in the army and came home at night to kill again on the bodies of their women, who had been hard brutal men without softness. That was how a man should be, not amenable to the wishes of a woman, not lured by beauty, not kind and compassionate with her weaknesses.

When they had caught him, his strength flowing out into the piles of soft hair at her feet, even then he had understood—he had looked at her with understanding and love and gentleness.

The last look before they gouged his eyes out. That was why she had trapped him and betrayed him and killed him. To put out that understanding, that challenge that she should be as strong, as good, as clean as he. She was a harlot, she did not want that softness. She despised it.

He was dead. And the dead whom he slew in his death were more than those he had slain during his life. That would have amused him. She could see the edges of his eye-sockets crinkle with mirth at the thought.

She had been wrong. The minute the deed was done, the moment the last of the seven locks had thudded gently to the floor she knew she had been wrong. That his softness, his willingness to share everything with her, even his weakness, his passions, his uncertainties; those were the things that a man should have, those were the things that were better than battle honours, which he had too. She had been given the chance to give her love to someone worthy of love and she had turned it down. She had betrayed him.

There was nothing left. No child in her stomach, no feeling in her heart. The waves lapped idly on the beach. Be-tray-al. Be-tray-al. It was herself she had betrayed, herself she had sold for silver, herself she had besmirched and stolen the strength from: because she had not been woman enough to meet the new and gentle man in him. The sun was too hot to sit here all day and get burned up. She might get freckles on her face, which would not be becoming.

5. AUGUST

She found she was watching Ian covertly. She pretended she did not believe Tim, that Tim was wrong, that Ian was fine and that everything was lovely between them. But she had made a habit of trusting Tim for so long that it was difficult to stop now.

She tested Ian out. "What did you do today?"

"Nothing much."

"I know," she said with an attempt at lightness. "You sat at your desk from nine to five looking out of the window in silence."

"Don't be silly."

"Well then, what did you do?"

"Couple of meetings, you know, the usual stuff."

"How are the new workers?"

"Not so new. They're getting on okay."

"How are the Stibblings?" The Stibblings were one of Ian's favourite families; they were wild enthusiasts for litigation, and were frequently consulting Ian about whom they could sue next and how to go about it. He loved them for their courage, their refusal to be defeated and for the endless hilarity that he got from them. He used to bounce home and regale Liz with their latest mad exploits and their stolid refusal to take any of his advice.

Now he said, "They're okay, I suppose."

She pretended to read while she watched him, kept an eye on him. He could move through his life oblivious of her greedy consumption. She needed him to be happy, she was only watching him to make sure he was happy. Was he more restless, less secure, threatened, trying to escape her? If he was late home, was it because he wanted to avoid her, needed to escape from the pain and intimacy of her demands and her failure? Would he stop loving her because she could not have his child?

One supper-time when he was out at another meeting and she had gone over to Nancy's house, she exploded into anger. "I feel like some damn black widow spider. He makes me feel as though I was trying to suck his flesh. I'm older, taller, heavier than he is. He carries on like some cautious male spider being lured into my culinary web. I can't stand it. He acts as though I was the enemy, as though I was trying to consume him, destroy him."

"Rubbish," said Nancy tartly. "You're projecting. It's too transparent. That's what you feel, not what he feels."

"Nancy."

"Well, it's true. It is simply not something that would ever occur to him and you know it."

"Just once I want to be the child. I want to cry out in the night and have Mummy come and offer me a nice warm breast to suck. I feel like Hughie did that first night you went out and left him, when I baby-sat. He woke up and he wanted you. There was nothing I could do. He was desolate. I feel that. That Ian has been there promising to love me and now when I need it, when I'm crying for it, he has just buggered off into his own world. Just cleared off. I envy him that. I know that when I go to work in the morning I carry him with me; but he can just go off and leave our whole relationship behind. I bet he doesn't go over and over it through the day, take it apart with his friends, measure and test it."

"But, Liz, it's men's loss that they can't do that. I don't know any men that can. They play chess and wrestle with each other, and make endless jokes, and they call it friendship. I don't envy them. I think they should envy us."

"It's all right for you."

"That's so unfair. You're always saying that, and it's nonsense. You think that some baby is going to solve your psychic ills. You are becoming a bloody obsessive, it's all you want to talk about. My baby. My husband. Give it a break."

All mothers go away in the end. Her own mother. Her father. Ian. Nancy. The baby is used to waking the mother with the smallest whimper in the night. Now the mother does not come: the baby rolls on to its back to project its voice louder into that infinite space, and sees the shadowy shape of the mobile hung over the bed. In the daylight that is a thing of pleasure; the baby, its tummy filled with milk and affection, reaches towards the pretty thing and gurgles with delight at the colours. But in the dark the shapes have changed, become menacing, dangerous. And where is the mother? Will she ever come back again? After the baby was born, shoved, squeezed, half-maimed, blinded with light, hung upside down, hit, left gasping for air, screaming with loss, it found a safe place at the mother's strong soft white breast; cuddled, cooed, soothed, loved. Now the mother had withdrawn, gone away, did not respond to the wailing in the dark.

"Ian, do you love me?" she asked him.

"What is this?"

"A question."

"Once you told me never to ask that question. Once you said that if I could not believe it without asking, we might as well pack the whole thing in. You said it was a question without dignity, or respect. You said it was a childish question, not worthy of a grown-up."

It was true, she had said that once, long ago, in the dark magic of a night when he had wanted to want her and she had simply wanted him. She had said it when she was in the position of strength. Had it hurt him as much as it hurt her now? She had meant it as the perfect assurance, the only way she knew of saying "I love you very much and always" without any exaggeration, and violence. She had meant, you know I love you, of course I love you, I am here, there is no need even to talk about it. His answer now might mean all that too. But it might mean, I don't want to commit myself, I don't want to have you demanding anything, pressurising me anymore; I don't want you to ask that because I don't want to hurt your feelings with my answer. It might mean, I don't love you and I don't want to be bullied into saying so.

Each evening when she got home before him she would make afresh her resolution. She would not lean on him, would not pressure him, would let him find his own pace, his own way through to her. She would respect his delicacy, his timidity, his reticence. It had always worked before, it would work again, it had to. All she had to do was be there and leave him alone: no demands. If she had demanded sex from him in the beginning, if she had hurried, been less than perfectly patient, they would not be where they now were. She would be there: calm, serene, ready, but not eager. No pushing and shoving.

Each evening her calm indifference was met by his calm indifference; her retreat from him merely increased the distance between them. He would not give, not an inch. Had he been like this before Tim had pointed it out to her, or was she making him like this by worrying about it? An hour later she would be pleading.

"Do you want to go to the pub?"

"I don't mind, what would you like?"

"I'd like to know what you would like to do."

"For God's sake, Liz, I'm indifferent, we'll do what you like."

Her anger mounting she would force herself to be calm, gentle, considerate.

"Did you have a good day?"

"Okay."

"What happened?"

"Nothing much."

Once he lost his temper. "Jesus Christ, Liz, don't be so fucking aggressive."

"Aggressive? Since when has it been aggressive to ask the bloke you live with if he could bring himself to decide what he would like for dinner?"

"God damn it. You know perfectly well what I mean. Now just shut up."

"Don't talk to me like that."

"There you are then."

She slammed into the bedroom, lay on the bed and tried to cry. If she did he would hear her through the walls and the self-consciousness prevented the tears. In the end she had apologised to him. Apologised. She despised herself. For the first time in months she did not go to her women's group meeting, ringing up with a facile excuse. How could she say to those sturdy complacent ladies that she was begging, begging him to love her. That she was running round performing for her man, so that he would reward her with a tiny taste of his personality. And that moreover she was not succeeding.

She tried to gain comfort from Tim saying that he would never leave her; but that hardly seemed to matter if he was going to be like this. Stubborn, distanced from her, he might as well be gone, at least he would not be torturing her like this. And it was all her fault. She had been so wrapped up in herself and her own problems that she had not noticed him, she had betrayed him. He could hardly be blamed. It was all her fault. Her guilt made her angry, she tried to be angry with him. Why should he expect all the attention, when the suffering, the failure, the inadequacy was hers? He had proved his manhood, if that was how he chose to think of it; he had brought a promiscuous woman to her senses, back to the path of virtue with his manly love. He had passed all the little tests that Dr. Marshall had prepared for him. His noble sperm swimming in their rich glue did everything they were meant to do, he could put them in the right place for their dangerous journey into the dark unknown where they had to die unfulfilled because there was nothing there but her desert. She was the one who deserved sympathy and love, she was the one whose personality was imperilled, who needed him. She should not have to foster his sense of security, it ought to be the other way around. But her anger only increased the feeling of guilt: it was not Ian's fault that she had made herself a sacrificial altar out of biology, that she identified her womb with her soul. Indeed she had told him otherwise with her own lying tongue: that she was a feminist and knew better than to be trapped in that biological determinism. Was he to blame because she had deceived him?

When she could bear herself no longer she took to her bed with a throat infection. It was a real infection, Nancy's Harriet had it, lots of people had it. But with her eyes puffed up, her temperature neatly recorded on her graph at levels that had no relevance there, her throat pounding and her flesh miserable, she was not able to deceive herself.

Illness had been the one way she could milk real love out of her mother. As a child, spots, pains, aches and fever had always drawn from her mother that hard-to-tap water from the well of tenderness. Aspirin—orange-flavoured, though with a nasty powdery texture—and cool drinks and forehead-soothing and attention had been hers for the asking. When she had been tucked up in her parents' bed, propped on her mother's special "armchair" arrangement of pillows, when she was weak and docile, she had corresponded to her mother's idea of a daughter. Her mother would sit beside her on the bed reading aloud. *Thomas the Tank Engine* and *Winnie the Pooh* when she was tiny, then *Swallows and Amazons*, *The Prisoner of Zenda*, *What Katy Did* and *Little Women*. Her father would come home at the end of the day and sit too, chatting and teasing. But soon her mother would come in and say, "Now come on, Daddy, she'll get over-excited." And he would be driven off downstairs, while she was tended to: lifted out of the bed and put in a comfy armchair, wrapped in a pink blanket while her mother remade the bed, pounded the pillows, tidied the table. Then she'd be lifted back into renewed comfort. Late at night after she was really asleep, she could remember being lifted out and carried back to her own little bed where a hot-water-bottle had taken the iciness away, and, half-conscious, she would snuggle down to kisses and endearments.

It worked less well now. Ian, brought up in a family where illness was nothing but a nuisance, had grown up almost disgustingly healthy, unable to remember any illness at all except German Measles which he and his siblings had enjoyed *en bloc,* with a flustered mother who had not wanted to miss even three days' work. At the bottom of his heart he believed that illness was self-indulgent, that the ill person, nearly always her (but even himself) should pull herself together, and until she had done so should be left alone as much as possible, so that reclining in bed gained her no social benefits. He was not really neglectful, but he went to sleep on the sitting-room sofa—"No point in both of us getting it"—and made long-suffering faces if she said she wanted her Ribena hot after he had brought it cold. He would come into the bedroom when he got in from work and instead of asking tenderly how she was feeling, would say, "You look a lot better" in robust tones which allowed no disagreements. Or say, "For God's sake, get better quickly, we're supposed to be going on holiday in ten days. I'm not wasting mine being a sick-bed Florence Nightingale."

And during the day when the flat was empty she lay there and wept. Slowly she reread sentimental novels, knowing that they would make her cry and indulging every tear. Weaknesses were fostered which she would not normally allow herself. She even found herself sobbing delightedly over Jenny's death in *Love Story*—and how on earth did they come to have a copy of that in the house?—and enjoying fantasies about how she was failing to conceive because of some terminal disease, preferably missed through the incompetence of Dr. Marshall. He would blush with humility and come to her bedside, making a long and extremely inconvenient trip across London from his clinic one evening after work. He would sit and tell her how sorry he was;

how he felt obliged to offer his resignation; that if it had not been for his incapacity and inability and ill-founded obsession with psychiatric causes for infertility, her condition could easily have been cured; and now that it was too late he felt obliged to go into a monastery, or work for the women's movement or some other appropriate and ghastly penance, about which he was looking to her for advice.

Ian would be sorry too. He would come each evening, noticing with pain the decline in her health, watching her slip gently away from him while she spoke so tenderly and wisely. He would hold her hand and repeat despairingly how sorry he was, how he had neglected and judged her, how he had blamed her for not giving him a child, but that now it did not matter, that no child mattered to him if she were to die. When she got to the point where she should smile softly and say, "Love is never needing to say you're sorry," she was brought back to reality with a giggle. And then she wept because it could not be true, because there was not going to be any soppy option like that, because she knew quite well she was suffering only from mild tonsillitis and acute self-pity, because she could see through herself and not much like what she saw.

By Friday she was getting better; she was up, though still droopy, when Ian came home from work, and that pleased him.

She said, "I should think I could go to work again on Monday."

"Why don't you stay home next week, then you'll be quite well for our going away."

She had forgotten to concentrate on their holiday. They were planning to travel down to northern Italy, stay in Tuscany for a while with some friends of Ian's who had taken an old millhouse for August, and then go on to Rome. Now she thought about it, she was happy. Travelling was something they did well together; Ian loved the sun, would relax in it, mellowed by laziness and warmth. Three weeks of sunshine and space. For one moment she had a sense of relief that they did not have a baby; holidays were a major complication for Nancy, needing detailed planning, careful considerations of so many different needs.

Ian said, "Look, are you sure you'll be okay for this weekend?"

"What?"

"Well, you know I'm meant to be going to this community worker thing in Manchester, but I could easily not go, if you need me."

He meant it too, he would stay home without a fuss if she needed him. His goodwill obliged her to offer at least as much.

"Rubbish, I'll be fine. I'm better anyway and if anything went awry I'm not exactly friendless you know. I can get some of the backlog of work done, then perhaps I really won't have to go to work next week. Of course you will go."

She had another thought.

"If this conference is in Manchester why don't you give Tim a ring and spend Sunday night up there as well?" He could not know the generosity behind the suggestion. Then she thought that as Tim did undeniably enjoy doling out advice to his friends it was quite possible that Ian would get the same little lecture as she had. Tim would certainly reveal to Ian the content of the conversation he had had with her the weekend of the demonstration—in loving interest of course; it was surprisingly difficult to object to Tim's intrusions into one's life. She refused to worry; drained of distress and energy by the warmth of her bed, she felt that it would not matter, might even be good for Ian.

"I don't know," Ian said, "I'll see how it goes. I'm usually so knackered by the end of these weekend conferences that the only thing I will want to do is return to the arms of my wife." He grinned at her.

She grinned back. A delicate restoring of balance, to which he would be attaching no importance. She would not ferret at their relationship anymore. If Ian needed to hide in his burrow for a while that need not hurt her. She did not have to wriggle in after him, her eyes bright, her teeth long and sharp, working for the jugular, driving him out. There was no need.

Saturday, with the flat empty and suddenly spacious, confirmed that easiness. She read a proposed synopsis, and wrote a letter to Amanda congratulating her on the birth of her baby, saying she had not come to visit her because of her bad throat, but that she was thrilled and so glad it was a girl after all those boys. They ought to get together and talk as soon as Amanda was ready, could they have lunch sometime? That salved her conscience about work. She wrote a letter to her mother, containing nothing of her life but the most carefully edited externals: a deed which always gave her a simple glow of virtue, driving away each time and at so little cost the vague guilt that she had not written for so long.

After lunch Nancy rang to find out where she had been and whether she was going to take Harriet swimming the next day. She almost said yes despite the lingering cold, because swimming with Harriet was such fun, and as neither Nancy nor Edward could swim, it was one thing that she could really offer usefully to do. The thought of Italy in the sunshine and the soft cool white wine discouraged her at the last moment.

"Is Harriet really better then? She's tougher than me."

"Have you been ill?"

"Where did you think I was on Thursday?"

"Sulking."

"Nancy! Why should I have been sulking?"

"You were sulking the week before and you know it."

They laughed, filling in the gap with commiserations about her throat and Harriet's. About how useless men were at responding to sickness.

"At least you're an adult," moaned Nancy. "Edward means to help when the kids are ill, but why should he miss a whole day of work, when I will only have to miss some of one, because I work at home? It sounds logical, and he can't realise that I can only work when I know I won't be interrupted, it's just impossible when a weak little voice is about, or even *may* be about, to call 'Mummy, I need a drink,' or 'Mummy I'm bored.'"

"Ian always acts as though I had got ill just to inconvenience him. He's really sweet, but in the most self-congratulatory way. Anyway I was emphatically not sulking, and I think I'd better say no to the swimming. We're going on holiday next weekend."

"Yes, I forgot. I do envy you, you know. Scotland with my mama is not quite the same as those unplanned detours to Turkey we used to get involved in so casually."

"What happened on Thursday?"

"Not much." And they fell into easy gossip about families and friends and books. The gap between them closed. Liz wondered why she had ever let it open. She felt good. Her cigarettes were giving her pleasure again, and she abandoned fruit juice in favour of coffee. She realised with amusement that Nancy had of course been lying to her about Edward, because it was the holidays and he could not possibly have been off to work while Nancy lovingly nursed their sick daughter. Far from making her angry, the knowledge amused her. She would not tell Nancy she had found her out. She went to bed early and slept well.

She was woken by the telephone. Struggling out of sleep, she had a fear of emergency, that something had happened to Ian, that something was wrong; but by the time she had crossed into the living-room and seen the clock reading half past ten she had suppressed the panic.

"Hello."

"Liz?"

"Mummy. Have you been ringing long? I'm afraid I was asleep."

"I guessed."

"I'm sorry."

"I didn't mean it like that. I'm just so glad you're there."

"I wrote to you yesterday."

"I wasn't worried about you; I'm worrying about me just now."

"Is something wrong?"

"Frankly, yes. I had a car accident."

"My God, are you all right?"

"I'm alive."

She knew her mother wanted something, and was finding it difficult to ask; the dry tone usually meant that. "Mummy, what's up?"

"Well, I'm in hospital at the moment. The thing is, I've broken my ankle, not too badly, and strained my shoulder a bit. But they won't let me out of hospital if there's no one at home. I hate to ask you, but I can't stay here, you know how I hate hospitals, and they don't want me because I'm not ill enough and I'm taking up a whole bed. It will only be for a fortnight or so, because Florence gets back from her holiday."

"Florence?"

"A friend of mine; but she's gone on a tour of châteaux of the Loire. Liz, please."

"Mummy, don't sound so plaintive, of course I'll come. Lucky for you my holiday time is just coming up."

"Were you going away?"

"No, no, our plans were still quite flexible."

"Oh good, I'm glad. How's Ian?"

"Fine. He's away this weekend. Look, Mummy, I'll have to wait till he gets back and fix things up. Can you stay put till Tuesday?"

"Yes, of course, that will be about right."

"Okay, I'll ring the hospital when I've found out about trains and things. How's the car?"

"Oh. I'm not sure. I'll find out."

"Don't worry. I'll be there."

"Thank you, darling."

It was not like her mother to say "darling," she was never one for the affectionate gesture. After Liz had said goodbye and put down the phone she could have wept with frustration. Goodbye sun of Italy, goodbye happy time with Ian. She could not have refused though. She could not have refused and left her mother languishing in hospital, which she really did hate, and given her mother yet another tool in the long war of guilt; she had not responded when her father was dying, she had not even remembered to telephone. It would take more than tending to one broken ankle to eliminate that victory of her mother's.

Before her father's funeral she had spent two days of panic because she had nothing appropriate to wear. She had kept telling herself that it did not matter, and she had failed to convince herself. She had borrowed a black velvet jacket from a friend and worn it, ill-matching with the black skirt they had had to wear for exams at Oxford, but the odd combination had had an air of frivolity that she worried might offend people.

The long, trying Mass of Requiem had flowed over her head, her only consideration had been that she would not cry. Beside her she knew her mother was locked into the same struggle. At the tea-party they had given afterwards some distant relative had said, "Liz, I never realised before how like your mother you looked." She did not look like her mother; it had been the expression of grim determination not to weep in front of the other that had deceived him. Neither of them were willing to ask any favour, any comfort, any gift of the other.

Now her mother had *asked*—it must have been difficult for her, she almost admired her mother for being able to. She would have stayed in the hospital sooner than ask her mother to rearrange valuable time on her behalf. Rather than admit she had any need of her.

Ian rang later to say that he was going to stay the night with Tim and Lenny. She did not tell him about their ruined holiday. He might as well have one evening of pleasure. She might as well have one evening not arguing about it. Ian was going to be furious, and sad.

She said, "What time will you be back then?"

"I thought I'd catch an early train, and go straight to the office."

"Don't do that. Come home first."

"Liz, why?"

"I'll tell you when I see you."

"Is something wrong?"

"No, I promise."

After he had agreed, and asked her to ring the office she had the most dreadful fear that he might think she was pregnant and travel south in that joyous expectation. She could think of no other reason that he could imagine for demanding his presence like that. Rationally he should be able to work out that there was no way she could have discovered anything in the two days he had been away, but people were not always rational. She nearly rang him again to tell him that she wasn't, but she became confused. If the idea had not crossed his mind there was no point in piling up the grief.

Instead she rang Nancy again and grumbled about having to go. At least Nancy would understand why she had to, there would be no dispute, only commiseration, just what she wanted. She was right.

"Oh poor you, what a bugger. We even have to mummy our own mummies. I bet if you were a son she would not think of ringing you up, demanding that you sacrifice work-time to look after her."

"I suspect if I had been a son, I would never have got away in the first place."

"I don't believe that, actually. You'd have had a much better relationship because she would have felt morally obliged to let you do what you wanted; she would have thought that 'normal.'"

"Well, I suppose she didn't break her ankle just to spite me. It's not fair to feel so angry with her."

"Mothers are funny. Do you know Alice finally told hers about the baby, much trembling and trepidation; and oddly enough she's over the moon with excitement. I suppose she'd given up hope of Alice doing anything as womanly as having a baby and not aborting it."

"Lucky Alice. Look, I had better get organised. I'll see you, probably in about three weeks."

"No, we're off in a fortnight. Send me a postcard."

"Of sunny Dartmoor."

"Don't be sour."

Ian was not angry; he was upset, which was worse. And he tried not to show it.

"Never mind, we can always sneak out and have it off in the rain."

She could not make love in her mother's house. They had been married five years, and that taboo still stood. The few times they had been down there for a holiday, a brief weekend was about as much as they could stand. She was moved out of her own little bedroom and installed in the guest-room, which made Ian laugh because he never knew what he was meant to do with a dressing-room. She knew the walls were solid and they could do what they liked in perfect privacy, but if he so much as caressed her she would become self-conscious, would push him off and either giggle or pretend she was tired. Her repression turned him on at first, it was the only situation in which he was more enthusiastic for sex than she was, it made him curious and excited. They usually ended up fighting.

"It doesn't always rain."

"Then we can sneak off and do it in the sunshine, better still."

"Ian, this is silly. You're not coming, you don't have to. Go to Italy. I never even thought of you coming. You know you'd hate it."

"I don't want to go to Italy without you."

"Liar."

"Well . . . I do want to go to Italy with you."

"Ian, I'm sorry."

"Darling, I didn't mean it like that. What a cock-up."

"Seriously, you know you don't want to go to my mother's. We'll never get a full refund on the flights anyway, it would just be a waste of money for you not to go. And your friends need you to pay part of the house rent anyway. I don't believe in the Equality of Misery theory at all. If you come you'll be miserable, I'll still be miserable, Mummy will be miserable, seeing how she feels about you, and the gang in Italy will be miserable. If I go alone I'll still be miserable, but you'll be happy, they'll be happy and Mummy will be happy too. So it's obvious. To say nothing of absence making the heart grow fonder, and separation being good for the young couple, bringing freshness to the tired marriage and so forth."

She knew he was happy not to lose the holiday. She tried not to feel resentful. It was the ideal solution to her resolve not to harass and pester at their relationship; the solution to her obsessions and worries about him. Five years, and apart from the time that he had gone to Glasgow for barely a week a year ago, and the occasional weekends, they were never apart. It was silly. Let her be generous, let her not spoil her generosity by feeling bad about it. Let her think about something else.

"How are Tim and Lenny?" she asked.

"Fine. Really happy I think. They're both over-committed and over-worked; I could never live at that pace. Tim was, as usual, full of marriage guidance techniques."

"He was, was he?" She would not be frightened. "I got the same when he was in London last month."

"So he told me. He also told me that I was betraying you by being so ready to avoid delicate situations, by playing up my psychotic past and by retreating up my own ass-hole, if you want to know."

"He said that?"

"Yes. Why?"

"Because he told me I was betraying you by retreating up my own vagina . . . more or less."

"Tim doesn't know the meaning of the word."

"That was only one of the difficulties in the conversation."

"He is an interfering old sod, he really is. Everyone's uncle."

"Luckily for us."

"True, but even so . . ."

Which was why they loved him, in the end. Laughing about him took the misery away from her. Why hadn't she told Ian in the beginning, spared them both these last dangerous weeks? And whatever he had said to Ian had sent him home to her in a new mood. Let the three weeks of holiday complete that.

Her mother was more badly hurt than she had said on the telephone. Liz arrived at the hospital in Taunton, tired from the train ride and angry at herself for still being ungenerous, for not wanting to come, angry with her mother for summoning her, already wondering if, after three or four days, she would be able to escape back to London, her duty cheaply done, and go to Italy with Ian.

The last time she had been in this hospital was when her father was dying. The intensive care unit had been hushed and frightening; he had lain in the bed looking silly and very old and faintly disgusting. As she went up in the lift she knew why her mother could not bear to stay even one more day here. She herself could hardly bear the hour or so that she might have to tolerate. At least a different ward, a different floor, but still the grunting breaths, the tubes running in under his blanket, under his striped pyjamas, the blankness in his eyes, the distance between that and her little room in Oxford where she had forgotten him. She did not want to come back here.

Her mother looked ghastly. Apart from the plastered leg and strapped shoulder, she had not mentioned the cuts on her face and hand, the extensive bruising. Liz was fiercely glad that she had come, and shamefully glad that her mother was ill enough to drive away the feelings of frustration and resentment she had been feeling.

"Mummy."

"Liz. I am glad to see you." Her battering made it easier to embrace her. Liz felt tender towards her, willing to help.

"I am glad to see you. Apparently the car is badly wrecked, but I've hired one for us. Perhaps you could pick it up. I hired it in your name, I hope you've brought your driving licence."

"Don't worry, Mummy. How did this happen?"

"Some silly maniac on a motor bike. I had to swerve to avoid him and went out of control. It's nothing. I think I was probably lucky."

After three days she wondered if she had ever been away, if her own life really existed somewhere outside. She hated cooking in her mother's kitchen, hated the feeling that she was intruding, feared all the time that her mother was about to criticise, to scold, to tell her the Right Way to do something that she did her Own Way every day. Her mother did not need nursing, she needed tending to, she could hobble from her bedroom to the sitting-room and sit there. She needed amusing and shopping for, and help getting dressed and undressed. She would call suddenly when Liz was in the middle of something else and she would have to stop and answer. Her mother was not demanding, but she was dependent.

Like having a child, Liz thought, and hated it. She did not find it amusing to have to give up the shape of her own day into the keeping of another. Perhaps Nancy was right, perhaps it was just one almighty drag for little reward. But her baby would not be her mother, would not have caught her in this web of guilt; she would not have betrayed her mother repeatedly, giving her up for the sake of different men. She had won her father's love away from her mother and she could make no restitution; she had abandoned her mother, widowed and alone, to live with Ian whom her mother hated, and had enjoyed the fact that her mother hated him. Surely a baby would be different.

Once chopping her mother's meat for her, Liz risked saying, "I'd have to do this for years if I had a baby, wouldn't I?"

"Not really, they learn quite fast. You mustn't compare them with sick old women."

"Old my foot." The ejaculation sounded funny and prim to her. Even her vocabulary was trimmed to meet the situation. Would she say "shit" when she had a baby?

"How old are you? Fifty-five?"

"Fifty-six."

"That's not old."

"Thank you. But it is getting to thinking about being old. Liz, I'm glad you've come down because there's something I've been wanting to talk to you about and haven't liked to discuss in letters. I'm thinking of selling the house."

She realised that her mother wanted her to be upset, expected her to be. She did not know how to say that she did not care.

"Why?"

"It's too big and expensive, and too isolated."

"Yes, I do see that. Where are you thinking of going?"

"I thought that I would buy a house near Exeter with my friend Florence."

"Live with another woman . . . You?"

"Well, why ever not?"

"But, Mummy . . . suppose it did not work out? I mean, you haven't known her very long."

"How do you know?"

"Well, you've never mentioned her before and . . . you might end up stuck with her."

"Liz, you sound like I sounded when you told me you were going to marry Ian."

"Mummy."

"Well, you do. You sound smug and know-it-all. You spend years criticising me because I don't have enough women friends, I don't trust other women, I judge them, I'm a failure, etc., and now I tell you what are my plans for my life you start criticising again. I'm not allowed to criticise you, your friends, your husband, your notions of family-planning which mean only planning not to have a family, but the same rules don't apply to you, do they? You're a bigot, a hypocritical bigot."

"Mummy, calm down, I'm sorry. I didn't mean it like that. You're old enough to live with whom you like. I don't care, why bother to ask me?"

"I thought it might be civil."

"For God's sake."

"Liz, please don't talk like that."

"I'm sorry."

"So am I. I know we've never been very close, but we've never fought either and I have no intention of starting with you now. And I'm grateful to you for coming down like this. I know Florence well, I like her a lot; she's just about to retire from teaching, she doesn't have a lot of capital of her own, but will have just about as much income and we think it will work well. I'm not asking you, I'm telling you. I did think you might be furious with me for selling Daddy's house, but I never thought you'd get upset about me living with another woman."

"As to the house, no I'm quite happy for you to sell it. It's yours not Daddy's. I was just surprised." She did not know what to say, she did not feel as though she knew this woman. Her mother saw the past so differently from her, maybe she never had felt the anger and jealousy and despair that Liz had read into all her actions. "Look, shall I make you a cup of tea?"

"Yes please, that would be nice."

After she had made the tea she went out for a walk. Looking back at the house, she noticed once again how beautiful it was and wondered why she minded so little about the thought of it being sold. It was her home. It had been her home and it wasn't any more; home was that god-awful flat near Parsons Green. Strange.

She liked her mother. She had not expected that; three days with her and although she felt drained and tired by looking after her, she found that she liked her, that all the tension had been in her mind, she liked the thought of her mother living in a cottage with another woman, growing a garden of her own choosing instead of her father's. Being with someone who would not find her stupid, who would not find excuses to compare her with other women. Her father must have been intolerable to her mother. Even the fact that she had been able to pick up bits of foreign languages on trips abroad—a skill that any small child has—had been used to put her mother down. The endless jokes about Liz's brains being from his side of the family.

The evening was long and peaceful, the fields through which she walked green and soft as the light began to fade. It was not she who had betrayed her mother, it was him. He should have attended to his own woman and not gone chasing after toddlers like her. She had no guilt to expiate. She wished she could ask her mother, "Were you happy with Daddy? Did you love him? Did you ever want to leave him?" She would not be allowed to make such intimate inquiries; her own unwillingness to talk about emotional difficulties was something she had inherited from her mother. She was not allowed to ask, she would have to guess as she had always guessed, but there were more options than seeing her mother struggling endlessly to win the love of her wonderful hero. Perhaps she had not cared.

She came back to the house, feeling light-headed. She beat her mother at Scrabble three times in a row and found that she did not feel bad about it.

"Do you want me to drive you to church tomorrow morning?"

"Why, do you want to go?" She sensed that her mother was mocking her, but she did not care.

"You know I don't." But she felt no aggression.

"Well then, I think I could give it a miss. We might drive to the seaside in the afternoon though if you'd like to swim."

"If the weather's good." It could not be so easy to repair a relationship, the whole thing was in her own head, good, bad; up, down. Perhaps her mother did not care about her either, only this woman who she was going to live with.

But in the morning nothing was repaired. She woke up happy in her small bedroom, nostalgic for a childhood where one woke while the dawn was still clean and untouched, new laundered, and pulling on shorts and sandals could roam the summer morning for hours before breakfast. Now she needed an alarm clock to arouse her, and the daylight had already been used by others. She stretched idly, wondered what she would give her mother for breakfast and reached for her clinical thermometer. It stood neatly in a cut-glass tumbler beside her bed. Convenient that her mother was unable to tackle the stairs or she would have had to keep it hidden: her mother would ask and she did not want to tell her. Perhaps things would improve, here without Ian, just the two women together in the big house, and she would feel free to tell her mother that it was not selfishness, or career, or fear that stopped her providing the grandchild. But still she did not want her mother's pity, she did not even want her sympathy. There was no sisterhood for them.

She stuck the thermometer in her mouth and lay back; it was always nice to start the day in this leisurely fashion. Once she had got used to it, she had enjoyed the *carte blanche* that it gave her to lean back and doze for the extra three minutes. At home Ian would boil the kettle while she lay back with her eyes shut and thought about the day. When she took the glass stick out of her mouth and reached for her chart she was not particularly concentrating. The beginning of the chart was so irregular from her illness that it lacked the usual ordered straight line, running neatly across the page. But last week the line had returned to that accustomed pattern. She looked again at the mercury; she twisted the tube, trying to make the reading other than it was. She shook it down and put it back in her mouth—perhaps the water in the glass had been warmed by the morning sun. She knew it had not. The tiny rise repeated itself on the second reading. A perfect ovulation reading, a textbook performance, she knew.

Dr. Marshall had said, "Well if you want to reject my psychological interpretation, what plausible alternative would you offer for the fact that the one time you have ovulated in all the months we have been doing this together was when your husband was out of the country?"

And she had said, "Coincidence."

"Well"—he had pretended to give this suggestion serious thought—"Well, that is possible. But I would like to point out that it is a very marked coincidence, taken along with all the other evidence."

"Lots of women do not ovulate every month. That's well known. That's a fact, as scientific as psychological repression of ovulation."

"You've been doing your homework haven't you, Elizabeth?"

"There's nothing wrong with that."

There had been something wrong with the feverish, selective perusal of journals that she did not have the methodology to analyse—*Fertility and Sterility, The National Journal of Gynaecology and Obstetrics*—stolen moments in a library to which she had gained access by "borrowing" Amanda's reading card . . . pretending to be doing research for Amanda's book. She had been reading only to disprove him; reading only authors who did not believe in psychological causes.

She had said desperately to Dr. Marshall, "There's nothing wrong with that. If I hadn't done careful background reading I wouldn't have found you."

"Of course there's nothing wrong with it. It's probably all to the good, so long as you recognise that casual reading of second-hand works by a layman, laywoman I should say"—kindly smile, patronising and pleased with himself—"does not make you an expert. Yes, it is true of course that a great number of women, even perhaps the majority of women, do not in fact ovulate every month. But you must also know that regularity increases up to about the age of thirty or a little over. You are nearly at that age of peak fertility, and you have ovulated once, once in ten or more months, and on that occasion your husband was in Scotland."

"It could still be coincidence."

"Of course it could, but I think you should ask yourself why you are so determined that it should be coincidence, why you are not prepared to assume that it was not coincidence and do something about it."

And now. Twice. Not coincidence. She was not so optimistic, so stupid, so blind, that she would be able to convince herself with coincidence. She leapt out of bed, rushed down the stairs and grabbed the telephone. It was only yesterday Ian was supposed to have left for Italy. He was indecisive, likely to change his plans, likely to have put off going for some reason that would seem petty and trivial to her, but over-riding to him, something coming up at work, or the inability to get organised into finding his passport. He had no plane to catch, he had been planning to hitch down through France; they had only bought tickets to fly home on.

She dialled their own number and found her hands were shaking. Dear God, sweet Jesus, Lord and Giver of life, here is a cause after your own sacred heart, a woman who wants a child, who does not want to abort it, a woman who is faithful to her husband. Let him still be at home, let him be there sleeping sweetly, his large nose poking over the top of the blanket.

He had given her up long ago, just as she had given him up. God could not care about a woman who married gays in registry offices, who betrayed fathers and did not respect mothers. But I do respect her. I have been respecting her for nearly twelve hours. Why won't you reward me for that, that breakthrough? A woman who marches in abortion marches and loves an unmarried woman who was going to have a baby, contrary to God's Holy Law and Ordinance.

The telephone bell rang and rang in the empty flat. With the receiver clamped to her ear she could see the flat, empty, tidy—because Ian would have tidied it for her return before he left—and with the sun coming in through the dirty window-pane, emphasising the worn arms on the chairs. After about eight rings she knew he was not there. The telephone always woke him, he was always sensitive to outside information coming in, he loved the telephone. But she hung on; if he was hung-over, if he had not got in till four this morning, if he were listening to music with the headphones on. At eight o'clock in the morning, she almost laughed at herself. After twenty-five or more of the double rings she hung up; she leaned against the telephone table twisted with pain. It wasn't fair, it wasn't fair. Her body knew, and had announced, that Ian had caught the last night's ferry. She could put out an international emergency; as he travelled southwards in someone's lorry, or squashed in the back of someone's car, would he hear on the radio? She knew she would not do it. There wasn't time—less than twenty-four hours. Even if she could persuade the police, even if he heard, even if he wanted to come home, there wasn't time, there wasn't time. Already that precious egg was beginning to die inside her, moving down the tubes towards despair. It was she, she who was the killer, she was the woman who deceived the world. Some dark part of herself was chuckling now, some inward corner of her soul was filled with perverse merriment, because it had achieved its evil ends. Where was that rottenness, how would she stamp it out? How would she kill it without killing her whole self with it?

"Liz," her mother called from her temporary bedroom they had organised in the old morning-room. "Liz, whatever are you doing?"

"Nothing, Mummy. I just remembered something I meant to tell Ian before he went away. About his passport. But it seems as though he's gone already. I hope he sorted it out."

"Gone abroad?"

"Yeah, Italy."

"Liz, come here a minute." She went reluctantly towards the voice. She could not tell without a mirror whether the pain stood out in lumps all over her face; but the mirror was way back down the hall in the loo, and if she went that way her mother would hear and want to know why.

She went into the morning-room; a pretty green-panelled sitting-room which was flooded with the sun. Her mother's bed was resting awkwardly between a sofa and some chintz chairs, looking temporary and out of place.

"Good morning, Mummy."

"Good morning. Listen, why has Ian gone off to Italy?"

"Well, it's his holiday, isn't it?"

"And yours too?"

"Yes, actually."

"And you never said, you just gave it up and came down here. You need not have done that."

"Of course I could have left you rotting in the hospital until the fair Florence returned from her trip among the châteaux."

"Oh Liz . . . Oh dear. I am sorry darling. I really am, I felt bad enough about calling you at all, I know how busy you are, how much you get through, but to take your holiday. I truly am sorry."

"There's no need to be, Mummy. I have had lots of holidays in Tuscany and you know it."

"That's not the point. I'm really upset. I wish you had said, I'm sure I could have made other arrangements. I am sorry."

"Mummy, please don't be. Don't upset yourself; you know how selfish I am, you are always saying so yourself. Don't you think I could have got out of coming if I had really wanted to?"

Her mother really was sorry and upset now.

"Look Mummy, let me make your breakfast. Don't get worked up about it, it will stop bones from knitting."

When she had broken her collar-bone falling out of a tree, her father had rushed across the lawn to rescue her. She could remember the pain in his face which must have reflected the pain in her own. He had taken one look at her face and put her right in the car and driven her to hospital. She must have been about ten: it was the summer when she had first been allowed to race her dinghy alone in children's classes. Her mother, probably relieved that the racing was off, as she had always thought Liz too young and too inexperienced to race alone, although she had been over-ruled by her father, had punctuated the whole following six weeks with that expression: "Fretting will stop bones from knitting." Liz had hated the very words, but looking at her mother now she saw that she remembered them with gentle amusement, pleased that Liz should have dredged them up from the past.

Liz went through to the kitchen, opened the lid on the Aga and put the kettle on. It was not fair that she should have to provide the comfort. Comfort Ian, comfort her mother. She was the one in need of comfort, of love. She hated them both. She refused Dr. Marshall's interpretation. Twice was not too much for coincidence. As quietly as she could she ran back up the stairs, collected her chart, ran down again, shredded it into little tiny pieces and thrust them into the Aga. She would tell Dr. Marshall she had forgotten to take the chart on holiday with her, she would tell him that it had been useless because of the high temperature she had run with her sore throat. She would tell him any lie that came to hand, but she would not tell him that he had more fuel for his theories, more evidence that she was mad, unfit, barren and alone. She would mother Ian, mother her mother. She would not care any longer about the baby; she would not care.

She made two cups of instant coffee, poured milk and sugar into her mother's cup and carried them with unnecessary care back to the bedside. She sat beside her mother chatting, she helped her dress, she drove them both to the seaside after lunch and she herself swam in the pleasant water. But it did not clean her, nothing could clean her, the filth was within. She would not tell anyone, she would not even tell Ian; she would cover her nakedness, because there was no more innocence.

And it was a lie, a cruel coincidence, there was no need to tell anyone because there was nothing to tell.

She almost managed to believe it. She was kind and patient with her mother, enjoying her company more than she would have expected. She was glad though when the mysterious Florence returned: a solid and, to Liz, unexciting woman, but she could see why her mother liked her. She was happy to think of them living together and tried to be helpful about looking at prospectuses for houses, although their tastes were never going to agree. She found herself suddenly reluctant to return to London and stayed on a few extra days persuading herself that she was being useful. She did not want the empty flat, her own empty thoughts and the awareness of her empty womb.

She finally left on the Saturday and travelled home through a hot empty-seeming London. In the morning she was bleeding. Of course she was bleeding, this month there had been no hope of otherwise, Ian had been far away and nothing could have interrupted the bleeding. But the grief was renewed with the wound opening. She was killing her baby, denying it in her flesh, there was the corruption. She was cursed from within. She refused the source of life, tricky and deceitful. What had she done that her body would do this to her? Aristotle taught, she had read in her secret delvings, that the woman provided the matter for the child, the man was only the congealing principle: "Compare," he wrote, "the coagulation of milk. Here the milk is the woman's body and the fig-juice or rennet contains the principle which causes it to set." But rennet cannot work on cold, sour milk; the milk must be warmed with loving attention, brought not to the boil, but to blood heat. She had curdled the milk of her flesh, no baby could congeal in her, in the blood which will not clot. She was a child murderer. Barren women murdered babies in their wombs, taking the children from their husbands and drowning them in the milky darkness, killing them in the hidden garden.

The mythology of science was safer, making both parents complicitous in the dark deed. But not for her. Science had found her guilty. Within the womb the morality of external genitalia continued. His vigorous active sperm did their best, penetrating further and further, rushing enthusiastically inwards, until somewhere in the upper reaches of the undulating river they encounter the passively waiting ovum. There, again, the sperm penetrate, he gives, she receives, the two are bonded by her submission, his penetration.

Ian's postcard which had been waiting for her makes her weep now. She has killed his baby, she has cursed it in the womb, with the curse that is upon her. She struggles out of bed, trying to refuse, struggling to reject these images. She goes into the bathroom, wipes the blood from between her legs and crotch, pushes the Tampax in again, cleanses her hands from the contamination.

The flat is empty. The blood flows on, invisible but still draining. Ian does his best, but the flaw is in her. Where is the magical power, the meeting point of female and male, the domination of her will by his strength, the masculine force that will stop that waste?

Wrapped up in the bloody rags of her shame, exhausted by

the washing and changing, embarrassed by the knowledge that her neighbours knew her shame, worn out by the curse on her, the woman with the issue of blood waited for her chance.

Each time she went down to the washing-place of her village she could see the gossips eyeing her washing with a delicate and half-discreet curiosity, with a tender fearfulness. If she could have afforded to she would have burned, evening by evening, each soiled cloth; but unmarriageable, constantly damned, displaced, avoided, always in a state of uncleanliness that would curse even the food she cooked, she had no access to money. Any that came through charity or fear she would spend on doctors who could hardly bear to touch her, who would blame her and fear her, who would not help her. Young married women turned aside to avoid her in the street, not wanting to catch the contagion of ill favour or bad luck. And what had she ever done to earn such luck; at what secret moment had she offended what unknown code, and called down this fate upon herself?

Twelve years. Twelve years. Four thousand, three hundred and eighty days. Each morning she would have to strip off the bloody clouts and wrap clean ones round her. The medicine woman, more friendly than the rest—knowing the dangers of being a woman and different from others—told her there was nothing she could do. Nothing any woman could do in such a case. Only a man could stop the blood, only a child hidden and tiny in her gut could consume so much spare blood.

But no man would come near her; afraid of the curse on her, afraid of defilement. And as she walked as privately as she could through the day she would feel her rage growing heavy, sodden with the gentle loss and her own flesh less fed, less rounded and beautiful. Bitterness flowed in to fill the spaces where the blood flowed out.

She examined her conscience, carefully going over each space of time to find out what she had done. She was innocent—there was nothing there; she had been not one jot more sinful than other women who now had four or even seven sons.

She had been betrothed to a fine man; his kisses sweetly demanding beside the well where the bonded couples might meet as they waited out their year. Sometimes the kisses had frightened her, promising more than they could ever fulfil. Was it that fear that had loosed the blood? He had been ashamed before the whole community when the blood had poured out unceasingly. No wedding then.

Once in four weeks the other women would join her, one by one. They tried to be kind, not to talk of home and family, but they were frightened of her; she exposed their fears, the fragility of the shapes that made their lives. They would hush their voices, kind but cruel.

When she heard of the Teacher, the man who did not despise women, the man that men said could not be a man, because he loved prostitutes and cuddled small children; she had known what she had to do.

When he had turned and asked who had touched him, she was ashamed. She should not even be here, defiling the whole crowd with the wickedness of her womanhood. The crowd was dense, she was not used to it, she had lived alone, she was frightened. The tightness of the crowd jostling her, overwhelming her, she could not breathe, could not think, the panic mounting, rising up from her pain. The blood suffusing her face, her neck, her whole being: the hotness and redness of blood covering her all over as though it had broken through the cloths and would run out and contaminate the whole world.

When she touched his long cape the bleeding stopped.

Afterwards she did not know what had happened. Perhaps all the blood in her ever-bleeding belly had been dissipated in the awful blushing, sweating panic, so that there was no more to come out. Perhaps when she touched the man she knew the wholeness of him: that all her blood was contained in him and if bleeding were necessary he would bleed for her. Perhaps her blood had rushed up to greet this man who was more of a person than she had guessed a man could be. In contact with his wholeness the bleeding stopped.

Had she bled because no man would allow her near him?

Had she bled because what she had felt in men had been bad and wild and dangerous and the blood kept them all away, kept her safe in her aloneness?

But the manhood she felt in the Teacher was yearning and tender and sharing. Needing.

Would the bleeding never have started if men were loving?

Would the bleeding never have begun if the men had not wished to put a separateness between themselves and the women they feared? The bleeding was not the curse; the curse was the bleeding.

The bleeding stopped. Her belly could fill up again, her flesh grow to the beauty the Teacher saw in it.

The bitterness and loneliness broken away there was nothing there to bleed. When she touched his long cape the bleeding stopped.

6. SEPTEMBER

It was a good evening at first. The empty flat seemed more spacious. She liked it empty, liked suddenly the idea that it belongs to her, that all the things in it are hers, chosen by her and not having to be shared. She wanted to be alone.

But things had been so much better since Ian, brown and relaxed, returned from Italy. She did not tell him about burning her temperature chart; he did not ask.

Dr. Marshall had asked and she had deliberately lied to him. "My dear Elizabeth, what very bad luck that you had to be apart for the holiday. Often I have noticed that sun and wine and relaxation is the very thing that is needed. How did you get on without him?"

"I had a pleasant time with my mother, I felt much more relaxed towards her than I have for years, I found that interesting."

"I do see that we don't have your chart for last month. Now why is that?"

"To tell the truth, I left rather suddenly for Somerset and I forgot to take it with me. I thought with Ian not there it would not matter too much and I didn't want to make a fuss because my mother does not know about . . . about my problem, and I did not want to worry her when she was unwell."

"Come, come. You must not think me such a fool; I may not be trained in psychiatry"—a nice shot that one, he was not going to forgive and forget—"but I am enough of a post-Freudian, and so are you, to see through a little 'mistake' like that. You weren't prepared to risk it were you? Why are you so determined to prove me wrong? Why should you rather do without the baby that you claim to want, than face up to the facts? We are reaching a point when I shall be forced to say that if you are not willing to be treated then I shall have to cease to treat you. I don't want you to see that as a threat, but simply as a fact; that we are wasting everybody's time. If you were really sure that I was wrong, you would have taken that chart and brought your nice straight unovulating pattern in with you like a banner."

He was right. She stopped her casual wander through the flat and acknowledged that he was right. If she had not marked and noticed that temperature rise she would have been in his clinic demanding, militant, about her rights to determine her future and receive drug treatment. She would not submit to their will to prove her wrong. Dr. Marshall and Ian, both driving down on her with their will to be right.

People never perceived Ian like that. She was used to the slender notes of pity that she could feel Ian receiving: the way Amanda looked at him with tenderness, beguiled by his apparent gentle charm. They felt sorry for him with his bitch-wife, his over-dominating woman. And it was not true. She could not even play Scrabble with him anymore, his desire to win burned all the pleasure out of it. He had had a good time in Italy, he was in a good mood, so he was being nice to her. She was dependent on his whim to civility and love. He could withdraw into his own inner security without a moment's notice and cut her off. She had no such refuge: always she had to be out looking for allies, forming defensive conspiracies. If he ceased to love her she would die.

Perhaps she did reject her femininity, perhaps that was what it meant. Ian was gentle and kind and loving and liberated, but she could still feel that power coming off him, and she knew that he was aware of it and enjoyed it. Perhaps that power was the real masculinity, and accepting it, rejoicing in it, was what she lacked, was what made her inadequate. When she felt the leaning of his will she ought to feel some excitement, some desire to be carried by him.

She laughed at herself; she knew why she was feeling like this and it was pointless to pretend. She made herself some coffee and, cup in hand, went back to the bedroom. She picked up her temperature chart from where it lay, on the floor beside the bed. Neat little Xs for the bleeding days, two little red rings, the night they had made love when Ian came back from Italy and the little row of dots—a completely straight line for fourteen days, and this morning a tiny dip. The line stopped. Tomorrow was tomorrow, she could not guess. She had read enough, she knew that the line was behaving like the standard, normal woman's line should. Two months running. Why now, after so long. Perhaps it was a delusion, perhaps she had not kept the thermometer in long enough this morning, perhaps the room had been a little colder, perhaps Ian had not pulled the covers back when he got out of bed before her. Perhaps she was going to ovulate. Perhaps tomorrow there would be the sharp little rise, the promise. Tonight was the night they ought to make love; tonight was the optimum moment, if she were going to ovulate.

Tonight is the night. Or might be the night . . . Ian would be home soon. She felt tired and uneasy. There was no fun in this conspiracy to seduce one's own husband. They were against each other. No, wrong, he wanted the baby as much, more than she did. Of course he would . . . cooperate. A horrible thought.

At the beginning of wondering when they would finally conceive their baby they had bought a book about infertility. It warned them against turning sex into something mechanical, against losing the romance of marriage. They had laughed.

"What a long way I will have come from my evil past," Ian

had said. "I give up work and gambol in a field of rich grass and when you're in heat you can come down and get the once-over. I should like the life of a breeding stud."

"You can see Dr. Marshall, sitting up late in his office with the turf guides in front of him working out whether our offspring will be 'son of champions' or some degenerate crossbred mongrel."

Dr. Marshall had been new to them then: still the great white hope, the guru who was going to lead them into the fruitful gardens of the promised land. They had laughed at him, and at themselves, but affectionately, and only because it was their habit to mock.

The chart still in her hand, Liz jolted herself. Jesus, they had thought it funny. Now she had become secret, hiding the chart, hoping Ian would not remember which night was which, planning to confuse him into bed. They had found it funny then. Ian's sperm count had been their dinner-party narrative for weeks. The relevant morning she had rushed out to the sleazy shop behind her office and bought expensive piles of pornography. The middle-aged attendant had asked if she were a journalist.

"Goodness, no."

"You're not one of those Festival of Light women are you, going to expose me? It's all quite innocent really."

"No, no, don't worry. I'm not the fuzz either."

"Just wondered. You're not our average client."

"I'm teaching my husband to masturbate," she had said primly and fled from the shop, giggling.

They had gone to the hospital together, still laughing at the poor man. Ian was ushered off into a cubicle, but he popped out again and asked if he could have the magazines. Only half-accidentally, she dropped them on the floor, and a splash of lurid pictures tumbled out of the carrier bag. A blonde in a schoolgirl's blazer and nothing else stared vacuously at the shocked receptionist. Some of the other waiting women looked distressed, and she caught a muffled titter from a very young man with his

arm round his woman. They did not look more than teenagers,
and she had felt a stab of shame. Ian picked up the magazines
and slunk off round the door, doing a very creditable imitation
of a dirty old man and shooting her the lewdest wink. She sat
primly bored, wishing she had kept some of the magazines for
herself. Time passed. More time passed. She thought suddenly
that she should have got pictures of young men, not girls, and
she blushed. To cover the blush she spoke very loudly to the
receptionist.

"Shall I go and help?"

"Help?"

"Help my husband?"

She put her foot up on a chair and leaned towards the nurse
in an attitude that was both aggressive and provocative. The
young man giggled again.

"Oh Mrs. . . . Er . . . where is your husband?" And after a
pause she obviously remembered and said, angrily, "Well, I expect he'll be along."

"I'm sure I could be of assistance to him."

The woman knew what she was implying and did not know
what to do. The waiting-room was filled with scandalised silence. Ian emerged again with a splendid smug smile and
quoted, "Thick and fast they came at last and more and more
and more."

Well, they did not joke about it anymore. She realised that
she would be more likely to joke at Ian's expense with women in
the clinic than to laugh with him at them, than conspire to humiliate them.

This last time she had been there, before she got her ticking-
off from the great Dr. Marshall, but not before she had known
that she would get it, she had been sitting in the waiting-room
trying to read a very messy typescript, when a woman had come
out laughing and crying, "I'm pregnant, I'm five weeks pregnant
and it never even occurred to me." There was a sudden silence
in the waiting-room. There must have been six women there and
they were all completely silent. The ecstatic woman looked

round, realised what she had done, and had begun to blush. "I'm sorry, I'm sorry, I didn't think, I just wanted to tell the world." Another woman stood up and said, a little stiffly, but quite clearly, "Well done, congratulations, I am pleased." Liz was shamed, organising her features she too tried to join in. "Yes, congratulations. Don't be sorry, it ought to encourage me." But she could hardly get the words out; the woman next to her began to cry and Liz knelt down and took her hand. She felt overwhelmed by shared tenderness, she was crying herself. The receptionist scuttled forward with easy sympathy, but Liz and this strange woman clung to one another's hands. They did not say anything, but Liz was seared with the thought that she had laughed with Ian at these women, had made a mock of them and deliberately embarrassed them with her own flippant aggression.

She could not laugh there anymore; there were less and less places where she could laugh. But after tonight . . . she went and had a bath, and began to cook the supper. She did not know how to set about seducing Ian; years of holding back, not pushing him, letting him choose the pace; surely she had earned a right to say, "yes, now." Just one night. If he were in a good temper he would laugh at her, if he were in a bad temper he would feel trapped, conspired against. He wanted the baby too; let it happen, let it flow, it would be all right, it had to be all right.

The pub is warm and hot. Noisy. Detached still, she looks at them as a couple. A skinny pair, both in blue jeans, both with badly cut, short hair. She is wearing a patchwork jacket, he a thin Shetland jumper. Two pairs of bony hands round pint glasses. His hands are nicer than hers; very long with thin fingers. The tops of her fingers are stubby and she bites her nails. He has another habit instead: he chews the loose skin over the middle knuckle of his right hand. The flesh there is very slightly deformed. She wonders if he did it as a child.

The summer that she was three her parents had taken their summer holiday in southern Italy, in the hills above Naples. She has seen the photographs: one of her in bathing trunks and nothing else. She had been skinny even then, with a long soft fringe like a baby donkey; her belly curved softly outwards, her shoulders even in the picture, mobile and winglike. No wonder her father found her enchanting. She has one real physical memory from this holiday: The Feast of the Assumption, August 15th. At some tiny village festival she sat high on her father's shoulders while the Virgin is processed through the streets. There is an excited crowd, incense, flowers in the roadway, the local nuns lead the little girls in white dresses, there is a band. The image, garlanded, sways, the crowd sighs, her father's shoulders quiver with repressed passion. She remembers her father's shoulders under her thighs, the texture of his neck against her bare legs, the thickness of his hair. That was the day that, back in rainy Leeds, Ian was born. It was not quite her earliest memory, she had been nearly four, but now it seems to have been the starting point in her life.

His mother says it was raining the day he was born. She had been trying to get the washing dry before her time was up. She was an old hand. Ian was her fourth child, her third son. Their problems are not from his side of the family. His mother has thought that ever since, on one desperate day, Liz had silenced her garrulous optimism about the grandchild by saying that children could not always be had for the asking. Whatever the London doctors might say, Ian's mother knew the truth. Barren women are accursed. She does not need to say so. She had hung up the washing despite the rain, it was likely to have dried before she could take it in again. She sent the two little ones who were not yet at school down to her neighbours with a request to send for the midwife and had gone upstairs to lie on the well-prepared bed. When Ian's father came home from work he had another son. As far as his mother was concerned Ian had brought his troubles on his own head, marrying a girl four years older than himself, when he didn't even have a job. It wasn't right; what could you expect? Not that she had anything against Liz herself. But you could tell.

Ian is drinking too much. She wants him to stop, because as Dr. Marshall says, "A little alcohol relaxes things and of course I can understand that that can become constructive, but too much drink usually relaxes them too much." She does not know if he is drinking too much because he has remembered which week of the month it is, or because he has felt her tension, or because he likes to sit in pubs and pour drink down his throat. She likes that too; between them they drink too much, simply for pleasure. But tonight she wants to keep things under control. In four days they will be able to forget all this, perhaps for ever. Perhaps this time it will come out right, but not if he drinks too much. He is a selfish bastard; he bloody well ought to remember.

He went to the bar for more drinks. She watched him finding a way through the crowd, small and compact; the back of his neck gave her a sudden stab of simple lust, the nicest thing she had felt all evening. She sometimes forgot how much she fancied him. He disappeared into the scrum and she unwound a little and looked around.

"Liz!"

"Alice, how nice. You're not here often, were you looking for us?"

"Hoping rather. I get so bloody restless and cooped up in the evenings now. Yes, I thought I might find you here."

"How are you?"

Alice put her hands over her stomach in a funny little protective gesture and smiled, but she said, "I'm tired, and I'm beginning to feel bloody conspicuous."

"Not long to go now, is there?"

"Nearly eight weeks. It seems like centuries, and I hate the sensation that I'm getting stupider and stupider."

"I think that's normal, isn't it? I know Amanda, my little author lady, says the same thing."

"That's the myth of motherhood woman, isn't it? I read her book. It made me feel guilty."

"What?"

"About not wanting to play Bach on the record player, and being a single mother I suppose, but anyone can make me feel guilty at the moment. I thought deciding to keep it would make an end to that, you know 'screw your courage to the sticking point.' You get it there and find it won't stick."

"You're not scared?"

"Sometimes. Other times I'm proud as a peacock." She folded her hands laughing over her bulge and grinned at Liz.

Liz thought, she's flaunting herself. Alice's bright red smock with its trailing green ribbons seemed like a direct insult to her jeans, and the enormous breasts threatened her. She tried to smile. "Ian's getting more drinks—do you want anything?"

Alice nodded at her glass and said, "I've got some thanks. If I have too much, this little bastard kicks at my tummy and makes me sick. Did you have a good holiday?" She sat down, her knees wide apart and the dress looping between them. Liz tried not to stare at her belly, but the baby in there seemed suddenly real to her, floating, splashing, dreaming in its own undersea world. A picture from her childhood edition of *The Water Babies*, golden hair adrift and water-colour bubbles. But Alice was oblivious, she wanted to hear about Liz's holiday, and how she got on with her mother. She wanted to hear about Liz's work and books and chat, she was bored by her own fascinating pregnancy, or else she was being carefully tactful; either way Liz found annoying.

Ian returned, two pints of bitter slopping in his hands. His face lit up when he saw Alice; of all her friends she was probably the one to whom he felt closest. The two of them had an immensely warm joking relationship tinged with admiration on both sides. Liz liked seeing them together because they brought out a richness in the other. But where she had stared she noticed that Ian carefully kept his eyes away from her pregnancy. Liz tried hard not to notice. Ian had met some people he knew at the bar: a guy she recognised called Bob and his West Indian

wife. They came over and joined them. It was an evening typical of their life, typical of what she liked, she did not know why
she could not enter into it, why she felt separated and confused.
Bob was full of some complicated plan for his tenants' association to withhold their rent in order to build a community centre.
Ian was arguing with him, dragging out obscure items of borough law and explaining how they ought to be pressurising the
council not the housing association whose tenants they were and
how to go about building up that pressure. Liz could not follow
the ramifications but she could sense and admire Ian's grasp on
the subject. The wife was trying to talk to her, asking her about
her work, and where they lived, but Liz was not able to concentrate. Alice and Bob's wife were quite suddenly engaged in a
mysterious conversation about maternity benefits and the horrors
of enforced induction and the callousness of the midwifery
system.

Liz watched them all with a nervous energy that surprised
her. She saw Ian and Bob as very other and different; their
stubbled cheeks seemed amazing, grotesque; the authority that
they wielded so casually by right of their baser voices and longer
legs made them seem miles away. But she felt as distanced from
the women, who formed as exclusive an élite society of their
own. The two powers, and she could partake of neither. She
drunk her beer. She felt lost.

Eventually the bell rang and the lights flickered. Alice lumbered to her feet and said she should be getting home, and Liz
stood up to kiss her. The other woman also rose and called to her
husband, "Time to move, honey."

"Hang on a minute, Sam."

Alice went, but she and Sam—at least she had acquired her
name—stood waiting for their men, something in common now.
They grinned guiltily at each other, wondering if the other
would be accusatory or would protest.

Ian said, "Liz love, Bob says why don't we go round his
place?" She noticed the tiniest and most rigidly controlled ex

pression of exasperation on Sam's face, but she did not need that encouragement.

"Oh, Ian, I'm really knackered. I want to go home."

"Okay then, I'll see you later."

"But Ian . . ."

"I won't be very late. We just want to finish discussing this and listen to some records."

And he and Bob pulled on jackets and started to move. Sam said, "Sure you don't want to come?"

"Thanks, no, I really am tired."

"Okay then, see you round."

She put her arm round Bob and the three of them went off into the night.

She lay in the darkness, on the floor. It made her back ache and she forced herself to lie still and feel the pain. She did not know what to do with so much anger. She could not cry. Her rage seemed to come in waves, drowning her. He had not remembered; he could not be expected to remember; he was entitled to spend an evening with his friends, that was their sort of marriage; housing rights in Greater London were more important than one single baby that would only add to those problems. She would kill him—the impotent bastard should face up to his problems and not disguise them with good works. He did not love her anymore because she could not have his baby. Barren. Barren, not just in her womb but beyond, devoid of attraction for him. For anyone.

And damn him. Damn him. Damn him. He was keen enough to screw so long as he could set the terms. She submitted to his inept embraces. He should have remembered, he had no right to forget.

It was her fault. She could not have his baby and he did not want to.

Down there, and her hands reached down, grinding at her belly till it hurt, down there was something so ugly that no baby wanted to lie there. So much filthy sperm had been packed in;

there was corruption, accursed blood. She was rejected; she had rejected. The doctor was right, it was her fault, her fault. She rolled on to her face, ramming it into the carpet, making it hurt. Ugly, ugly. Her soul was ugly and her body followed it. She banged her face onto the floor, hardly able to breathe. She would kill the bastard. If he rejected her she would die. She would not die, she would kill him. She refused him. The rejection would be hers. She could set herself up alone; feed off men. She did not need him. She would kill him; castrate him. Black widow spider.

That was a femininity that she would not reject, as she ground her face and her claws into the carpet, as she fed her anger with visions of power and aloneness. She had had a lover once briefly who had loved the taste of menstrual blood; for five days he had fed off her dead babies. She had lain on his college bed and gripped the iron frame above her head and writhed in delight, and guilt and the delight of guilt overcome, while below he had sucked and licked and moaned himself to orgasm, and her too. She had hardly touched him while he ministered to her. That was a power she would not reject either.

But Ian. She would knife him in the dark and drink his blood; reversing the shape of the old relationship in a new blood bath of her own. Still lying on the floor but excited by her anger and her memories, she reached down to her own crotch with one hand, forgetful of why she was there. Masturbating slowly and carefully she thought with a thrill of victory, I don't need him, I don't need him. I will go alone into the barren desert and take delight from myself, unexposed to betrayal, or need, or generosity. But it was her own body that was guilty of the betrayal. For the sake of a craving in her own gut she had given up that easier sexual life, had bound herself to one man, had given him the power of love and demand over her. Her body had lied to her in that painless, inconvenient monthly bleeding; had deceived her into believing that as she was cursed as a woman, she might enter into the privileges of a woman. It was she who drove herself into these pains and confusions, like the one she had just enjoyed, which were sterile lies, solipsistic inversions.

While Alice, who had made no sacrifice, who had lain casually with some man some night, was filled up with fruitfulness.

When Ian came in drunk, a little stoned and thinking happily of a bed already warmed and the softness of her sleeping—he found her there, lying on the floor in the dark. He did not want her awake, scarlet-faced, swollen-eyed and filled with hatred.

"What are you doing?" he asked.

"Waiting for you."

"You needn't have done that, silly."

"I did need. I wanted you. I've been wanting you since you got in from work this evening."

"Wanting what?"

"Wanting to fuck, you silly idiot."

"Liz, it is nearly three in the morning. I've got to go to work, you've got to go to work. Why the hell aren't you asleep?"

"Because, as you have, luckily for you, seem to have forgotten, this is the time of the month when sex might actually have some meaning for us."

"Liz, don't say it like that. Yes, I had forgotten, I'm sorry. But come on now, the morning will do."

"No. Now."

"Love, I'm sorry, but I couldn't get it up now even if I wanted to. I want to go to bed. I'm smashed, I'm stoned, I'm bloody exhausted."

She got off the floor, forcing down her fury and hatred, disguising it, knowing it, hating herself. She wound her arms around his neck and tried to kiss his mouth. She had no desire for him, no love, only anger and will.

"Darling," she murmured.

"Darling nothing. You don't want to darling me, you want to bloody rape me. I've said No." She could feel his anger, but did not believe that it could rival hers. She reached for the zip of his jeans, rubbing herself against him, trying to remember the devices of her youth, unused for so long. Her hand nuzzled into his groin, pretending a tenderness and love.

"You'd love it if you got started, wouldn't you?"

"I would not. Take that silly sexy stuff off right now." He pushed at her shoulders. She knew he was right, that her whole performance was counter-productive, dangerous, that she ought to stop. She knew too that she had to assert herself, her own needs. She was sick to her stomach of him and his. He pushed at her shoulders again, a motion of refusal, of rejection. Her mood changed, she was pleading, begging him.

"Ian, darling, please. Tonight matters. It matters to me and it should to you. For the first time in months, my thermometer is behaving like it should. Please, Ian, please try. Just try, I won't be angry if you can't, I promise, but please try."

"If I can't . . . just what are you saying? What are you, some bitch in heat?" His anger was rising as hers declined.

"Ian, that's not fair. I thought you wanted this baby."

"Of course I want a baby, don't try throwing that in my face. But I don't want a baby at the expense of a whole sodding relationship. Why can't you face the facts, sweetheart?" She could feel his animosity, the kindliness and care buried under drink and anger. "Dr. Marshall has told you—you are the one with the problems, they're in your head, not in my prick and you know it. Open your eyes. You won't get a baby by making me perform. It's there, there." He jabbed at her forehead with his finger. "I'm not going to be blamed for your fucked-up head. And I won't be your stud."

"Ian." She was stricken, not even angry, appalled. "That's not fair. You've got no right to say that."

"Right, right. Who are you to talk about rights? Jesus, you only married me because I was the first bloke you thought you could wind round your little finger. You don't love me; you just want a male victim on the altar of your mystical motherhood; you just want some damn prize bull."

Her head exploded, her voice was icy. "My dear Ian, if that was true I would hardly have picked you—you lapsed faggot with a guilt complex. Talk about facing up to the facts. You impotent queer."

Even as she said it she knew she had gone too far. Her hands were already shielding her face when he hit her the first time. He pushed her back on the couch, smashing at her head and face. She had a moment of clarity thinking, "more drink than dope then." He shoved his fingers into her hair and banged her head up and down against the sofa arm. She was frightened by the maelstrom of his fury, she had thought herself stronger than him physically. That was a joke—his will to hurt her was beyond any strength she had ever encountered. He slapped her face and then hit her breasts. She did not even try to fight back.

Terrified, appalled, she heard herself apologising, begging for mercy. "Ian I'm sorry, Ian stop it, please. Don't. Don't." She was screaming. This did not happen to women like her. She cowered. "Ian. Ian. Ian." She could even feel sorry for him. But how dare he?

He stopped hitting her as suddenly as he had started. "Get out," he said. "Get out. I never want to see your stinking face again."

"You don't have to tell me," she said, almost sulkily. "I wouldn't stay if you begged me."

She was shaking all over. She walked into the bedroom. She must not say anything, she must not acknowledge him, she must not admit that she would and could forgive him, but she would never forgive herself for not fighting back, for begging him to stop, for not resisting him. She was shamed and dirty. She picked up a comb, her toothbrush and a clean pair of knickers, stuffed them into her bag. She washed her face. She went back into the living-room: he was leaning against the wall, his face hidden, his shoulders shaking. She would not notice; she would not be with a man who reduced her to a blubbering wreck, who vanquished her own self-esteem.

She walked out into the dark.

She walked until there were early-morning cafés open. She did not know where to go. She could not go to Nancy's and admit what he had done to her, what she had done to herself. She was too ashamed. And she knew that Nancy's anger at Ian would be so intense that she would be forced to defend him. She did not want that, she wanted to be able to hate him, to transfer the hatred she felt towards herself on to him. She was the victim, he was the aggressor, she had nothing to be ashamed about. She could not stop seeing herself, cowering on the sofa, begging him to stop. She was bigger than he was, she should have bloody well knocked him out. She was disgusted. She could not stop seeing Ian leaning against the yellow wall of the living-room with his shoulders shaking. She loved him. She knew they had gone too far to go back. She walked shivering with cold.

She drank a cup of coffee in a working man's café near Charing Cross Station. She realised that she had walked a long way. She began to cry. The tears rolled down her face and she had nothing to do with them. She did not sob or strain, she made no noise. The few people already there, eating massive breakfasts and talking softly, did not seem to notice her. She could stay here all day if she wanted, weeping into the heavy white china mug of coffee. It came out of a bottle. Camp Coffee—there had to be some irony there somewhere. At least she was getting warmer. She bought another round of the stuff. The tears continued to flow, she waited patiently for them to stop, not really knowing why she was crying. Her back ached. If she could stand drinking coffee with sugar in it perhaps she would put on weight. There is a median weight, which if a woman's body falls much below she will not ovulate. Not a weight exactly, but a proportion of fat weight to other body weight. Dr. Marshall said she must put on weight. She even reached for the sugar jar: a glass one with a dented tin top and one hole. But the thought of the sweetness in her mouth made her retch. She held the warm mug against her bruised chest, trying to stop the shaking. The thing to do was not to think. Just try to get warm.

Just try to sit upright at the desk, try to get through the day. Try to decide how to apologise to Ian for provoking him, without apologising because he hit her. He hit her. Even there

where she had felt safe at last, the violence lurked; there was no
way out, no breaking of ancient patterns. The curse of Eve was
on her, like on other women. The long years of patience and
giving were for nothing. She had not taught a man to love her;
she had taught a man to feel safe enough to do to her what none
of the casual lovers of the past had dared to do.

Tony came into her office, and said, "I've been stood up for
lunch."

She disciplined her smile. "Oh, who by?"

"Editor from Mathesons. Do you want to eat?"

"Not much."

"Ah, come on. Do you good. Put some weight on you."

She did not want his sympathy. Did not want him to be sorry
for her, be kindly and avuncular, and expose her to the enormity
of what Ian had done. She did not want to have to tell. She
began to cry again.

Not the gentle tears of the cold breakfast, but racking violent
sobs, edging towards hysteria, where she would not be able to
control them, or the world that contained them. She put her
head down on the desk and began to wail. She gasped that she
was sorry, that he should go away, that she would be all right in
a moment. But also she began to bang her head up and down on
the desk, the wails gaining in pitch and ferocity.

"Liz, hey, Liz love." Tony came round the desk, picked up
her head and transferred its wilder gyrations to his shoulder. She
hid her face in the folds of his flesh, and even in her misery
smelled the rich flavour of his after-shave and the warmth of his
skin. He stroked her head, held her tight. She pushed her face
further into his body; he pulled her round, encompassing her,
letting her sob there.

"He hit me. He hit me and hit me."

"Susha, susha." Motherlike noises; he kissed the top of her
head, soothing her like a child with a hurt knee. His solidness
comforted her like her father had done. Big men both of them.
The kisses became more determined. "Liz. Liz. Liz." She was
beginning to indulge herself, here with this daddy.

Once when very small she had had a fight with her mother.
Exiled to her bedroom she had longed to say she was sorry, but
waited, biding her time, already skilled. She heard her father
come in; she heard them talking; she heard his feet on the stairs.
When her father came into the room she had been ready,
thrown herself into his arms, been embraced there sobbing,
while he petted her, loved her for her grief and sorrow, loved
her because it was to him, not her downstairs, that the contrition
was directed. That sense of safety, and of something beyond
safety: a victory because her mother was excluded from the passion of the reconciliation. He had carried her tenderly downstairs; had said to her mother, "There, it's all over now, she's
said she's sorry." And her mother, to whom the apology should
have been made, was unable to protest, had been outwitted. Liz
had been triumphant; and lain in her father's arms, already too
crafty to crow her victory, but knowing it. Betrayer of her
mother, she had won the more important victory: she had stolen
the pure love of a man.

But Tony's love was becoming rather less pure. She knew it
and did not resist it. The kisses on her head were becoming less
paternal, more demanding. She knew that he wanted, that he
planned to make love to her; that the desire had always been
there, biding its time. His will was strong, hers to resist negligi-
ble. And desire breeds desire. She turned her face up to his
kisses. Slowly, not crowing his victory, always leaving a place to
stop if he was not welcomed, his tongue found her lips, her
teeth, and the deep places of her mouth. Something exploded.
She had forgotten, if she had ever known, that sensation of
drowning in lust. She had heard all that stuff about the drum-
beat in the mountain, the fountains of blood; and she had not
believed in it. This was a new sort of passivity—a passivity of active consent; incapable and exultant. He picked her up effort-
lessly, never releasing her, removing the necessary minimum of
her clothes, turning her, handling her. She was powerless even
to want to resist. Somewhere her body cried out and she could

not even pretend not to hear it, her skin sang to her that this was the Man, this was what bred children, sent women weeping through the world in joyfulness. It was not what she wanted, and now she wanted it totally. She consented to the certainty in his hands. Dripping and desirous she spread her legs out for him without consciousness of it and welcomed him into her. She accepted the rhythm of the storm, let it overwhelm her and leave her resting.

It took less than ten minutes. They both lay on the office floor, not sure what to do next, what meaning they might give to this foolishness. The lower half of her body pounded as her head and shoulders had pounded the night before. And she knew what she had done.

Lie. A denial of what had happened was essential. He had comforted her. He had been the father. He had kissed her better, well again. She must not weep, must not thank him for the sex; must thank him for the forgiveness he had offered in the name of his sex. Deny the passion: only a friendly re-creation of her, a kindliness to protect her from loss and despair. The act of a friend: he must not know that how much she had felt him in her flesh, only the friendship in the heart.

"Thank you, my dear."

The words were thin and pale, not adequate for what she had received, but he must not know. She was married to Ian, Ian was the Father of her Child, the man of her heart. Satisfaction had to reside there, it had to. Tony must not find out that what he had made her feel she had never felt before. She must forget it herself.

"I do feel better for that."

It was important that he too should consent to the imposture, that he should acknowledge that he was the Father, not the Lover. The wise king, not the younger son who wins the maiden. The good friend, not the adored adulterer. Tony had re-created her in his approval, had been kind to a sad little girl. She must repress the fact that she wanted to do it again, right now and tomorrow and the next day, until she was sated by the extravagance of such richness. She must also suppress the fact that she had acted like a whore and he like an opportunist, that they had used each other thoughtlessly. That it had been fun.

They went out to lunch; he took her somewhere improbably respectable. She was grateful. She did not know what he knew; but she was glad he was willing to pretend. She worked all afternoon, with great clarity and care. She wrote three letters, made four telephone calls and tidied her desk twice. She knew she was going to go home when it was time to leave the office. She knew she was not going to tell Ian what she had done.

He was there when she got back. She opened the door to the flat, walked into the living-room, and he said, "Where were you?"

"At work. Where do you think?"

"I didn't think you would go. I didn't go."

She felt a minor victory; for the first time she had been the one able to walk away from a fight, he had been trapped within it unable to move. The realisation made her tender.

"I'm sorry, I should have rung. You could have rung me."

They stood the width of the room apart; nervous of each other, unsure what to do next. He pushed his hands upwards over his face, he looked desperately tired.

"Liz, I was so worried."

He had probably stood there all night after she had gone, all day waiting for her, wondering if she would come back.

She said, "There was no need to worry like that. I'm sorry."

But she still felt disconnected. Detached, not just from him, but from everything that had happened. She wanted the film to move on, away from this awkward moment, on to whatever came next.

He risked a grin. " 'Love is never needing to say you're sorry.' "

She wouldn't then. She loved him, the small pixie head, the tensed-up hands, clenched still against whatever was coming. She would not say she was sorry; she would never tell him what she had done; she would blot it out, a compass error, leading her to the wrong part of the jungle, endangering their whole expedition. She smiled at him, remembering that she loved him.

He wanted her to know how worried he had been, that he had tried to find her. "I rang Nancy's."

"I wasn't there." The conversation was becoming impossible, something had to give somewhere, but she did not know how to move. Her mind flitted off—now Nancy would know something had happened; would she have to tell her? Would she want to tell her? Not sure what to do she repeated herself. "I didn't go to Nancy's."

"I know," he said.

Another pause spread out. She wanted to put down her bag, take off her jacket, establish firmly that she had come home. She waited.

"It is not true what I said," he said at last. "I don't feel it to be true."

"Perhaps it was true. Perhaps you should feel it. Perhaps I don't love you enough. I should not have said what I said either. Perhaps I am just using you."

"Don't." He moved now, at last, towards her, but stopped with his arms on the back of a chair. Looking down at his own hands, he said, "Liz I love you. I love you very much. Quite separately I want us to have our baby. I believe that we will have her. I don't think I have recognised the strain on you enough. I want you to know that it doesn't matter. I love you."

She could hear the right words and the pressure in her head to say them; to say that she loved him and that the baby did not matter, that she loved only him. Almost the truth. But she wanted to try for more than that, to tell him the whole truth. It was not so easy. She had cast him in a rôle in her life. The husband, the daddy for the child. That was his unique claim. If there was no baby, what was there that would make the relationship special enough to give up all the other things, to give up what she had enjoyed on the floor in her office? Why had she come back to him? What was she going to say about him in the end? This is the man whose baby I never had.

She was frightened. She called out to Ian, "Darling." She was in the dark, a dangerous wild place, the beasts howled at her, there was no pathway. Out in the desert, filled with the curses laid on barren women through the ages. The curses of their husbands and the curses of the children who could find no resting-place in their dark innards. John the Baptist had gone out into that desert, wailing with guilt and loss. Repent, repent. Half-naked and totally mad, the offspring of a barren womb; born from a dark pit which had already accepted its own damnation. He knew what darkness there was to repent of in there. She was wanton. She was barren. She no longer believed that she would ever have a child.

"Darling."

And he crossed the room, held her as she sobbed in his arms. So different from Tony; she knew Ian wanted nothing but her comfort. She could be generous too. If he wanted to interpret her tears and screams as "I want *you*, I need *you*, I love *you*," he could and it would not be a lie. He could translate as he chose so long as he held her, uniting her again to the real world. So long as he kept the monsters away, so long as he staunched the bleeding wound, so long as he loved her. Her child had rejected her body; Ian had not. He was better, far better, than nothing.

He was petting her, soothing her. They were lying on their big bed together. It was a lot later, they had eaten, and joked and pretended nothing had happened. His hands were suddenly shapely, gentle, purposeful. His lips were on her breasts, her arms round him. He fed from her flesh, from her nipples, he was her child. Gently, with her hands supporting him, he climbed into her. He was her baby. Her trembling stopped. She spread her hands across his shoulders, rubbing them. She patted his back as she had seen other mothers do, his head tucked up over her shoulder. Long firm upward gestures from the flat of his spine up between the spiky shoulder blades. He was so small, so light, a comparison that filled her with guilt, because she had noticed it for so many years. She did not feel that wild danger, did not feel him overwhelming her. She rubbed and pat-

ted him tenderly. With a tiny sigh of contentment he came into
her. They lay there, warm, comfortable, while he dozed and she
petted him.

The next morning she took her temperature and registered
the new higher level. She dressed, leaving Ian still sleeping, and
set off for work. Not until she was riding high on the bus, swaying over London, did it occur to her that she had ovulated and
might well be pregnant. It was possible, and she knew it was
possible, for sudden and intense sexual excitement to stimulate
ovulation. In normal women. Damn it, in normal women, not in
her. She is the whore; the emotionally inadequate woman who
cannot give real love to any man. She is the dark woman who
haunts the periphery of the world; she is the witch of the night
who in secret trysts with the hairy devil swallows his icy semen
into her flesh and spews back the succubus. She is the desert
where the valiant struggling tribes cast their seed, but which
will never give them a harvest. She is branded with the Scarlet
Letter.

Dear God, for once let her be branded in secret with that scarlet mark. Let that dark blood flow. She does not want any child
to be born out of yesterday.

She sits in Nancy's kitchen. She is not speaking. Nancy is
concerned—her long hair falls forward on to the table opposite.
Liz is moved by the sight. Here is her safety and her love. The
children are both asleep: Liz has been and looked at them. Harriet on her back, naked, the delicate tendrils of her fingers, the
softness of her palms spread out; her golden hair soft, as soft as
her skin. The baby is curled face downwards, his nappied bottom stuck up in the air, his blue towelling stretchsuit shows the
wrinkling of his vest through it. Warmth comes off from him as
his whole body rises and falls subtly with his breathing.

Nancy with her dark hair, her bare brown feet curling round
the pine table leg, with her long flowered pinafore dress,
is a madonna, in the Franciscan mode—not enthroned in gold,
distanced by jewels. A friendly madonna who will carry the silly

little messages of foolish girls to her almighty son. Liz cannot approach Him, only supplicate with the mother for the favours the father and son can give. Holy Mary Mother of God, I have sinned exceedingly, please help me, please show me what I can do to regain that love and security that you have eternally.

"I was so upset. He shouldn't have said that, and then I told him he was an impotent queer. I can't think why I said it."

"That's no bloody excuse for hitting you. Ian. Of all people. He's the man who's always on about the renunciation of power, the sex-treachery that all men have to commit. Liz, you mustn't feel guilty because he hit you."

"I was so upset. Cold, tired, I hardly knew what I was doing."

"Exploitative bastard. I never really liked that Tony. He's a sexist pig. Nicely dressed up of course, but I really hate sexual opportunists. Taking advantage, to use a rather outworn concept."

"But Nancy, I asked for it. I didn't even try and stop him. I, damn it, I enjoyed it, I was unbelievably turned on."

"So? Everyone enjoys being wanted like that. You were the distressed one."

"Supposing I'm pregnant?"

"You want to be."

"Not like this. I thought I had got away from that, finished with selling my body just to gain attention. I can't go back there; back to my cunt in exchange for your love."

"Don't be so puritanical. One night, one bad shitty night, when you were feeling like that, when you had every right to feel like that."

"Ian . . . sex with Ian is so strange. It always has been, I just forgot to compare. He hits me over the head like some machismo king and then he just wants to be my baby. He wants to be the baby, he wants me to be the mother. In bed."

"Okay. He uses you. Tony uses you. That's real. Edward uses me. At the moment his wants are being fulfilled so we have what's called a happy marriage. But it's not easy, not cheap, there are bad, bad things with us. There are bad things with everyone."

They are bastards our men. We cling together. Nancy extends the forgiveness of women to Liz. Liz accepts it. They bolster it by hating Them. Daily they are abused, used, made over.

"Liz, sometimes I'm frightened of Edward. He doesn't even need to hit me; just this force, this will to win. We say we have equal responsibility for the children, but when it comes down to it, when I look at what we do and how we make the choices, he wins. He gets good-Daddy points for bathing the kids a couple of nights a week when he gets in from work. It's bloody cheap."

"But Nancy. I love Ian. When all is said and done and screamed about, I really actually love him."

"Okay. Me too. But I love Harri too and she behaves appallingly and I shout at her and I tell her so and sometimes I even lose my temper and spank her. But I can't do that to Edward. I can't even get angry with him. I redirect all that: abortion campaigns, equal pay marches, battered women's refuges. But Edward fucks me about—doesn't bring the car home when he knows I'm waiting to go out or morally blackmails me with the spectre of being a bad mother; which means that he gets to go to his conference next weekend. And I can't say, 'You bastard.' I can't say, 'I'm so angry that I want to kill you.' I go into the kitchen and cook a lousy supper, or go and chat with Alice and get a buzz off the fact that she's doing it all without a man. Or make a heroine of Jane and romanticise about gay women living in communes down the Mile End Road. Or get in the bath and pummel at my horrible fat. . . . I love Edward too, and I don't want and don't need to go and 'come out' or acknowledge the homosexuality that must be latent in me too, I suppose. But I have a more equal relationship with my two kids than I do with Edward, because I don't dare to be angry with him."

"I can't have that relationship."

"Oh, Liz."

"I like to mummy Ian. It's true. My little boy who I, only I, can introduce to the beauties of heterosexual love, who I can keep safe from the dangerous world of his own nightmares. But he can't have it both ways; he can't want to be my baby and then smash my face in like some mediaeval baron. I feel he betrayed me, and I can't tell him; but he betrayed me."

"Then stop feeling like you betrayed him. One fuck. It doesn't matter."

They hold hands across the table. Their wedding rings clink against each other. They both notice and it makes them smile. They know why they are smiling, they smile some more. Nancy's hands are smaller and plumper than Liz's but her nails are just as badly bitten; her wedding ring is signet-shaped with a blue enamel plate. Liz's is plain silver. They feel close to each other.

Jael fondles the tent peg, one hand wrapped firmly round it, the other stroking the pointed end, caressingly. She feels the weight of the hammer in her hand, resistant, heavy, beautiful. She looks at Sisera asleep, his noble head turned sideways on the pillow she has laid for him, his hair is stroked back from his forehead—by her, by her. Between the thick dark tresses and the silky growth of his beard his temple glows sweetly in the moonlight. He is a king, bred on royal food. He is the most powerful, the most beautiful man she has ever seen: he is more beautiful than her husband ever dreamed of being, more lordly, more manly, more virile. He had asked for water and she gave him milk, she brought him curds in a lordly bowl. For the first time in her life it is a joy to service a man. Before she places the point of the peg against that soft glowing skin she kisses the spot with a tenderness she has never felt before. She goes out of the tent and looks at the roughness of the mountains, hears the warmth that seeps out of the goats through the night, and looks at the stars glowing far up in the desert night sky. It is very silent. She is very joyful.

Back in the tent she does not hesitate: the weight of the hammer is with her now, the pointed stick is no longer alien but a part of her person. With her first stroke she breaks the skin, penetrates the bone, the point is finding its own pathway into the depths of the man. He groans once, unable to resist the strength of her stroke, she has heard that groan before. She goes berserk; long after it is necessary, bang, bang, bang, rhythmical, powerful she bangs, in and in; the blood and the flesh flow out over the sheepskin coverlet, over the pillow, she is delighted with her power, her strength. Bang, bang, bang. Her moment in history, her song, her story, her revenge.

After, she sinks exhausted against the bed, lying close to the bleeding hulk, that had once been a king: she sees that with his last reflex he has shat himself, and, worn out by her own excitement, she giggles. Looking at the mess, she has her greatest moment of triumph; when her husband returns from his war and sees what she has done he will be very, very frightened, of her, of her.

Deborah the Prophetess looked at the slaughter on the field and laughed. She had looked so at her husband but had never before felt the freedom to laugh. This was her doing: she had called Barak, her leader, to her and made him prepare an army; she had led that army, had been his courage and the courage of the army. It no longer bothered her that she was an ugly woman; she had wept over that throughout her youth, but now it did not matter anymore. Her words had delivered Sisera into the power of a woman. Barak is frightened; the battle had not frightened him, not in the least—there he had felt a king, there he had felt the admiration of his enemies, the strong wind of carnage that encourages a man, builds him up, reminds him of his birth-rights, of the noble blood that flows in his veins, of his place in history. But now he looks at the tent standing so mild by its stream, the goats and sheep softly picking the barren mountain, and he feels sick with fear, he does not want to go again into the tent and look at the bloody mass, the remains of a worthy enemy. Deborah and Jael look at each other, they smile at each other—they are friends. They look at the smashed head of Sisera, the tent peg still firmly standing in the bloody remains, and they grin. They reach out hands, almost shy with excitement and touch each other very gently. They know their husbands will not want to touch them, they know they are the enemy. They laugh again, breathing in the stink of fear that comes to their nostrils; when they walk out of the tent they rejoice because the whole army, the whole victorious, exultant army is silenced with fear.

Deborah the Prophetess, takes the arm of Jael, just above the wrist, and holds up her right hand for all the army to see. She laughs, Jael laughs, but the army watches in silence. What is the source of the joy that lights up these two women? What are the words of the song that they will sing together? What power drove the hand that drove the nail? The men cannot help seeing the women, they cannot help feeling the hatred, and the joy. They are sick with fear.

OCTOBER

"Well," said Dr. Marshall, with a warm smile, from which he could not totally exclude his surprise, "we seem to be getting somewhere, don't we?" He looked at her chart again, while she sat at the other side of the table. "Perhaps I should threaten you more often." He laughed at his little joke; she managed to laugh back.

"It didn't work though, did it?"

"Not this time, but there are the clearest signs of ovulation. Not that we are out of the woods yet. I hope it is not just this hopeful sign that has raised your spirits so."

"I don't think so," she said cautiously. There was only one X for the relevant day on the chart; she did not mark her intercourse with Tony, no one's business but her own.

"No, I must say I don't think so either. You do seem to be coming to terms with yourself, don't you?"

How could he possibly hope to tell in one fifteen-minute interview? He just liked to talk; liked to have an opinion and show it off. She was not afraid of him anymore. She said, "Oh. What would you mean by that?"

"Well, there seems to be a great deal less of your anger, and . . . er . . . impatience this month, wouldn't you say? Actually

I can assure you that is a good sign, medically speaking. Often we find, that once the point of acceptance of sub-fertility problems is reached, then point of conception is not far behind. I think that this spirit would be the most healthy one in which to view this, I must say unexpected, evidence." He tapped the chart with his pen. He looked bemused. If he knew her sexual adventures of the previous month he would quickly be able to devise a psychological interpretation, and she was not sure that he would not be right.

When she told Nancy what he had said, Nancy giggled. "Liz, you must give a party where I can meet this amazing man."

"What?"

"As soon as he thinks you don't really care about having a baby he starts to promise you one. The man is the most convoluted thinker I have ever heard of, I'm surprised that he doesn't recommend going back on the pill as a guarantee of pregnancy."

Liz laughed.

"I must say though," Nancy said, "I can't help but see his dilemma. Why are you so suddenly cheerful about not having the baby you've been beating your breast about for so long?"

"You know why. It's only this one month. I feel so free."

The blood flowing, the wall of the womb, the complicated web of matter there, falling inwards, collapsing away. A bloodletting, a purging. Once a year the Goddess Hera and her nymphs came down to the fountain of Canathus in Nauplia—and there the Queen of Olympus shook off her clothes and was bathed by her handmaidens in that icy water. In the fountain, bubbling sweetly into the pool below, surrounded by ferns and small trees, an oasis in the deserty uplands, she washed away all the impurities of the year and was restored again in her full virginity.

The nuns on a Shrove Tuesday go one by one into the privacy of the confessional; they strip themselves of the pride they have in their starched white wimples and their Christian virtue.

There, naked before their priest-servant, the blood of the Lamb washes them clean again; makes them whiter than snow. The water from the fountain of the Sacred Heart restores them to the spotless purity of their baptism.

The blood coming out of the most inward part of her, the soft blood which does not clot, washed her. The contamination of adultery and lust is not going to grow and take shape in her, so entangling delight and self-disgust that she would never be free from the guilt.

"I don't understand," said Nancy cautiously, "why you take it so seriously."

"Neither do I. It's part of my obsessive make-up I expect."

"Liz, do be serious. It certainly seems rather crudely biological."

"But it is Ian's baby I want, not just a baby."

"Well, I can understand that."

"Do you think you can? It has become the pivotal point of our relationship."

"It would be that relationship which created the baby even if Tony had been its technical father. You were only sleeping with him because of your relationship with Ian and you know it."

"I'd feel I had cheated him of something important to him."

"But Liz, he need never have known."

"Nancy, that's a cheap comfort and you know it, however kindly you mean it. Both your kids are Edward's too. Think about that. Then imagine if Edward had staked some major part of his identity on having those kids with you."

"But Ian would have them with you even if . . ."

"I'd have to lie to him."

"But you're lying if you don't tell him about Tony anyway."

"But that was nothing important. A misreading. Anyway it doesn't matter now. I ought to mind so much—the best chance I've had for months. Rats. But I woke up that morning and felt this loss of weight. I felt liberated."

She did not tell Nancy that she had gone to the bathroom so

that her relief and delight would be hidden from Ian. She had lain in the bath and watched with passive curiosity as the water coloured faintly between her legs. Nancy could say she was crudely biological whatever that meant, but she knew how differently the same signs could be read. Not this month a sign of her curse, of the barren and unwelcome desert of her gut: now a new sign that the Gods had not abandoned her, a sign that she was forgiven.

The forgiveness extended to Ian. Her voracious eagerness for his tanned flesh must have confused him; but she could not stop to explain. For a year she had been teasing him, keeping desire as light as possible—not very light—but saying wait, save it up, keep it for the magic moment in the month, contain yourself until my body is ready to contain our baby. She did not care now: she wanted only to be with him, to celebrate that they had found each other again, that they were together; that the awful spectre of betrayal had been flushed down the loo with her Tampax.

She lured him to the cinema; they played on the swings in the park; she bought him a skateboard. She wanted to have fun with him to help her forget the excitement she had tasted, along with warm flesh and expensive after-shave, in Tony's arms. She would not be a slave to that sort of passion, she wanted to forget it. She wanted to remember the playful tenderness, the sense of control and completeness she could feel with Ian which was worth a thousand hysterical orgasms. She wanted the intensity of care and attention they had to pay to each other. She could not use Ian's body and he would not use hers. She would deny completely that heady and unthinking lust. She knew too well where it led.

James had battered her flesh into orgasm. He would take no refusal from her body. He would regard such a refusal as an assault on him personally. He would make her enjoy it. She did at first: she had never experienced this before and she knew it was because she had never had it demanded of her. James would not take no for an answer, not from her, not from her submissive flesh. His pleasure might be in giving her pleasure, but it was still his own pleasure that he sought. If he had caught her masturbating he would have killed her. The exhaustion she had carried out of that relationship had been physical as well as mental. He could not accept that she might want to control her own pleasure; he saw that only as one more sign of her inadequacy and immaturity.

"Woman," he would say, sitting naked and attractive on the bed beside her, before or after one of their acts of consenting rape. "Why don't you give in for me, float with me; are you afraid of yourself?" Yes, she had been afraid of, and for, herself in the end; afraid that she would lose, had already lost, control and choice and dignity in bed with him.

But she had found it difficult to explain what frightened her. When she had once tried to speak about it to her women's group she did not think that they had understood. She hated that loss of control, that floating riding submission, where she feared she would drown. Now Tony had opened that fear again and she had enjoyed it. She wanted to forget, she wanted to play.

Nancy listened as patiently as she could, but Liz knew she did not understand the lavish release she felt. Liz felt a closer sympathy to the children than to her grown-up friends. They were in bed now, but Liz had given Hugh his bath. Naked he was plump and smooth like the women in Chinese pictures, but in the water he took on a new shape, graceful, fish-like, dancing his body in the water and looking at her for approval of his beauty. There was water everywhere: his hair, still thin and babyish was sleeked down to his skull, making him look different, older. She had hidden down under the side of the bath and popped out on him making noises like a tiger; hovered, pounced and disappeared, leaving him screaming for mercy and for more. She disappeared, pounced again, more water splashed on to the floor as he bounced with delight and thrashed. He lost his balance, slipped under the water. Panicking she pulled him, nervous that he would be drowned or frightened; he emerged from the waves, gasping in amazement at his own fear and courage. He was slippery, hairless, with a soft white belly and preposterous, floppy genitals. "Out, now," she said, but he knew she did not mean it and splashed her. She sprayed him with the hair shower and they both collapsed with laughter. The invisible voice which usually commented wryly on her boyish charm or affected manner when she was playing with children was silenced. Later he went gentle and cuddly as she wrapped him in a towel, dried him, put his nappies and sleep-suit on, tucked him into bed and called Nancy to come and kiss him.

Now he was asleep. Nancy said, "It's not fair how much more fun other people are allowed to have with your children. He and I may have a few moments like that in the whole week. But you and Harriet can do it every time you pick him up. Edward too. No wonder he thinks Daddy is more fun than Mummy, that everyone is more fun than Mummy."

"But why's that?"

"I don't know. My puritan conscience I suppose, rears up its ugly little head and thinks, 'He'll get over-excited,' or, 'I'll have to wipe up the mess' or 'I ought to be cooking the supper.'"

"Nancy," Liz said, stung, "I did clear up the floor."

"Oh, love, I know you did. It's not that. Hughie adores you anyway. But I seem to find so little time when I can really let go with him, without worrying about the consequences. Really I think it must be nice to have children under the old middle-class nanny system, where the mother can be the special guest, the source of delight and newness, and not just be the old bag with the responsibility if he's whiney all morning or won't eat his greens."

"But the responsibility is half the point. I have a pretty good relationship with your kids, and some kind of pleasant friendship with Paula's boys too, but I'm dependent on your kindness."

"No, no. I on yours."

"Look, I take them to the park some Saturdays or Harri swimming once a fortnight if she's lucky. It's nice, but it hardly helps you with the whole shitty reality of the dirty nappies. And if you and I fell out, or even if you wanted to move house, or job, the last thing you would think of—quite reasonably—would be my relationship with your kids, my loss of their friendship."

"We should all live in more communal situations I suppose."

"We probably should; but I don't think that would change this thing much really. I mean you feel a responsibility for those kids and sometimes resent that you can't share it. I feel friendship and resent that it doesn't earn me responsibility. But I don't have any control. Even if we lived in an ideal commune, I might have more daily contact and stuff, but it would still be because you chose it so, and could unchoose it any day you wanted. That you and Edward chose it I should say."

"Should, but don't. That's interesting. Personally I think that paternity is over-rated. I think it's just an act of choice not a biological thing like motherhood."

"I thought that was meant to be an act of choice too."

"You're not listening. At least that's not what I'm trying to say. I'm saying that a mother can't have a child without noticing. A father can. What does the word mean in relation to Alice's baby? We don't know who. Alice may not even know who, and I bet he doesn't know. Can you use the word father?"

"What word do you use for a mother who gives her baby up for adoption?"

"Yes, fair enough. I don't know. But it's not the same as fathering."

"Are you still trying to absolve my conscience for me?"

Nancy grinned at her, and Liz went on, "Because, O kindly earth mother, you are miles off course. I'm not pregnant. I'm the lady who doesn't get pregnant, remember?"

"Liz!"

"What?"

"Well, it's not like you to joke about it."

"Oh, I'm following the great doctor's advice. As soon as I convince you that I don't want a baby I shall swell up with triplets. You wait."

But she was puzzled herself by the light-headedness she felt.

Baffled by the joy that rose in her throat every time she realised that this month she was not pregnant. Frightened by the waves of real tenderness and concern that she felt for all the pregnant women who she saw in the street. Alarmed by the fascination and open interest with which she watched Alice in this last month of her pregnancy. And nervous of the loosening of strain that she felt towards Ian: the open lust, the sudden inability to be careful of him, protective towards his feelings. She was finding herself forgetting to take her temperature in the mornings, or to record it on the graph. Suddenly she did not care.

She had a letter from her mother. It arrived one morning when they had actually woken up in time to be sitting drinking coffee together before going to work.

Dear Liz,

As I told you in my last letter, Florence and I have found the house that we want. It isn't large and I think I may miss the space that I'm used to, but otherwise it is exactly what we want with a good deal of garden which seems to me to have a lot of potential, especially for some extension of the shrubberies. I hope the buyers of this place won't mind too much when they discover the extent to which I'm planning to denude this garden here. And in these buyers lies the point of my writing. I have got a rather fabulous sum for this house: I suppose one forgets when it becomes so familiar, just how beautiful and desirable a residence it is. Certainly I have got far, far more than I shall need to buy my one half of a small, rather ordinary cottage. As you probably remember when your father died he left everything to me for my use in my lifetime with an obligation to hand it over to you. I don't expect he imagined the house being sold really and the idea was that you should have it, and live in it, but this wasn't a term of the will and I don't feel obliged to act that way. Nor do I really see that you and Ian are ever going to want a large country house in Somerset. Even if you should it is now too late. I can only do what seems best to me, and when you were here you did not seem heartbroken at the thought of selling it. Anyway, as I can't see that I need anything like all the proceeds of the sale it makes sense to me and to Mr. Timms, who will write to you about all the legal things, although as your father's family solicitors I don't think he approves of what I'm doing, to give you a "cut" if that is the right word now instead of waiting till I'm dead. So I'm arranging for you to have about £10,000 as soon as we have completed the sale. Liz, I want you to spend this on a house. I think your flat is horrible, as I have said, and with this sort of down-payment I understand that you will be able to get a mortgage for the rest without any problem, which will work out much cheaper than renting for the rest of your life. I know you don't like me "bullying" you about it, but I am sure that if you had somewhere decent to live you would not feel so nervous about starting a family. I am not going to make getting a house a condition of having the money, you can give the lot to the Marxist-Leninists or whoever you are supporting at the moment, but I shall be very upset and rather angry if you do. There will be plenty for them later, if you are still of that mind.

Florence and I hope to be moved in by Christmas if everything goes smoothly. If there is any furniture and stuff that you would like from here, can you write *soon* and say what, because obviously I shan't want a lot of the stuff and must organise a sale for it otherwise, but I could keep back things you might want and store them until you know how big your new house will be or what you might like to put in it.

I hope things are well with you and your job is still fun and so on. You don't write very often, please let me know what you are planning and how you receive my usual "interference" with your life.

With much love and kisses, Mummy.

"How is she?" Ian asked without looking up from his *Guardian*.

"Fine." She hesitated. "She says she's sold the house, and found the cottage she wants."

"Good for her."

"Ian. Ian, do you like this flat?"

"What? Well I thought we had decided . . ." He looked up now. She watched his face for some sign of pain, some reflection of her own nervousness at suggesting a move. There was nothing there but curiosity.

"Ian, she's given us £10,000 to buy a house with."

"What?"

"You heard."

"Well at last it has paid off."

"What has?"

"My crafty plot to marry into the upper-middle classes. I was beginning to despair; I plotted for long hours through the night on how to snare an heiress, and after all these years I was beginning to think that I had wasted my options on you."

"Idiot."

"Now at last you can begin to keep me in the style to which I wish to become accustomed . . . yes, I think a smallish place in Mayfair, not more than six or eight bedrooms, we don't want to be weighed down by the responsibility for the servants; they are all so feckless nowadays, you have hardly got a girl reasonably trained when they seem to want to get married or something ridiculous like that."

"Ian, stop fooling. Would you really like to move?"

"Sweetheart, I have wanted to move since the second week we were here. I just haven't wanted to mention it because I thought you might be upset, because . . . you know why because."

"Oh never mind about that now. Listen, I must rush, I'm going to be late. How does one go about finding a house?"

"Try the Yellow Pages."

"Under Houses?"

"No, you half-baked moron, under Estate Agents."

"I know, I know."

She was late, she had to hurry; she got up, dropped a kiss on his head, swept up her bag and ran down the stairs. She would write to her mother later, she would say, yes please and thank you a lot and I have notified the Marxist-Leninists that their subscription will have to wait upon your funeral. Out of that flat where she had gone mad, out of that flat where she had let Ian hit her, out of that flat where there was not enough room to swing a cat; away from that place where she had been unfaithful to her husband. A new life. A new start. And Ian had not been neurotic about it, had not looked at her as though she had killed their child dead with her impatience. So what if they had planned to conceive it there? Planned to take its timing into consideration, its need for nursery and yellow walls and mobiles swinging? She did not care. Let it do what it wanted. She was going to have a house where she did not feel trapped, where she could lock herself up for an evening and not have to walk the streets.

A home, she could make a home for Ian and for her, a place where her friends might like to come, a place of space and beauty; she was tired, sick and tired of being disgusted by her house.

When she was about eight her parents had given her a dolls' house for Christmas. Not an ordinary dolls' house. They had had it made by an old man in the village, a scale model of her own real home. On Christmas morning she had come down to see its vast shape covered over with wrapping paper. She had not been able to guess what it was. When the time came to open it she had been overwhelmed with excitement; she had swung back the hinged front almost nervously, but inside even the furniture was correct and tucked up in the little bedroom on the top floor was a tiny doll with a blond fringe: "a me-doll, a me-doll." Her mother had even found a bonsai cherry tree for the front garden, had painted the rooms in the right colours, had used minute scraps of her own furnishings for the curtains, had painted wooden doll plates to match their own china. Magical, delightful. Liz would write to her mother and ask where the dolls' house was now. But it would no longer be the right house.

There would no longer be that sense of magic when she could move the daddy doll through the bedroom into his dressing-room and lean him against the basin to pretend to shave, march him down the stairs and disappear him from the house while the mummy doll made breakfast for the me-doll. Sometimes she would put the mummy-doll outside in the garden and let the model of herself indulge in all the things she was never allowed to do: walk on the dining-room table and play with her mother's dressing-table, go into the kitchen and cook on her own or climb out the attic skylight and play on the roof.

Liz shook herself; what had happened to her, that she remembered things from her childhood like that? It was so rare that she remembered herself doing anything girlie, but now she could see and feel that dolls' house and sense the magical thrill that she had taken in it. Were her imaginings of herself, as her father's substitute son, all a lie? He had given her the house, he and her mother together and had laughed with pleasure at her pleasure. She knew it was a real memory, but she could not fit it into the other pattern of memories that she was more accustomed to. What had Tony pumped into her with his semen that morning on the office floor; what had Ian beaten into her head and body with his angry hand?

It was a surprising amount of work, buying a house. She had not known it would be like that. She felt impelled to hurry, to consolidate the joy she had felt at the idea. Evening after evening, when they had finished work she dragged Ian out to look at the most unsuitable places; she talked with mortgage companies, accepted that they were not going to take her full earnings into consideration, felt unable to stand up to their calm logic, unable to say that she did not have a child and would not have one, unable to say to them, I am barren, I do not conceive, I will not lose my earnings looking after some baby. She just tolerated their assumptions because it was less effort than trying to argue with them. But with her mother's cash they had a lot of buying power.

Ian found the house, and she felt jealous. She had wanted to be able to give it to him as a present, to say I have found a house for you from me, but he rang her at work and said, "I think I've found our house."

"Ian, where?"

"Not far from here; it's a bit slummy and needs a lot of work, but it's got a garden and steps up to the front door, and it's the sort of place that I want."

She wanted to carp, she found herself having to bite back criticisms of a house she had not even seen. She said she would come straight after work to his office and they could go and see it together. She was sure she would not like it, that it would be intolerable in some way that she could not actually work out in advance. It was not. A Victorian terrace on the fringes of a nasty part of North Kensington, with a lot of noise and a good deal of dirt in the street, but there was a garden of sorts in the middle of the square and the houses had iron railings round the front area.

"It's too big, Ian."

"Rubbish. We can knock the two front rooms together and have an enormous living-room, and that great big kitchen."

"I love it."

As soon as she had said it, he started apologising for it.

"Well, it's in a dreadful mess; it will need a lot of work."

"That's nothing. It will be so handy for you and you know you've always wanted to live in the area where you're working."

"I might want to change jobs."

"Ian, don't. I heard how much you wanted it on the phone. Now I want it too. Don't try to spoil it for yourself. Ian I like it, I love it. I want us to live here."

"Really?"

"Really."

Suddenly everything went smoothly. Their friends kept telling them there were bound to be hitches, that they would be gazumped, that the mortgage people would decide it was too old, or too run down, or it would be squatted and they would be paralysed. But it did not seem to happen. They might even get moved in before Christmas.

One night in bed Ian said, "Liz, it is rather large you know."

"Ian, we've been through that. It's not too large—we can have someone to live with us."

"Yes, that's what I was thinking about. Liz, why don't you ask Alice if she'd like to."

"Alice?"

"Don't sound like that."

"I think she likes living alone."

"But she probably won't after the baby is born. You could ask her anyway."

"Why Alice?"

"Well, I like her, you like her, and I should think that she would like some sort of companionship."

"Yes, of course, but . . ."

"Liz, I would really like to have a baby living with us in that house. It's the right sort of house for a kid, it needs a kid to live in it."

She had been hiding her head in the sand. The ostrich does not really hide its head in the sand when it is frightened, any more than the unicorn is drawn by the scent of a pure virgin, or the pelican feeds its young with the blood from its own breast, or the phoenix rises again in the flames of its own destruction, or the woman has an extra rib. The ostrich has long, ugly, skinny, powerful legs on which she can run away across the veldt, she does not need to hide her head in the sand. But if she did she would feel the hot prickliness of the desert grains, faintly pink against her translucent eyelids; sound and clamour and danger and desire excluded by the warm weight of the sand. She would be safe, in that silence, from her own fear. She would perceive the warmth and peace; not the preposterous long legs and the silliness of the posture.

Nothing is changed, just because she has refused to worry about it. Nothing is different, she is still the barren woman who has betrayed her husband in the bed of another man. She is still the whore. "The reeking steam of her fresh villainies would spot the stars and menstruate the skies." Ian wanted his baby and would go anywhere to find it.

"Yeah, it's a good idea. I'll ask her."

Alice was getting very tired. Liz could not help noticing it at their next meeting. The graceful fullness that she had carried before seemed to have collapsed into a massive mound of flesh.

Nancy said, "Well, you ought to stop working."

"I have basically, but I can't turn down money. Nancy, I need it, I can't live on maternity benefit, can I? I'm not doing much now, but I really thought I could do this last little job okay. I don't know what it must be like for other single mothers who can't get freelance work at home. You're always reading about these women who work until they go into labour, but I just can't understand it."

"You're too old," Paula said with a smile.

"I know, it's funny that. I'm only just over thirty and I'm a senile parturient or something, it's extraordinary. I should have done it ten years ago."

"Or not at all," said Mary-Ann. "But it's not long now."

"Shit, I don't believe it. Another fortnight and I'll be dead. Even walking downstairs from my flat has me puffing like a grampus."

Jane said, "What is a grampus anyway?"

None of them knew. Liz said, "Ian and I have found a house."

"Where?" "What's it like?" "What's it going to cost?"

"It's a too big, rather disorderly place in North Kensington. Mildly slummy, very nice. Actually it really is too big. Ian said, Alice, why didn't I ask you if you'd like to come and live with us after the brat is born."

"Really?"

"Yes, really. Why are you surprised?"

"Put bluntly, I'm surprised that, what with one thing and another, you want a little baby in your house."

"No, no; that's why."

"Was this Ian's idea or yours?"

"Does that matter? I think he brought it up first, and I agreed. I think it's a great idea."

"Liz, if it's just for Ian, I mean, wouldn't you feel a bit sensitive about another person with a small baby?"

"Jesus, Alice, don't be so bloody tender with me. I wouldn't have asked you if I didn't want you, would I?"

"You might."

"Up yours."

Jane said, "Now girls, no arguing."

Alice said, "Look, Liz. If you're sure, I'll think about it. My immediate impulse is to say, yes, great. But I haven't lived with anyone else for years. I've been thinking that I didn't want to be alone with the kid and wondering what to do. But only if you're sure."

"Think about it. Come round one evening and we'll show you the house, and talk it over; we're quite easy to live with."

Not on the nights they were beating each other up, of course, not on the nights when she did not notice Ian's needs and he was furious with her for hers. Not on the nights when she was screwing her boss and her husband was weeping against the living-room wall. She had asked. She had not wanted to, but now the thought of a small child, a real baby in the house was turning her on, a baby she could legitimately hug and depend on, whose mother would not suddenly appear and push the pram away. A baby that was not hers to remind her of what she could not have. She had asked, she would not be held responsible for everything.

The others had gone back to Alice's pregnancy. Alice herself had had to struggle out of the chair and go to the loo. The rest were discussing whether Alice and Liz could or should live together, whether it would be good for them, whether Liz could cope, whether Alice would mind being the only mother. They could not mind their own businesses for ten seconds and let her mind hers.

Alice came back and sat down again. "When this hulk first moved down I thought that was great, I would be able to eat again. Now I can get it in at the top only in order to have to relieve it at the bottom every two minutes. I can't even sleep at night. The next time I see the doctor I'm going to ask him to induce it."

Nancy said appalled, "You're joking, aren't you?"

"Not entirely."

"But you can't do that!"

Nancy was a natural childbirth fanatic. She and Edward even watched home movies of Hugh being born. She had failed to persuade Alice of the importance of this, but she was still unable to stop trying.

Alice said, "I can and I will—or I may. Now lay off, Nancy, please. All I want is to have the damn thing over, and I can remember you saying just the same thing the last weeks with Hughie, didn't you?"

Jane said, "I'll be there to hold her hand anyway."

"You?"

They were all a bit surprised. Jane laughed and said, "Didn't we tell you? I was really curious so I asked and Alice thought it would be nice. She knows I won't have any morally uplifting advice. That is, assuming the hospital will let me stay, and they say they will at this point."

Liz could tell that Nancy was hurt. As far as this group went Nancy was the mummy expert. Paula's children were bigger, but they had been born before Paula was in the women's movement, and Paula resisted strongly any attempt to involve her as a mother. But Nancy had chosen her children within the context of her present life. If Jane was, as she so often challenged them "their token gay lady" then Nancy was equally their representative "feminist mother." Liz watched Nancy trying to work out why Alice had done this to her, why she was not wanted in her most cherished role, why her expertise should be dismissed.

Liz knew that she would have to try to point out to her later, that it was precisely because of her expertise which she had so kindly poured down Alice's throat throughout her pregnancy. Alice wanted to be in charge of her own birth, not hand it over to Nancy's ebullient bossiness; she could quite understand why Jane should be a more sympathetic hand-holder. She shied away from telling Nancy that, from the fact that Nancy would be bound to ask her and would not let her wriggle out of answering.

She felt as tired as Alice looked. She wanted to go home. They all cast themselves as the star in their own interpretation of the play, and then expected everyone else to play supporting roles. She was probably as bad. Would Nancy love her less when . . . if . . . she could no longer pity her as a childless woman? She was valuable to Nancy: women like Jane who did not want children, who proclaimed them as oppressors, destroyers of freedoms so hardly gained, or women like Mary-Ann who found them boring, not worth consideration, were a threat to Nancy's self-image. Other women who did have children, might be seen as rivals, might be better at combining motherhood with feminism, might create jealousies. But she, poor Liz, dear Liz, was someone who wanted what Nancy had, who enhanced Nancy's sense of achievement by trying to emulate it; and never threatened her authority, because she failed. Nancy would have something to forgive if Liz had a baby or if she gave up trying to have a baby. What was a friendship worth?

Her father loved her when she was a child, because she had been a woman who did not challenge his authority. He had stopped loving her when she stopped acknowledging his power. Ian loved her because she was a woman who did not threaten his timorous sexuality, Nancy loved her because she was a woman who did not encroach on her territory, but sat on the boundaries looking enviously in. That was her own power; she bought love by being inadequate as a woman. Perhaps that bloody doctor was right: she did not want the baby because she had noticed, subconsciously of course, that it was precisely her failure that earned her that loving concern on which she depended for attention. Even Dr. Marshall himself would no longer give her his important time if she were a real woman with long curly hair, who creamed her babies' bottoms and washed her husband's football socks.

But her mother was certain that her father would have wanted her to have a baby. Her mother ought to know, Liz's father was her husband, she ought to know him better. Liz knew she must give up the delusion that she knew her father better than anyone else ever had or could, that he had loved her so specially. Memories deceived, changed shape according to the context, according to the need you had of them. When her father had died she had seen him for weeks afterwards walking ahead of her, coming out of doors, waiting in bus queues, even sitting at lectures. She had been furious with him: he was meant to be the grown-up, he had walked out in the middle of their fight and had subtly won a victory; she would never defeat him now, never establish herself as her own person and make him love her for whom she really was. She thought of those of her friends who had worked through their adolescent power-struggles with their parents and entered into richer, gentler friendships, and declared that it was not fair. Once when she imagined that she saw him walking down St. Giles's outside St. John's College she had run after him under the plane trees to tell him that he was a bastard, that he had cheated her repeatedly, and now, finally, by escaping from their relationship.

But when she could not bear the pain of her own anger any longer the memories had changed completely. She recalled not the bitter fights and hysterical battles of the last few years, but her whole childhood through a rosy haze. In her first years at school she would get dressed with him in his dressing-room. He had always refused an electric razor and had a brush made of badger-hair, and a little tub of lather. He would stand at the mirror, watching her and himself in it while she got dressed in the big leather armchair, and he taught her the times-tables, barking the questions from behind his Father Christmas beard of foam. Or they had learned poetry together. *Hiawatha* and Macaulay's *Lays of Ancient Rome* and the longer speeches from Shakespeare. She had tried to tell herself that this was not the whole picture, that this was not the reality of her father, but her memories would give her nothing else to play with.

She did not need to be afraid of what was in her head. Sort out the memories, put ropes on them. Sort out her feelings about the baby. The problems need not be desolating, they might be interesting. And it would make Ian happy. She would go and see the psychiatrist; not to get herself a baby, but to look at herself through someone else's eyes, to get a guided tour of her own muddled head, to explore those hidden corners. Something beautiful might be lurking there to surprise her.

One of the first tests they had done at her clinic had been a microscopic examination of her cervical mucus. She had thought that it would be horrible, but the process was neutral, neither painful nor uncomfortable. Dr. Marshall, still her idol, smiling, chatting, had withdrawn his sample from her, spread it on a microscopic plate, dried it briskly under a fan, put it under the microscope and hummed at it thoughtfully while she lay on the table with her jeans and knickers beside her on a chair. She had thought of getting up and putting them back on, but she had not liked to move without his permission. He had explained in the most general terms what he was doing, but she did not know if he would be needing her body anymore, or if he had finished with it for now. He called the young student doctor who was with him to come and take a look, and the younger man went and peered and hummed likewise over the microscope. She was forgotten, ignored, like the young nurse on the other side of the room. They had taken their pleasure from her. With no explanation but a brisk "Wait here" to all of them, Dr. Marshall suddenly left the room. She had lain there thinking, "Oh God, I have cervical cancer, and he has gone to get his knife and chop me up, or a trolley to carry me away to an operating theatre and I will never see Ian again"; or Ian and she did not make love right and he had found it out; or worse. The student doctor suddenly, without warning, said, "Hey, do you want to see? Quick then." He grinned at her invitingly. "It's something pretty." Startled she looked over to the nurse, but she was busy with something at her table. Liz leapt from the couch and ran across the room. She felt foolish in only her socks and jersey with nothing in between but the tuft of pubic hair, and the fading mark of her bikini from the summer before. She had a sudden realisation that her legs were very hairy. But the young man hardly glanced at her.

"Look," he said, and she looked down the little telescope. The most beautiful pattern: elegant like ice on a window-pane; irregular fernish fronds crystallised on the glass plate. Her mother had once had a pot of miniature ferns—it had stood in a pot on their dining-room window-sill. She had looked at it often, entranced by the delicate tendrils, the careful tracery against her nose, dampness clinging to it, moss embedded round the base. And here again, the same tangling, the same delicate but sturdy stalks, the magical fronds. But cleaner, colourless, still.

"Is that me?"

Her amazement sounding, even to her own engrossed ears, like a child who has seen a conjuring trick, convinced by the eyes, unconvinced by the marvel. She bent down and squinted again; it was still there, the lovely patterning had come out of her own vagina, she had made it herself.

"It's called ferning," he said, almost unnecessarily. "Isn't it pretty?"

He had not told her, bless him, that it was in fact a bad sign. By that stage in her menstrual cycle it should have gone away, that the hormonal changes leading up to ovulation destroy the patterning, just as the warmth and glow of the morning sun destroy the same pattern on winter-morning windows and leave them beaded and ordinary and cold. He had just let her look at this miraculous biological stunt-act for a moment or two longer and then said, "You'd better hop up on the bed before his Lordship returns." They had grinned at each other. She had said, "Are you a caste traitor?" and he had said, "Oh Lord, does it come over like that?"

She had clambered back on the couch and he had added, "I think it's an amazing thing. When I first saw that I knew I wanted to specialise in gynaecology, even at the risk of appearing to exploit women. Oh yes"—he said, seeing her surprised face—"I get told. But I think everyone should see it, especially if you've made it yourself. Marshall is more old-fashioned. Mind you, he is bloody good." "Yes, I know," she said quickly to reassure him. And then Dr. Marshall had come back from wherever he had gone without a word of explanation or concern that he had left her on the bed with her knickers off for ten totally unnecessary minutes.

The student and she had exchanged a conspiratorial wink, but she had never seen him again since then. He had made a difference. She had never minded any test procedures after that, curious only to know what strange and exotic side-shows her inner flesh could put up for her next. The memory of that unexpected loveliness delighted and encouraged her. She meant to remember to find out more about the technique of showing up the pattern; whether it would be possible for one of the women and health groups to stage this marvel for themselves. But if what came out of her body could be so fascinating and beautiful why should she be so frightened of the hidden matter in her head?

If that garden were better tended perhaps she would find strange flowers growing there too. Not just evil weeds to be eradicated, but unexpected blossoms, unremembered dreams.

"Ian," she said, "I've decided that I want to go into therapy."

"He wore you down in the end, did he?"

"He? No, no, it's not Dr. Marshall, at least not directly." She could not say, "You told me to get my head sorted out." She did not want to remind him in any way of that night, she did not want him to remember it, she did not want to remember it herself. "I've been thinking about it and I've come to the conclusion that I'm curious, that I want to explore that, and if I get pregnant out of it so much the better."

Ian grinned at her affectionately. He also looked worried, puzzled, but she could not attend to that now. She did not want him to believe that Dr. Marshall had frightened her into a conviction that she was insane, she wanted him to know that it was interest, simply. Ian said,

"Well at least you will be able to get the best treatment on the National Health, via the despised doctor. You might as well do it now, rather than some other time at ten quid a session."

"Do you think it's a good idea?"

"Well, I don't believe you need it, if that's what you mean. But you should do what you like. Do it if you like. But it'll be very time-consuming."

"Meaning the house? Did you ring the agent today?"

"Yes. It's all going ahead fine. But I've asked around, and I think the mortgage people we've talked to are in line with everyone else. No one is going to let us take your full salary into account."

"You should have told them I was barren."

"Well, I did think of it. Then I thought that was mad. We can get enough anyway, I reckon, and if we did commit ourselves to your full salary, what would happen if you did, when you do get pregnant?"

"True. It's just the insult. I mean I earn more than you. Perhaps they should take the whole of my salary and only a part of yours. When we have the baby you could take care of it."

"They don't think that way."

"No, I know. It's not your fault."

Supposing she had got pregnant. Supposing she was pregnant now, not knowing which of them. Would they be buying a house? Would they even be together? She was washed in the blood of the lamb, the unborn lamb in her gut which had forgiven her, cleansed her and restored her. She loved him. Loved Ian. She was forgiven, freed, liberated in the bleeding. He need never know. It need never come between them.

She rushed into his arms, wanting to insist on their closeness, wanting them to be together.

"Hey"—he was surprised, amused, looking back over the conversation, trying to work out where sex and arousal had come from—"I haven't even had my supper yet."

"It can wait."

They were giggling together. He had to love her. He had to go on loving her. She had to have him in her arms, in her cunt, she had to have proof that they were still together, that she had not ruined everything. That she had been forgiven.

At first she had meant it only as a joke. She let down her long mane of golden-red hair, which she had used to bleach blonde, but which was now growing in a more beautiful, rich colour than she had ever hoped or expected. She bound a red ribbon round under her breasts, between them and crossed over her shoulders, so they stood out high and tight. She meant only to tease him, to shake for one moment his impeccable composure, as he ate dinner with those respectables. It might shake some of them too, ex-customers for all their smug self-righteousness. Afterwards they would all laugh together, and Simon Peter would try to be shocked, and the others would laugh at him. It would be a good joke: she spent the last of her savings from the trade on the alabaster pot and the ointment. She waited till the dinner was well under way, till she was sure he would be bored by their prim moralising and conceited manners.

When she came in, he smiled at her, leaning at the table, talking as always; but he glanced round and saw her costume and smiled warmly. She enjoyed the shocked faces of those others, that she a sinner, a woman of the town, should penetrate their dreary fastness, should challenge their precarious safety. And yes, as she had thought, some of them she knew. That greasy slob, who had taken a whip to her and refused to pay extra for the privilege, who claimed she would not do it if she did not enjoy it, that she ought to pay him for pleasuring her.

It was meant to be a joke, but when she bent over his feet—

dusty, tired-looking feet—when she caught the gentleness of his smile, she began to cry. The tears eased their way out softly and fell on to the feet; she tried to wipe them away with her hair. He had saved her. Saved her from the shame, saved her from the disgust she felt at herself. He had called her a very loving woman, because of her profession. She had thought he must be innocent beyond belief at first, but it was not that; he knew that the body and the soul were not as separate as people tried to make them. He knew that she could be a whore and so be a loving woman.

The tears fell over his feet, not tears of sorrow, but tears of joy. He had bought her back, paid her price to her pimp, paid for the doctor that dosed her for the foul disease that clogged her gut. He had introduced her to women who liked her. His own mother: he had not been ashamed to introduce her to his own mother, to ask her to take care of his own mother who was often confused by the noise and the movement and the late nights and the mixed company. He had asked her, a sinner, to use her rich experience of the world, her knowledge of the moods and timing of people to help his mother. He had not been ashamed that she had been a whore, he had seen the talents she had gained there as things to be appreciated. He even found her beautiful—she had enough knowledge to know that—he found her beautiful, found her desirable.

The dust was washed from his feet now and she opened the pot of ointment, soothing it down between his cracked toes. None of his other friends would know how to choose an ointment with so rich and delicate a scent. That knowledge was special to her too and she knew he would like it. She did not desire him, he lacked a certain animal roughness that would turn her professional duties into a real pleasure, she suspected he was probably a virgin: something she had never much enjoyed. But she liked him, it was new that liking for a man, that richness and freedom, that not having to watch the timing, wonder where the snags lay, wonder how soon he would move away from chatter and into demands. She liked his world, she felt at home there, with his mixed bag of friends; some of them made her positively respectable; all of them accepted that easy friendship; accepted that she had talents and worth outside of her past, and inside of it.

Someone at the dinner was protesting now, protesting that he should even let her touch him. She felt his fingers come down gently on her head, soothing her against the pain she was immune to. He said her sins are forgiven because she loved much. Simple. Love was everything, could buy everything, could excuse everything. He said she is a loving woman. He said Run along now, everything is all right. He said, Thank you for what you have done, thank you for your present, thank you for your sense of humour, thank you for your friendship. Don't worry, he said, don't worry about anything. Everything will be all right.

She wept again. Later she wept in the arms of his mother, who could not share her humour but could share her tears. There was no need to wash away the past; the past made you who you were. There was no need to apologise for an unloved childhood, to apologise for poverty and beatings, to apologise for seeking love wherever and however, those things made you what you were, made you the person who could have these friendships now.

She never braided her hair again. She never wore a veil. She was not ashamed of being a whore. She was proud of the hair which was long enough, beautiful enough to wipe his feet with, which would be long enough to cover the worst of his wounds so that his mother would not have to touch them. She was proud of a past that made her tough enough not to be afraid of his dying, not to be ashamed of him when he was hung for a common criminal.

She was a whore and he loved her. There was nothing to be ashamed of. When she recognised him in the garden, it was a meeting of friends.

8. NOVEMBER

"Well," Ian said, curled against her on the sofa, warm and relaxed. "What was he like?"

"She."

"She?"

"She. You can have lady psychiatrists you know, you sexist pig."

"I'm sorry. Just . . . Dr. Marshall being who he is."

"Yes, I know. I was surprised too, actually. She's probably his fifth column, a spy in enemy places. I wondered why he looked so smug when he gave me the name and address. When I next see him he'll crow with self-satisfied mirth."

"Back to the beginning. What was she like?"

"I don't know, Ian. Pleasant enough. I found it faintly farcical: her place was so like a film—big couch, antique chair for her, that stuff. I felt I didn't know what Dr. Marshall had told her, I felt I didn't know whose side she was on. I felt trapped. I went in, right, and we sat and looked at each other in silence, and I thought I'm not going to be bullied into starting this, it was never my idea in the first place and the silence just got longer and longer; I felt I was being bullied into saying something, but it worked because I did, I just started to blether, and then I felt foolish and genuinely mad. I felt manipulated. But that may be more the situation than her, as a person, or as a professional. Just me being neurotic."

"I shouldn't think so. I think they're all like that. I don't trust them an inch."

"Three evenings a week minimum, she said. I don't know if I can hack that, I don't know if it's worth it. I don't know whether to go back again. Even Dr. Marshall said that if I didn't like her there was no point going on. I do have an out."

"Of a sort. Presumably he'd just suggest someone else, wouldn't he?"

"Yes, I suppose so. If only I knew whether his whole theory had any substance. If it was a miracle door to pregnancy I could just go through with it as honestly as I could manage; but it might just be a waste of time. Ian, you've been there. I do think you might give me some guidance."

"That's against my principles. I think you're sane, I don't think you need to go into analysis; but like you say, maybe if it is problem-related . . . it's hard for me to understand how it could be. When you decided, I thought it was curiosity, a new game to play. That's okay." He nuzzled his head into her shoulder so that she could not see his face. "I'm prejudiced, you know I am. They made me go and see a shrink; the price for escaping from the nut-house. I didn't go for long. I've told you. Maybe I needed it then, I suppose I was quite sick, in anybody's terms. But he didn't like me. I never felt that he liked me, what I needed was for someone to like me. I didn't like me much, I admit, but I didn't want to be made over into someone else. I don't want you to be made over into someone else. But it might be different for you, different person, different problems. That's past anyway. I got better. A bit."

She pushed him back and put her face over his mouth.

"You are okay. Tough. Lovable. Don't worry about you. I love you."

"I hit you."

"That doesn't matter."

"It does. Matters to me. Ought to matter to you. I think it does matter to you. You've been different since."

"Ian."

"You have, Liz. I can't say I blame you. You were glad you weren't having a baby. Glad. I noticed. You don't want my child anymore."

"No. No. Ian, it wasn't that. It's your child that I want."

"You were glad. Each month you've been heartbroken. I know. I've tried not to see how much you've minded, I can't cope with how much you care. But now you're glad. I know you've tried to hide it. Suddenly you want to move house. Suddenly you agree to see a shrink. Suddenly you are glad not to be pregnant."

"Look. It's true I was glad. I just didn't want the baby to be conceived out of that night, when there are so many good ones."

"So it did matter. It did matter to you enough for you not to want our baby. And you're right. I wouldn't want to risk having a baby from someone who could behave like that."

"Ian, two months you've been thinking this and you never said. Darling, it wasn't that."

She thought she would have to tell him about Tony now and she could not bear it, he might stop loving her. She would not add to the burden of guilt they carried between them. He might hold adultery against her, but knowing him he might equally, probably would, hold it against himself: one more proof of how vile he had been, one more sign of how much she minded him hitting her. And she did mind, it would be silly to pretend that she did not mind how he had reduced her in her own eyes to that blubbering, begging indignity. They had to forget. They had to move as far and as fast as possible away from that night, had to travel together to some different place. She would tell him about Tony, spread the guilt. They had to carry each other, and the whole weight of their insecurities and fears and lusts and passions and needs. There was no way out but through. She had to try.

"Ian. Ian, you are way off beam; that was not why I didn't

want your baby. I do, I do." She waited but he would not respond to her, looking away dumb and despairing, as eaten by guilt as she was. "Ian, I love you." But that was too cheap, an easy spell—name the thing desired and you can create it. The source of all magic lay in naming. She said, "I love you," trying to conjure the words into the feeling, trying to remember that they were true, that she had been so certain of their truth. It was not enough. "Ian."

There was a knock at the door.

Ian said, "Bugger," but he still sat there numbly.

"Let's not answer," she said, but she was already on her feet, tugging her jeans down. She glanced at the clock; it was only just after ten, really not late. Lost in the muddle she had created between them, she had thought it was the middle of the night.

It was Alice. "Liz, I'm sorry. Can I use your phone? Mine seems to have broken down." Even so she had come past at least one public phone box, to say nothing of the still open pubs to get to their house. Alice could see that Liz was surprised. She said quickly, as though embarrassed, "I think I'm in labour. I didn't want to be alone."

"Well, come in."

Alice came through the front door and they started up the stairs. She said, "Am I disturbing you?"

"Shit, Alice. Not so it could possibly matter."

They went into the flat. Ian had returned to a more normal expression. "Alice. Hi. Come to discuss our new house?"

"Not really. We could though. I'll come if you really want me."

Liz hated them for spoiling her sense of drama, of excitement. She had not expected to be so close to this event. She wanted Alice to infect her. Alice was still embarrassed. She said again, standing in the living-room doorway, "I am sorry."

"Idiot."

"No, sorry that it should be you. You were the nearest, but it's not fair. I'm sorry."

"Shut up, child. I'm not that delicate. Now what shall we do?

Look, come in and sit down anyway." She put her arm round Alice, tender, wanting to participate, not sure what she was meant to do.

"Ian," she said, "Alice thinks she's having her baby."

"Christ."

"I don't know. I'm confused. I thought I had the whole thing sewn up, and now I'm in a panic about going to the hospital on my own. I thought if I could find Jane, she could be there. I'm afraid that if I go on my own they'll somehow keep her away, not let her in. I don't want to be on my own." She pulled herself together and said, "Quite apart from anything else, Jane would be furious to miss this treat."

"Ian," said Liz, alarmed by Alice's apparent insecurity, "make us some coffee, love." Something ordinary and safe while she worked out what to do. But Alice said, "I don't think I'm meant to eat anything now."

"Shit. Oh dear, we're not much use are we? Surely you're not going to have the baby just yet?"

For a wild moment she hoped that Alice was, here in their flat with Liz to hold her hand; to be given the magic key to the realm of motherhood. She would deliver the baby, Ian and she; would gain the power, would grow and stretch towards claiming the moment for themselves.

Alice said, "I bloody hope not. I've only sort of started. Classical pains in the back and sudden contractions, not very heavy, but they've taken me off-balance. I had kind of settled in my mind that the baby would be induced tidily on Friday according to the medical profession's plots."

Ian asked, "Are you excited?"

Alice grinned at him, feeling better now she was not alone, now she could share the deciding what to do with her friends. "Yes, actually, now you say it, I am. Listen, can I use your loo?"

"Sure."

"And please, yes, I would like some coffee; there's bound to be plenty of time. But I'd like to find Jane and ring the hospital and those things."

Ian went into the kitchen. Liz picked up the phone and dialled Jane's number. She was not in. Liz felt a moment of panic, punctuated by an odd exhilaration. Then returning to details she asked if they knew where Jane was. Alice was nearly a week overdue, surely Jane had made some arrangements. The woman at the other end of the phone went off to ask. Came back, said she thought that Jane was at a meeting. Where, she asked, and yes it was important, she had to get in touch with her, right now. Almost reluctantly, Liz felt, the woman gave her another number to try, of course she could not be sure that Jane was there, but she might be.

She listened to the receiver purr for just long enough for her to wonder what she should do if no one answered it. Then it was answered.

"Hello."

"Hello. Is Jane Burton there?"

"Jane Burton?" A puzzled man's voice. "No one called Jane Burton lives here. Are you sure you've got the right number?"

Of course she wasn't sure, silly bugger. "No, I know she doesn't live there. But the woman at her flat thought she might be at a meeting. They gave the number."

"Hang on, I don't know. There is some meeting going on upstairs. Would she be at that?"

"I hope so."

"Who is this?"

"I'm ringing for Alice McLeod, tell her."

"I'll go and see."

The phone made silent noises, after she had heard him put it down. She waited. She tried to imagine him running up the stairs of some strange house, looking into the meeting, nervous, as it was probably an all-women thing if Jane was at it. Please let her be there, please let her not tell him to push off, she was busy.

"Alice?" The phone was picked up again, and she recognised Jane's voice. Thank God.

"No, it's me, Liz. But Alice is here. She reckons she's started having the baby."

"Oh sod it. It would be tonight, I'm the other side of London. Is she okay?"

"She seems to be. I don't get the impression that there's masses of hurry. Not that I would know."

"Look, I'll get a taxi, if you've any money in the house for a loan. It's bloody freezing and it will take all night to bike. Perhaps Pam'll give me a lift. Hang on." She moved her mouth away from the phone but Liz could hear her calling up the stairs, then her voice back close again.

"They say you're not to go to the hospital until your contractions are regular and about ten minutes apart. That's what they said at the classes."

"Did you go to classes?"

She could feel Jane's grin. "Yeah. They're called fathers' classes. I wore a big yellow 'Glad to be Gay' button and you could see the good ladies doing a double-take."

"And you're the feminist who said I should express my solidarity with the motherless women at my clinic."

"So I did. I suppose we can none of us resist teasing them. Very bad. Hang on again." Liz could hear her talking to another woman, and then, "Right, Pam's going to bring me over in her car. Okay? About twenty minutes I should think. Listen Liz, can you cope?"

"Yes, of course."

"I am sorry. I'll be as quick as I can."

"Don't worry about me. But Alice wants you here, so get moving."

"See you," said Jane and hung up.

Liz tried to find the telephone directory to ring the hospital. The blue volume was not with the others, and she could not see it. "Ian, where's the telephone book?"

"Mmmm. Have you tried under the big chair? I think I may have shoved it there yesterday."

She felt angry about the chaos, shoved at the shabby red

armchair and located the extremely dusty directory. She rang the hospital, tried to discipline herself against apologising for bothering them, failed, but managed to explain.

"All right," said the crisp woman at the other end. "We'll expect Mrs. McLeod later on."

"Not Mrs."

"Don't apologise, we don't discriminate. One name for everyone. Perhaps we should go over to this Ms thing. Don't bring her earlier than necessary, this seems to be happy birthday night for half the children in London."

"Thank you." At least it was not the same hospital as her clinic. A place for everything.

Ian carried in the two cups of coffee, and was about to go for the third. He put down the ones he was holding, Liz's beside her on the floor and Alice's on the mantelpiece. Squatting on the floor beside her he put his hand on her back, gently.

"Liz, are you okay with this?"

"Sure."

"I thought you might find it a bit painful."

"Not yet." He got up and went back to the kitchen. She rose and followed him.

"Ian, do you?"

"What?"

"Find it painful."

"No. Yes. Sort of butterfly-ish, I think."

"Jane's coming."

"I heard. That's good. How's Alice?"

Liz went through to the hallway and banged on the loo door. "Hey, are you okay? Your coffee's ready."

"Yes. I'm just coming out." The door opened and Alice came out. "This is the real thing all right. I'm bleeding."

"Is that meant . . . is that okay?"

"Yes, I think so. There's this thing they call a 'show.' Not real blood. It's like my first period, just a sort of staining."

"Was your first period like that?"

"Sure. I really felt sold short. My mother had described it, all

this blood and gore and embarrassment and horror and certainly
pain. When I took my knickers off one evening there was this
sort of reddish stain. I thought I must have cut myself, or wiped
too hard with that crinkly school loo-paper. I didn't put the two
together for about three days."

Trust Alice to do things with so little drama. Liz's first period had been a source of panic and fear. She had been the last
girl in her class to start: sometime after her fifteenth birthday
she had begun to worry. Her girlfriends said, "Lucky you," but
she knew they did not believe that. While they had been entering the mysterious rites of adulthood, discussing bras and Tampax in a knowing way, she had been left outside, isolated by her
flat chest, by the light, almost invisible fuzz around the tops of
her long skinny legs, free to vault over the horse in the gym
week after week, while the others took their ritualised turns at
sitting off to one side once the floor exercises were finished. Excluded, cut off. She had never been popular: cut off by her family's richness, by her own cleverness and sharp tongue, and now
by her freakish body. She wanted to ask her mother if she ought
to see a doctor or something, but she had not even known how
to phrase the question. Night after night she had pored over her
body in the secrecy of her bedroom, disgusted and amazed by
the difference between herself and the other women she knew.
With her finger she explored the entrance to that dark world,
not knowing what she was meant to find, and finding only
softness and pleasure. And guilt: she was appalled that so inadequate a body could give her so much pleasure in exchange for a
casually investigating finger.

But she was punished. She had not even noticed. At the end
of one class she had gathered her books together to go to the
next. Sensed the staring eyes, the horrified awe. No one had
even giggled, but she had sensed their dumbstruck disgust. Finally someone had said to her, in a half-whisper, "I think you
should go to the bogs." And she had said, "Why?" She had wondered if it was some elaborate practical joke against her, and it
was. Not played by her school friends which she could have

borne, but played against her by her own body: the whole of the back of her pale green skirt had been drenched in blood. She had walked all down the corridors with that give-away stain marking her out; she had not expected the blood to be like that, liquid, flowing as though a long erected dam had burst, the scarlet wave covering her. There was no hiding. She had groped for her coat and run, run home. When her mother had seen her and asked what she was doing back at this hour she had not known what to say. And when her mother had seen her skirt there had been no moment of commiseration, no understanding of her shame. Her mother had said only, "Go and change at once. At once."

The girls at school had hated her because she had exposed them all, down the long beige corridor she had carried the shame, the curse that was on them all, for every boy to see. Every boy in the school had had a chance to learn the horror that flowed out from that scarlet place that the girls had been trying to make into a temple of promised delights. Her mother had not even let the skirt, which was one that Liz had liked a lot, be taken to the cleaners; it had been thrown away, forgotten not forgiven.

Now Liz said, grinning, "Lucky you. I started in the middle of a French lesson, and had to hobble home on the bus hoping the blood wouldn't pour down to me ankles."

"Well, perhaps in compensation that's why you never have any period pains."

"Dubious. Funny that one should have less pain when the system is not working, isn't it?"

"What?"

"Didn't you know? Period pains are a sort of possible sign of ovulation."

Alice suddenly grimaced, and put her hands on her stomach. "Feel, feel," she gasped and nervously Liz put out a hand and felt the long ripple of tension spread across Alice's enormous belly.

"That's a contraction," Alice told her.

"Does it hurt?"

"More than the last one. Give me period pains any day."

"Well, for goodness' sake come and sit down and drink your coffee."

Ian came out of the bedroom with the clock with the second hand. "Here, you can time them."

"Thanks."

"And you are meant to put your feet up and breathe out with the contractions."

"How do you know?" Alice asked smiling at him.

"I've read the books."

He brought out a pillow and put it behind her back. He made a note of the time on a little piece of paper, and put the clock on the table facing so that they could all see it. Liz looked at him and realised that he was enjoying himself, his face curious and alert, watching Alice with tenderness. She felt the first pang of jealousy that she had been putting off since Alice had arrived at the flat.

Once Ian had kept pictures of newborn children, their faces like ancient buddhas or curled away in sleep. They had been pinned up round the house. He had devoured birth literature; tearing the beautiful smiling faces out of Leboyer's book. He had bought a series of poster pictures of the baby growing inside the womb, had pored over them like a traveller over a map of a new land. Taking the maps as a guide but knowing they were only the beginning, the outline of the country that he and Liz would explore together. The pictures had gone now and the posters were hidden away somewhere, if he had not destroyed them. She never asked, they had been his territory. Hers had been the babies in prams in the park, the babies in back-packs on the street, and sucking at their mother's milk-filled breasts at women's conferences. But while she turned in pain now from such sights, Ian had clearly lost none of his enthusiasm. She had denied him what he wanted, the whims of her gut and mind were driving his tenderness to other sources.

They timed another contraction for eighteen and a half minutes. Then Jane arrived. She kissed Alice, hugged Liz and said brashly, "I can't think what I'm doing here. Gay ladies don't have to go through with this. They were not pleased with me at the lesbian cell meeting." She laughed and they laughed with her, but Ian looked, for the first time, nervous.

Alice said she thought she ought to have a rest, as the hospital were no keener to have her than she was to be there, before it was necessary. Alice asked Ian, quite bluntly, if she could borrow his razor as she would rather shave herself than leave it to some knife-happy young resident. Ian went into the bathroom to find it; Liz yelled to him to bring some talcum powder too, as she had heard somewhere that it made the job easier. The three women looked at each other, seeking for some response to the situation they could all use.

Ian came back, said he had put his razor and the powder in the bedroom. "Why don't you do it and then have a lie down?" He reached out with both hands to pull her to her feet.

Alice grins at him, a grin of tenderness shared, and Liz cannot avoid looking at that grin, although she cannot see Ian's face. She is shocked to find herself grateful that his expression is hidden from her. Alice reaches her arms up to Ian's hands and he pulls her firmly. As she balances herself upright, a gush of water springs from between her legs and splashes on to the carpet, spraying even the bottom of Ian's jeans. In a moment of shock he unbalances her and she sits down again suddenly and bursts into tears. Liz looks only at that water.

Jane says, "It's okay, it's just the waters breaking," and Ian laughs with relief. But the three women look at each other shakily, embarrassed and marvelling that something so unexpected should pour out from where they have become used to blood and stickiness. Alice stops crying almost at once and says, "Christ, I'm sorry." Then another contraction changes her expression, as though her face had been wiped over by a maternal but invisible face-flannel.

Following a mysterious rule-book, that Liz knows she has not read, the others agree to ring for a taxi, because now Alice must go to the hospital. Jane sits holding Alice's hand, and Ian notes the timing of the contraction on his paper. As though in a dream Liz hears herself offering Alice some dry underclothes. Alice has withdrawn for a moment into a silence from which both her fear and her excitement glow out almost tangibly.

After a while the taxi arrives; they have recorded another two contractions, and written them on the paper. Liz and Ian have gone out into the bedroom while Alice has shaved her pubic hair, and put on some dry knickers.

At partings they are more accomplished than at watching the magical water in which the baby has swum and sung for so long. Kisses they exchange; Alice says thank you so much and sorry; they say it is nothing and good luck. Ian goes down the stairs with Alice and Jane, his arm round Alice. Liz hears them stop on the stairs for a moment, then Alice's voice: "Cow, that one hurt," and Jane's louder: "For God's sake let's get a move on. The taxi bloke will have a fit if you have your baby in his cab." And finally Ian's: "Now good luck, and be sure to let us know." They move out of hearing. Liz stares at the damp puddle on the floor, it has soaked in somewhat now but it is still visible, darker on the already dark carpet. She thinks she will get a cloth to wipe it up, but instead she kneels fingering the wetness, disgusted at herself, embarrassed lest Ian find her here, and yet still reaching out with her finger.

When she was a child her father took her to church. At the beginning of the Mass the priest would come out with a little silver bucket and walk down the aisles sprinkling the congregation of the faithful. "You shall purge me with hyssop, and I shall be clean," sung the choir. "You shall wash me and I shall be whiter than snow." At Easter time the chant changed. "Behold I saw water, proceeding from the right side of the temple and all to whom that water came were healed everyone and they said Alleluia, Alleluia." The body, she was patiently taught, is the temple of the Holy Spirit. This was the water from the inner temple; she would be purged, healed, would obtain the powerful magic from Alice, would glut herself on the water and say Alleluia, Alleluia. Fertility charms did not come from the wounds of that ascetic purity which Christ had poured out on the cross; she did not believe in his magic anymore. But this mingled blood and water, from the source of fertility, that had to be believed.

Quickly, nervously she rubs her finger into the pile of the carpet, her other fingers curled in tightly as though afraid to touch the untouchable. She grinds her finger into the dampness, feeling the weave of the wool. She looks at the finger for a moment, horrified and exultant. She raises the finger to her mouth and sucks greedily. Dr. Marshall is wrong; she is not coming to terms with herself, not to his terms with herself. The psychiatrist, whom she saw only hours ago, will never know of this. She is creating new terms—she squats there on the floor muttering her spells. Alleluia. She looks up suddenly. Ian is watching her. Her finger is still in her mouth, like a shy child, like a mad woman trying to re-create the image of an innocent childhood. He opens his arms away from his side a little. She does not know if it is an invitation or a gesture of despair. She takes her finger out of her mouth and moves towards him. They are both crying. Huge tears pour down their faces: salty water that kills crops, that sterilises. In each other's arms, their faces pressed against each other so that the tears become confused, comingled, they weep. They weep there for a long time.

In the morning Jane rang from the hospital. She sounded tired but still excited. Alice had had a daughter. Ian laughed and asked, "Do all feminists have girls?"

"Nancy didn't."

Which reminded her, and she rang Nancy. They agreed that they would both go and visit Alice that evening; Liz when she finished work, Nancy when Edward finished work. She wanted to tell Nancy about the night before and started to, but Nancy cut her off: Harriet was meant to be in school, Hughie was screaming for his breakfast. Liz smiled, knowing that Nancy was still put out that anything so mother-minded should have happened without her, that it was necessary now for her to insist on the burdens of motherhood. She rang off.

Throughout the day of work she kept tasting her finger again. The flavourless water, gritted with the bits of carpet; the excitement on Ian's face while Alice had been there; the tears when she had gone; the roughness of the wool pile against her fingertip, against her tongue. How could she have thought she had come to some peaceful place, where all that mattered was to forget about screwing with Tony, to remember that she loved Ian? She wanted a baby, there was no other desire, no other love. She had to find a way.

The maternity wing of the hospital frightened her. There was no one at the reception desk although it was marked with an enormous notice, and the businesslike nature of the whole place made her nervous of asking for help. She thought of the familiarity of her own clinic, where visitors never came and the whole procedure was designed to comfort the nervous; the carefully thought-out consideration which greeted new arrivals, the stylised informality which was meant to make you feel relaxed. It was probably like that here for the mothers, but visitors were treated with contempt; signs demanded your consideration and thoughtfulness, though without much hope that you would pay attention as they were repeated at every turn. Other notices ordered you off the premises if you had a cold, a cough, wanted a cigarette or were under thirteen. Her clinic was a shrine of intercession where women must go to beg for their heart's desire, where the medical profession could set itself up as the giver, the generous purveyor of blessings. But here the professionals were even stronger: the mothers here could be lured into the rôle of priestess collaborators with the magical medicine gods. Here the visitors were forced to be the suppliants, made to beg to see the holy places where mothers and doctors together had created these new power-points, these babies. She wandered the labyrinth of passages: red arrows with Way Out on them representing the thread she would have to uncoil to escape. But now she had to push further in. She found a nurse, asked where she was likely to find Alice, was given some inadequate instructions. She followed a long passage with rooms off it; she ambled, peering into small chambers where women lay in frilly nylon nightdresses. She decided that she was not going to have her baby here ever.

Nancy had had Hugh at home. Her pregnancy had been enlivened by her fight to achieve this: week by week she had been ready to entertain the group with the newest version of bureaucratic silliness and shilly-shally through which she had been forced to struggle. Throughout the early part of her labour she had talked to Liz on the phone for hours, repeatedly telling her how much nicer, better, more constructive, less painful, more natural, more feminist, it was to be having a baby at home. Liz had thought then that she was scared, had never said so to her, had wanted her only to get off the phone, to stop describing her every physical tweak. When she had seen her the next day propped up in bed with Hugh curled beside her and looking pale and exhausted she had still not believed it when Nancy had insisted on how marvellous it had been. But now as she tried to find Alice in this bland hospital she was at last convinced. It really had been important and liberating for Nancy to escape from this prison and have her baby in her own way.

She found Alice finally, without help from the hospital system, simply by looking into every room. She paused outside the glass door, and watched Alice for a little while. She felt suddenly and strangely shy, remembering the pain and desire she had felt the night before, remembering Ian's face as he watched her suck her finger. Remembering that she hated visiting people in hospital.

When she had been about five her mother had had her hysterectomy. To repair finally and forever the ghastly damage that Liz had wrought on her inner flesh. Her father had taken her to the hospital to visit her mother. She did not believe anymore that she could really remember the incident, but she still carried it with her. Her father had lifted her on to the bed so that she could see her mother. But it had not been her own mother she had seen, but a crumpled doll of her mother with a long tube sticking out from the side of the blanket which she had been warned not to touch or joggle with her foot: it looked as though her mother was being drained away into the bottle at the end of the tube. She had been frightened by that. Her father had told her to kiss her mother gently, gently. It had not seemed beyond her abilities to kiss the flat bundle of blanket and face. Her mother had been in a private room, there was no one to see, but she had not been perfectly, absolutely sure that it was her mother. The hesitation made her clumsy, as she leaned towards the face at the top of the bed she lost her balance and fell heavily against the blanketed shape. Her mother let out a cry of pain. Her father snatched her up quickly, so that his hands missed her armpits and hurt her. She had seen her mother's face drained grey and rigid. She had hurt her mother. Liz had not cried, she had let her father put her down from the bed and she had explored the rest of the room, but she could not forget.

Her mother had been there because of what she, Liz, had done to her, because she had hurt her. Her father died wanting her in a hospital bed, wanting her, while she had enjoyed unenjoyable sex and had not heard his voice. She was glad that she had not known Ian when he was in the hospital. Out at the end of the Oxford No. 1 bus route the walls of the Littlemore hospital greeted the visitor; Ian had been there for over a month. She was glad she had not had to visit him, it would have killed her love dead. She had a rottenness inside her that made her hurt people who were already hurt.

Alice did not look hurt or vulnerable. She was lying back reading a book. There were two other women in the six-bed ward, they had flowers by their beds and cards massed together on tray tables at their feet and bowls of fruit and frilled extravagant nighties. She ought to have brought Alice a present; they ought to be celebrating, welcoming their new sister, welcoming Alice after so intimate and female a journey. Alice looked calm enough in a pair of shabby blue pyjamas, her long brown feet sticking out at the bottom, laid abstractly on the pale yellow counterpane.

"Alice," she said, breaking through the invisible barrier and entering the ward.

She was going to bend over the bed and give the gentle kiss that she had denied her mother, but Alice sat up at once and leaned forward so that their heads bashed into each other. Alice roared with laughter and said, "Bugger," and then looked round guiltily at the other women in the ward.

"Are you all right?" Liz asked ruefully, feeling idiotic and inadequate again.

"From that bump, or from my big bump?"

"Both. Either."

"I'm fine. I tell you something though—all those books I read, none of them said how long and boring and tiring it was going to be. I'm knackered."

Liz wanted to say Did it hurt? Did it hurt very badly? Was it exciting and important as I don't want to have to believe that it was?

But Alice said, "Jane was so marvellous. Tough and funny all through and just so *there*, you know. I loved her. And you and Ian were great. I was getting scared on my own and then there you both were. If you're really sure about my sharing the house, I'm really turned on to the idea. Thanks."

Liz was embarrassed. "It was nothing. We could hardly have thrown you out on the street. Anyway you could see, Ian loved every moment of it."

"I felt unfair. I thought it might be very painful for you both, or something, but I had to be somewhere. I'm sorry."

Liz said, "What is she like, your daughter?"

"Do you want to see her?"

"Of course I do." She did not want to be asked, she did not want to be excluded like that, she felt sure that Alice would have pushed the baby on to anyone else. She was tired of such tenderness.

"She's in that one," said Alice pointing to the left of two cribs that stood by the window. "She's asleep."

Liz went across the room and peered into the transparent sided fish-bowl. There was the top of a very round head, lightly covered in downish stuff, dark, still clinging to the side of the head in a wave-like pattern; a huge red forehead and beneath it two screwed-up eyes. She could see nothing else except the tightly tucked blanket. The baby was asleep, but without her head moving suddenly a tiny hand emerged from the blanket and flexed itself; the skin loose like an old woman's but the fingernails minute, perfect, glowing. This person had come from so far away, the lack of weight round her hand must seem strange after her long journey through the waters. She had crossed over safely, the waters had parted, she had been brought through triumphant. Now was the time for sleeping. Now was the time for rejoicing. They should be singing and dancing for this child. Liz reached out a tentative finger and touched the head; she could feel the warm mobile skin and beneath it the soft feeling bone; she ran her finger down towards the ear. This was a person she was going to share a house with, who was coming to live with her. It was strange. The child responded to her touch with a tiny juddery movement and the eyelids flickered. Liz took her finger off.

Her gut churned. She was more turned on than distressed and she noticed it with curiosity. Once, coming away from Dr. Marshall's clinic, she had gone to a supermarket to do some shopping and seen the babies in their prams outside. She had been furious with their mothers for leaving them so rashly when there were obsessives like her around. She had approached one pram, a smiling infant in a yellow wool costume, propped up against the pillows had gargled and waved at her, its face split into a manic grin of joy, its toothless gums glowing pinkly. She had put her hands on the pram handle, feeling the neutral smoothness of the dark blue plastic. She tempted herself. Did she want to steal the child? She did not. She let go of the handle and grinned back at the baby; it waved both its mittened paws in an ecstasy of delight. She turned away and the baby howled with annoyance, turned back shocked and the grin had magically reappeared. She was trapped there grinning and now waving herself, for every time she turned away the fury would mount and she would feel cruel. After a few minutes the mother came out of the shop and loaded her bag on to the carrying shelf under the pram. She did not seem to notice Liz, but nonetheless Liz felt embarrassed. Suppose the woman took her for a nutter, suppose she accused her, or worse still, was gently understanding? While legitimately protecting her baby she might offer Liz her pity. She must be at least five years younger than Liz was. Liz said, "Hey, that's a neat baby." And the woman, glancing up at her, said darkly, "She'll do anything for attention, even make herself agreeable." But she turned her attention away from Liz and focussed it on her daughter. "A little horror, aren't you, my precious?" she said with great goodwill and, flicking up the brake with a practised foot, wheeled off leaving Liz with a sensation of having just parted from a close friend. But the yellow mittens transferred their attention happily away from Liz on to the mother, who chatted friendly and meaningless words and waved herself with a hand spared from pushing.

But this new sleeping baby had a look, not of trying to please, but of deep thoughtful concentration. Tell me what it was like in there. Tell me your story, tell me how you grew in your tent and how you struggled out, trailing clouds of glory. Why Alice's body, not mine? What did you find there that was pleasing? She did not welcome you as I would welcome you; she did not even stop smoking, not though we all told her, and even Mary-Ann dug up obscure articles on birth weight, and slow development of reading skills. I would stop smoking, I promise you I would stop if you were in me. Was it dark? Warm? Rich? Did you want to come out? The baby did not respond, gave away no clues. She just lay there sleeping and looking as though the whole of heaven was under her intense speculation. Liz wanted to stay there quietly by the baby with her hand hovering over her head, while she drew water from that ancient well. But Alice broke into the charmed circle. "Isn't she ugly?"

Liz laughed and said, "Well, you said it not me." But she was outraged by Alice's insolence. "What are you going to call her?"

"Miranda, I think. A thing to marvel at."

So she was under the same spell, despite her flippant tone. Liz noticed. That was all she wanted to know.

Jane arrived, with two purple chrysanthemums, long-stemmed, elegant.

"All I could afford to offer at the shrine of motherhood, but better than nothing. We couldn't let the other women's blokes do all the gift-giving." She wandered over to the baby's crib and looked at her with a casualness that Liz felt as a physical blow. "Do you know," Jane said to her, "that this place is so rife with sexism that it is almost unbelievable."

Alice said, "I have given up being shocked by it."

Jane said, "The minute she was born they said, 'It's a girl' and before we had time to comment or express our unilateral delight, the younger midwife woman, no older than me said, 'Much better for a mummy on her own.' And she said it in this kindly consoling way. Although they asked Alice at the beginning what she was hoping for and she said a girl quite decidedly; but they still thought she might need comforting. Weird."

"That's nothing," said Alice laughing. "This morning some doctor came round; they had to take a prick from her heel for some blood test. He picked up the chart, right, and saw she was a girl and he said, 'Well better luck next time.' Sort of jokingly, you know how men can. Then he must have seen at once that I wasn't married and he got unbelievably embarrassed; muttering 'sorry' and all that. He could hardly wait to get away. Anyone, his kindly face implied, could make one mistake but to wish another on them, even for the sake of a son. He was quite upset, got tangled in knots and finally left without doing the blood test. He sent a mate of his back for it, obviously better prepared."

Jane said, "It really does begin here, you know. Not joking, I mean. I wanted to buy a card, or rather about six cards, because

I don't want there to be anything apologetic about this baby; but all the cards are really blue for a boy, pink for a girl, or if in doubt a floppy-eared bunny looking up at a grinning stork doing a fly-past. I wasn't prepared to buy them. We really must design our own cards or something. We ought to be celebrating, and it is practically impossible to do so without being sucked into their assumptions."

Liz asked Alice, "Do you mind not having stacks of cards and a pretty nightie?"

"I know I shouldn't, but I minded early this afternoon. They have a fathers-only visiting-time, and I did feel lonesome. I wanted to draw the curtains and hide."

"Damn," said Jane, "if I'd known I'd have come."

"Tell you what, what time is that? I'll send Ian tomorrow. Better still we'll see if we can send Ian and Edward and get them really goggling."

"Don't do that," Alice said. "I mean do send Ian, because it would be nice to have someone, but I don't want to antagonise other women here."

"What?"

"No, honestly, it's funny, but there really is a closeness. A sort of intimacy, and I wouldn't like to spoil that by showing off. I'm not ashamed of Miranda having no daddy, but I wouldn't want to embarrass the other women more than the truth demands, because it does seem such a good opportunity to talk with women, be close to them really sharing something."

"Maternity wards as the consciousness-raising meetings of the century."

"Jane, you can laugh, but there is something in it, you know. You were the one who told Liz she should be expressing solidarity with the other women in her clinic. Here is just the same, and the sexism here is terribly blatant. One woman was telling me that they have a rule at the desk, the reception desk I mean. They have to describe all newborn boys as fine and bouncing, and all little girls as sweet and little unless the baby's in the special care unit and then you call it brave and little. Isn't that extraordinary?"

Liz said, "I'm not surprised really. My opinion of the medical profession is practically unprintable. As you know. But all their assumptions are so masculist. Nothing has the power to shock me anymore. I can take it in my stride."

"Liar," said Jane affectionately.

Nancy and Paula arrived together, while Jane was off finding a vase to put her two flowers in. All of them consciously avoided looking at the sign which proclaimed "Only two visitors to a bedside." Nancy went at once and looked at Miranda, then pushed the crib over by the bedside so that Paula could see her. That was nice, Liz thought, to include the baby in their chatter. Nancy, Paula and Alice went into obstetric details together with a ghoulish delight that made Liz feel excluded and ignorant. The baby was clearly put out too because it began to wake up, stirring under the blankets as best it could, and opening its tiny mouth to squeak angrily.

Nancy said, "Do you want to feed her?"

"Oh dear, I'm not sure if I'm meant to."

"You're being institutionalised."

"No I'm not, I'm being ignorant."

Nancy dismissed such fears, scooped the baby out of its crib and held it while Alice undid her buttons. A woman on the nearby bed called over, "Don't let them catch you. No one but mothers are supposed to touch the babies."

Nancy refused to be intimidated but did hand the baby over as soon as Alice was ready. The baby nuzzled in, not enthusiastic to feed but clearly contented to be there.

Jane came back with a vase and stood watching for a minute. "Something that really surprised me was her enthusiasm to feed last night. There she was, bright red and unbelievably small, but when they gave her to Alice it was as though she was a thing inspired, she really laid into those breasts, knew exactly what she was about. It was funny and touching, to see her so small and so tough."

Paula said, "That's the worst of a Caesarean. You don't get to see that, you don't get close to the baby so quickly. I wonder if that's why I could never breastfeed Tommy."

Jane organised her flowers into their vase and put them beside the bed. The other two were reminded of presents; Paula fished out a bag of tangerines, and Nancy unwrapped a bright red baby suit. Liz felt worse about her own negligence and said, "Look at the three wise women from the east, who come bearing gifts."

Nancy said, "Well we're not going to fall down and worship."

Liz was prepared to do that. She would prowl for days in the hospital, touch the stitched wounds of the mothers and the wet heads of the babies. She needed their magic and she would find some way of stealing it. Animals eat their own placenta for the rich protein supply they find there. She would salvage the hospital garbage for that strong inward flesh. Alice was a priestess who could initiate her into the cult if she proved yet more diligent in her postulancy: if they believed her a true seeker after the tiny baby-god they would lead her through the rites and she could enter the domain. She would light a votive candle as her father had done at so many shrines; she would eat the flesh and drink the blood until she lived dead to her old self and born again with the new life inside her. She would pass through the waters of regeneration, tasting them, drowning in them, and be restored to fulness. She wanted to touch Alice's swelled breasts, where the baby was now playing, and the flesh of her stomach, which Alice was at this moment carelessly describing to her friends as wrinkled like an elderly prune.

She touched the baby, even as it fed, as a talisman. It did not stir. She was willing to pay the price. She hated the other four: for their laughter, their casualness, their ease. They were blasphemers. Desecrators. She hated them with a poisoned jealousy.

"I have to go now," she said.

"Oh, dear." They were all sorry, but not unduly. She gathered her things, kissed them all, promised to come again soon and walked off through the glass doors. She just heard Paula say, "Poor old Liz," before she began to run. She hated them for the easy pity, for the easy superiority. She would steal their power and store it up for herself. Ian should not be tender to another woman because his was barren. They should not mock and pity her, because her flesh was sterile; her womb a desert that swallowed seed and gave back no return. Her finger felt the tingle of the baby's warm head, and the dampness of the amniotic fluid from the carpet. There had to be a way.

Leah's good and handsome sons found some mandrake roots one day in the field. Women's roots they knew, but the most ancient powers; the ugly bi-form roots can give fecundity to the most barren women when they are carved and spelled over by the women who knew such magical devices. Their power is great, older than Eden and stronger than Egypt. They gave the roots to their mother.

When Rachael heard that her sister and enemy had the mandrake roots, she tried not to cry. When she cried, her eyes swelled up, weak and puffy and she looked like her sister whom she hated. It was not fair. Rachael the beautiful, the beloved, was barren: and she knew that Leah, ugly and unloved, mocked at her in the evenings; mocked her and took greedy delight in her barrenness.

In the end Rachael swallowed her pride and went and asked her sister for the mandrake roots. "Give them to me," she said. Leah called her sons the better to laugh at Rachael, whom she hated. She appeared to consider the gift, and thoughtfully denied it; the boys laughed with casual adolescent cruelty; but Rachael fixed her eyes on the magic she needed, on the spell she could make, and begged, "Please, Leah, please, please, be generous; you can afford to be generous, please."

How dare she beg so? How could she have the nerve to beg from Leah? From childhood upwards Rachael had been the favoured one: more beautiful, more clever, more loved. The bottled-up hatred and jealousy of the years welled out of Leah, her eyes narrowed with poison and she told her sister how she had always hated her, hated her when she crowed in her father's lap while Leah herself was thrust into a corner, hated her when Jacob had been willing to serve seven years for her beauty, hated her when her father had seen a way to get ugly despised Leah married off by a trick. She told Rachael how she nourished her hatred on Rachael's monthly bleeding, fed it on the tight swelling of her own belly. Hate. Hate. Hate.

And at the end, when Leah leant back exhausted and saw the eyes of her sons no longer smiling but struck with fear, Rachael only lifted her rigid face, as though she had not heard one word, and said, "Dear Leah, kind sister, please give me the mandrake, please, please."

Leah was disgusted; that a woman so brave and beautiful as her sister could beg and winge before someone as hateful and unloved as herself. That she should flatter and fawn to a source as dangerous as the well of Leah's hatred. She liked humiliating Rachael; she would humiliate her further.

"I will sell them to you, sister."

"Thank you, thank you, dear wife of my husband, dear daughter of my father. Name the price and I will pay anything, anything, please, anything."

Leah had not needed this dark magic, this inner rotting to bring forth her sons, just a night of pleasure and lust. She did not just hate Rachael now, she despised her as well, and was glad of her disgust. What was beauty and love and brilliance gained at the price of a slobbering pathos? Her husband might not love her, she might have been tucked into her husband's bed by a trick, but she kept her dignity, her self-respect, her womanhood. She would not beg like this. She tried to get her sons to grin with her at Rachael humbled and reduced. She said, "My husband is my price. Send him to me for the night and I will give you your wretched shrub." She would lie with him and enjoy it and rub her sister's face in it. If Rachael would pay the price of her husband for a child, Leah would make sure Jacob knew of it. She would rub his face in it too. She hated both of them. "I will sleep with him and while you are still whittling at some little pieces of weed like some age-maddened crone, I will be bearing him more sons."

Rachael was beyond all pride now, only she wanted the mandrake roots, she wanted the magic to get her a child and fill her empty arms. But when she had agreed to her humiliation she began to rant, hardly audible she muttered into her arms, "Do what you like. I don't care, because when I have my son yours will bow down to him like stars before the moon; they will bow down to his power like skinny sheaves to his full harvest." But it was only a mutter, she did not dare to let Leah hear her, she did not dare to anger her or retaliate, because she wanted the magical roots.

Leah screamed now, "You are barren, barren, Rachael. All your famous beauty and charm won't help you. I could give you every damn mandrake in the world and it would not help you. You're not even a real woman."

And then she did cry. She did not care if Leah and her sons laughed; she did not care if Jacob was disgusted by her ugliness and went and slept with her sister. She only cared that she should get her hands on some magic powerful enough to fill her belly and her breasts with meat and milk, and make her feel like a woman.

9.

DECEMBER

The people who were putting in the new wiring and tearing down the wall of their house thought they would be finished by the New Year. Ian kept saying that he did not believe it, but nonetheless they gave their month's notice on the flat and spent as many evenings as they could painting the upstairs rooms, and arguing about colours and curtains. The furniture that her mother had promised them arrived from Somerset along with an invitation to spend Christmas in her mother's new house. They could not decide what to do. Ian's mother was equally urgent in her invitation.

Christmas carried different memories for each of them. They had to decide between the semi-teetotalism and delicate disciplines of her mother's house and the overcrowded tenseness and fights of his family. Liz urged the latter, more able to cope with Ian's noisy drunken mob than with her mother's chilly disapproval and the unknown quantity of Florence. Ian though preferred her mother's, because of the luxury and because she was too well-mannered to criticise openly. Both of them felt some vague nostalgia for the Christmases of childhood, and both wanted the other to enjoy what was left of their own magic.

Liz's parents would wake her at eleven. Her sleepiness vanished into shivery excitement as she got dressed all over again. She would glance nervously at her stocking, but it would still be empty. Later she grew to admire the administrative efficiency of her parents who had two identical stockings; one already filled, days in advance, and craftily hidden. No midnight groping and pretending for them, just a quick switchover after Midnight Mass. She remained surprised that this solution never seemed to have occurred to other parents: it was a device that she stored up against the day.

But in the darkness of the winter midnight she would dress and then be bundled into endless layers of outer clothes. It was supposed to be frosty, even if real snow did not convert the landscape to Christmas-card magic: a little child rendered spherical with jerseys and coats, just a pink nose poking out under a striped bobble-hat was part of her parents' Christmas. The service was long: the church vibrant with flowers and decorations after the blank penance of Advent purple. The choir boys and altar servers giggly with the unusual lateness. Peace on Earth, Goodwill to Men, Hark the Herald, *Mater ora filium, ut post hoc exilium*. The Gloria long and complicated after the accustomed brevity of the Kiries, always seemed to her like a waste of time, longing only to get to terms with *Come All Ye Faithful* at the end. And after back-slapping and Christmas greetings, the relief of back-to-bed, the sheets pleasantly cooled down and welcoming after the piles of clothes had been removed.

For Ian it was different. None of that middle of the night stuff, except the disturbance of his parents coming in from the pub. He and his siblings lay pretending to be asleep, while, half-drunk and wholly cheerful, his parents giggled their way through the muddle of stockings. And before the grown-ups were awake, a dawn swap shop, so that the chaos they had created would be thoughtfully smoothed out by their children.

But neither of them wanted to go back there. Last year they had divided the time with scrupulous care: Christmas Day with

Liz's mother, but New Year and one extra day, in compensation, with Ian's family. A reversal, exactly, of the year before. The pattern could be repeated indefinitely, the only seemly way to break it would be with a child of their own, when they would be free to start the whole mechanism off afresh.

"Couldn't we stay right here and sleep?" Ian suggested.

"Your mother would be hurt."

"I doubt it, she'll have the rest of the gang. Yours might."

"No, no. She'd rather be alone with her lesbian paramour and two distressed gentlefolk dug up for the occasion."

"What is it that distresses gentlefolk so particularly? I've always wondered and, being one, you might know."

"It's not kind but quantity, you see. It distresses them more."

"Quantity not quality?"

"Being quality themselves they want to expand."

"If they were real quality, they should have gathered some quantity around them, shouldn't they?"

"Stop it, Ian." He was painting elaborate pound-signs on the new bedroom wall.

"You encourage me." Even thinking about Christmas filled them with goodwill. Perhaps they really should not waste it, let it be dissipated on either set of parents.

Ian said, "You'll hate it if we go to my home. My mother will say, 'Of course it isn't really Christmas without little ones' with a meaningful glance which will ignore the seventeen grandchildren fighting by the stove. And she will lure you into the kitchen, pretending to need your help with the mince-pies and grill you about whether your intentions are honourable."

Liz countered that one. "Well, my mother will say, 'I do think you young things are right not to burden yourself with children. I think that's a frightfully good idea. We never thought of such things. But don't leave it too late will you,' and she'll lure you down the garden to dig potatoes and tell you that you mustn't let my selfishness ruin your life, and what I've always needed is a strong hand. And later, after half a glass of dry sherry, she'll tactfully send me off to visit some old dear, who is just longing to meet me, and she'll get you over the kitchen table and enquire whether you think her awful experiences in childbirth have put me off the whole idea."

"Yes, then I can say, I don't really think so because only last month we practically delivered a friend's baby on the floor in our flat and we thought the whole thing was absolutely thrilling, really super. Then she'll clap her hands together and say, 'The things you two get up to.'"

"Only I am allowed to be rude about my mother."

"I'm sorry."

"Anyway, our accounts take no account of the fair Florence. It may be quite different now."

"We must decide, we really ought to let them know."

"Ian, I think we are meant to paint the ceiling before the walls."

"Damn, yes you are right. Never mind, we won't do it. Then we can learn modesty by keeping our eyes down and not looking at it."

Next Thursday, feeling a little guilty at leaving Ian to wrestle unaided with the bathroom, she told the women's group about their Christmas dilemma. Nancy said promptly, "Don't go to either. Stay in town. Come to us. Alice is."

Paula said, "Jesus, why are we all so hung up about Christmas?"

"If we use his name to swear with, we can at least celebrate his birthday. Look how many words he has given us to be offensive with."

"It's easy enough for you, Jane. You can take Midge and yourself down to Chelsea, where your lovely liberal parents will think it is pretty cute to have their gay daughter and her lover for lunch, and you'll get some reasonable conversation and some really good nosh, and you can be home again before five. The rest of us if we want to go home, or if we simply can't face the hassle of not going home, have to travel billions of miles on overcrowded trains and put up with a minimum of three days of being rigidly restrained at best, quarrelsome at worst, and either way end up being told that we're bigoted, rude, immoral and wicked." Mary-Ann laughed, "My father has a specialist line in saying, 'your friends' whenever he refers to the current government, and I hate being put in the position of being a dangerous traitor for defending the Labour Party. It's very disorienting for a good lefty."

Paula said, "Well, you can all count your blessings. My dear ex-husband has just invited himself to Christmas lunch with us."

"Tell him to stuff himself."

"How can I? He asked, quite politely, in front of the boys, for their sakes, he said."

"Holy cow."

"I tried a deft counter-offensive by suggesting we all went to his place, which meant that at least he would have to do the cooking, but he wriggled out of that with psychologically flavoured mutterings about normal home environment. He wants a bloody free meal and a groovy number about how liberated he and his ex-wife are. He makes me sick. I just get this feeling that he gets off with everything scot-free, and I have to carry the can. I feel guilty and bad about our marriage, I feel the hatred, I feel the pain, he can just run around and not feel any pressure, he can even invite himself for sodding Christmas."

Alice's baby slept quietly in her corner. She recognised that the carry-cot was Nancy's old one. Nancy had promised to keep it for her. Well, Alice's daughter would have grown out of it by the time she had any use for it. The baby was wearing a woollen hat; there was nothing to be seen of her except a bit of nose and two tiny fingers sticking up over the rim of the cream-coloured blanket. The fingers moved vaguely, like seaweed in a pool. Upstairs Hugh and Harriet were likewise asleep; and a mile away Paula's boys were probably watching the television, preparing for bed.

And it was not just the children. She was not that blinded. This was her family. This was where she was both nurtured and disciplined. This was where she was at home: if there were tensions, anger, spites, it was only to be expected in family life. If rôles like mother, child, good, naughty, were played here it was because they had come out of the womb of other families, been given baffling pasts and unresolved presents. But these were the people who were the focus of her caring, her yearning, her loving, her growing. It was nearly Christmas: if she wanted to be sentimental about them, now was the time.

"Ian, about Christmas . . ."

"Not again."

"Last time. Nancy says why don't we go there? Alice is."

"Do you want to?"

Bold now. "Yes, I do."

"Great, I think that would be a good idea."

She could hardly believe her ears; after so much hassling around the idea they had resolved it without tension in thirty seconds.

Ian went on talking: "I didn't want to miss our tenants' association party anyway." They lay in amicable silence for a while, then Ian said, "It's funny. It seemed like a vice somehow to spend Christmas on our own, but all right if we're going to share it with other people."

"Christmas on our own is like masturbation."

"But I like masturbation."

"Hum. But you don't tell your mother about it."

She knew he was smiling; she could imagine the secret glee at the idea of telling his mother that he was too busy wanking to come home for Christmas.

He said with obvious relief, "No going down to the pub and choosing between toasting the Queen or having a fight about why not."

"No martyred mother making me cook food I don't want, which she is making me cook because she will have to cook it if I don't, because it is Christmas and therefore I ought to want it."

"Your guilt-cycles are too complex for me."

"It's because of the inner conflicts in my libido."

Dr. Marshall had gone away for his holiday. He was taking his three sons skiing in the French Alps. She pitied the sons.

Before he had left she had explained to him that she would go and see the psychiatrist properly, but not until after Christmas; she didn't want to start and then have a gap almost at once, it sounded very sane, but she knew she was procrastinating. She had been convinced, even as she spoke that he would see through anything so obvious, would give her another ticking-off, would leave her feeling small and inadequate. She told him about the house and how much time it was needing to get it habitable. He approved of the house as she had known he would. "Aha," he had said, "developing a bit of nesting instinct are you?"

"No. We got some money."

"There are other ways to spend it. A year ago I don't think you would have bought the house, do you?"

He had told her about his skiing holiday, relaxed, waxing eloquent, more interested in it than in Liz. She had not minded. He told her about the skills of his sons, whom he had taken skiing annually since they were toddlers, and were now beating him hollow at his own game. She had been skiing once, as part of an exchange with a French family and she had hated it, it had made her feel inadequate and cold and homesick. Her French was not up to the vicious instructor who had yelled at her night and day to "*Flexez les genoux*" and "*Allez-y*," and other more mysterious things that she had no way of obeying. But despite the hatred of the activity it amused her to think of Dr. Marshall in so domestic a rôle; she hoped his sons were badly behaved, rude to him, and left him struggling on simple *pistes* while they took to the mountain passes and laughed at him. But her dreams were without substance: it turned out that not only had he skied for the King's Hospital Team and been a runner-up for the National Team, but he had even met his wife on a German mountain. When she checked him out in *Who's Who* there it was under hobbies: "Family recreation and winter sports." She consoled herself with the thought that family recreation almost certainly did not include washing-up or helping his wife with the housework. But it was hard to feel superior to someone who not only held the key to your future happiness but could also manage ski-jumps and complicated slaloms.

But with him safely out of the country, she found that she could laugh about him again. It worked like magic, sure that Big Daddy was not watching, poised to punish and condemn, she was able to joke about conflicts in her libido.

"I don't think I shall go and see that Dr. Marshall anymore next year," she said.

"It won't work," said Ian, following her mind's detour surprisingly fast. "You'll feel just as bad about missing appointments. Delight only in the thought that he may break a leg and have to be in traction for six months."

"Perhaps his wife will seize the golden hour and push him down a glacier."

"Poor doctor, as the green ice closes over him he will recognise the pressure on his libido."

"How strange to be a witch doctor and not know it."

"Shaman is the posh word, Elizabeth—what was all that education for? Actually, he probably does know anyway. If you were a bright young doctor and wanted power, where could you better seek it? No wonder so many men want to go into obstetrics and paediatrics and gynaecology. They can pretend there it is all kindliness; but you've got already submissive people and you claim to give them what they want, so they do exactly what you say and are grateful afterwards. I bet when you get pregnant you fling your arms round his neck and kiss him."

She would too. She was glad Ian was prepared, even if he did not agree with her, to stop challenging her interpretation of the great doctor, to enter into her convictions. It might just be generosity, kindliness, an unwillingness to hurt her, a recognition of how important it was to her to put the master down, but he played it along most convincingly. She was glad that Ian had said "when" and not "if." Casually like that, in the middle of a different conversation.

He was alert tonight too. He recognised what he had said and grinned. "You see, despair does not gnaw my vitals."

But that was going too close to the pain for her, too close to the heart of her fear. She shied away, annoyed with him: what would happen when . . . what would happen if . . . if despair did gnaw his vitals, when he gave up hope, if she did not conceive his baby? Not tonight, she refused that possibility for now, she would not talk about it, would not even look at it. If it is not named it has no power. If it has no word it cannot exist. The word creates. The name holds power. To move over the face of the water and call them into shape; to give her fears the name of despair.

"Do you surrender, do you surrender?" One of the few fights she had had as a child. She had been beaten. In the playground of her primary school, down on the hard tarmac, with the victor crowing over her, banging her head up and down on the hardness, forcing her wrists harder and harder, and chanting "Do you surrender, do you surrender?" The victory was obvious to all the audience, a large one, because fights between girls were unusual and because the fight had been long-drawn-out and vicious. But until she surrendered, until she admitted it in her own words, the victory would not exist, would have no reality. "Say it." Bang. "Say it." Bang went her head. "Ask me to stop." She would not. Her head hurt and she knew she could not win, but she was not going to say so. The bell rang, the teacher came out and the fight had to stop. The other girl had not won because she could not make Liz say that she had won. Liz believed in the power of silence. She would not name her fear, she would rather drown in the waters of chaos than name even the possibility of despair, even secretly, because then it would exist.

How could she come to terms with the truth if she would not confront it, if she would not drag it out of the slime and look at it? Perhaps if she did it would not seem so bad. A temptation. Get thee behind me Satan. Don't even think about it, don't get involved in conversations, situations, emotions, that might risk bringing it to the surface. Don't talk about it.

There are other words to conjure with. "Love. Love. Love," murmurs Ian to her ear later while his hand stirs gently at the cauldron of her stomach. And his word creates the love, the desire, the melting into each other. "I love you," she says in response, and it is immediately true; and her hands, too, stir, stroke, murmur the same spell. The other things can be driven downwards, banished. There is no need to conjure with the black spells, the dark words. They can still work this white magic for each other: love, lust, energy, pleasure, orgasm. That is the magic for them, a white Christmas magic: the desert has rejoiced and blossomed as a rose, their land would not more be called desolate. Use those words, the good words. Mother, sister, lover, child, friend. Solidarity, love, delight, friendship. Hope.

So Dr. Marshall was away and she put off till the New Year seeing that stately woman shrink. They were not going to be anywhere near any grown-ups. If they wanted a season of Peter Pan, they were entitled to it. She refused to be afraid. She bought an early Victorian cane bathchair for their house: it was comfortable but difficult to get into, with the long metal handle rising up between the legs, so the invalid could steer while someone else pushed. She bought Ian an Edwardian grotesque sideboard with seven mirrors and eleven shelves all too small to put a dinner plate on; but it was painted with birds and papier-mâché fruits. Ian, entering into her mood, bought a picture in the primitive style, of Noah struggling to load pairs of recalcitrant animals into his Ark, while Mrs. Noah looked on with resignation, her hands on her hips and her eyes raised despairing to heaven. Ian painted a jungle on their bedroom wall, which was rather good, and she painted the bedroom that was going to be Miranda's with an underwater scene which was not at all good.

She bought tickets to the circus, for Ian and herself, then in

an unexpected moment of embarrassment she bought one for
Harriet as well. Surely they could go to the circus without a real
child if they wanted to? She wanted a child so that she could
remain a child herself, to go to the circus and find it wonderful,
to scream loudly with ecstatic fear when fireworks went off. She
told Ian she had bought the three tickets and he looked askance
at her for a moment. Then he asked if they could bring Bob and
Sam's little girl as well; she was about the same age as Harriet
and she would enjoy it. She had not even known that such a
child existed; did he too go courting children like she did? Did
he bath them before his meetings and splash water in their faces
and feed them puréed baked beans, while they dribbled down
their fronts and oozed the delicious goo out of the corners of
their mouths? Did he watch himself with other children and
wonder how soon he would be judged worthy to be a father? It
both pleased and distressed her. But by good luck she was able
to get a fourth ticket, in a block with the others.

The two little girls were so similar it was startling. Marguerite
had the same leggy, unself-conscious elegance, the same physically conscious charm, the same rapid retreats and openings out
as Harriet did. Her coffee-coloured skin and tightly braided
fuzzy hair oddly seemed to emphasise the similarities she shared
despite Harriet's blonde, cropped pinkness. Ian and she sat either end of their group of four seats with the children between
them, and they glanced at each other over the top of the intent
heads. She had seen that glance before, she thought guiltily: a
very married glance of pride and self-consciousness. Half the
parents there would exchange some version of that glance tonight looking at each other over the heads of their children, and
muting their simple pride with worries that the candy-floss
should make one sick or another would get lost in the crowd on
the way out and be untraceable. "I love you," she mouthed over
the heads to him as the seals balanced balls on their noses and
smirked at the audience. But he had already looked away and
his eyes were fixed on the ring. His delight seemed simpler and

purer than hers; she could not look so hard, had to see the acts through the pleasure of the girls. If she had her own daughter would she be able to see the circus as she had once seen it: actually believing that there was a possibility, a real one, that the highwire man might fall off, that the trapeze artist might miss her hold and crash, broken, to the ground, that the lions might go berserk and kill their trainer, or escape and consume some member of the audience. That had been the real thrill of the circus: that something could so easily go utterly wrong, and that it hadn't was only because of the most miraculous luck and the almost unnatural skill of the performers. Now she did not believe any performer was likely to run a real risk of death and disfigurement. But the girls still believed it; one day she would have a child who would believe it.

At the end of the act Ian looked back at her again and she realised that he was a little embarrassed by his own enthusiasm. It was the interval. He told his guests that when he was their age the circus would come to their town in the summer; they would set up in a big tent in a field not far from his house, and they always had a small fun-fair which travelled with the circus. His father used to give them the tickets for the show itself, but if they wanted to spend money on the fun-fair they had to save it themselves from their pocket-money.

Liz knew more to the story than Ian was telling the girls. Ian and the brother nearest to him had stolen some money from their aunt's purse in order to indulge in the fun-fair rides and had then fought about whether to spend it on the dodgems or the Ferris wheel. Ian's brother, just sufficiently older to have an edge, kept telling him that the Ferris wheel was for sissies and people in love; and in the end he had given in rather than be branded with these awful stigmas, and had sacrificed, at least that one time, the beautiful terror of swaying loosely at the very top, seeing the lights of the city around him in the darkness while he prayed that the machine would not break and crash him to the ground, while he prayed that it would break and he would be stranded, floating up there for hours and hours.

Ian told the little girls about the real Victorian merry-go-round with its own steam organ, and the wild prancing ponies attached to the roof with spiralled poles that seemed like seaside rock. Liz went on thinking about Ian and the Ferris wheel. He had had his very first sexual experience up there in the gondola of the Ferris wheel when he was thirteen; lured up by a man who had paid for the trip and who had asked him, swinging secretly up there to jerk him off. He had told her that when they had been to a fair together and as their little basket had swung higher and higher she had realised that he was getting turned on. Now concentrating on the children, she knew that he did not even remember the incident, that his mind was quite free from it. He told them only about the wall of death, and the fat lady, and how he and his brothers and sisters had scraped and saved and done extra chores to raise fun-fair money, but that he had usually done best because the fair came just after his birthday and he was usually able to cash in on the fact.

"Didn't you have to share?" asked Marguerite, her eyes wide with the thought of such luxurious wickedness.

"No, we never had to share a single penny of money that was given to us, or that we saved or earned." Then, more consciously, jerked suddenly back to his adult and high-minded socialist principles, he added, "But I think it would have been better if we were made to."

They did not bother to hear this last bit, either of them. The idea of not having to share really appealed to them. Harriet said, "Lucky for us then it's not like that now. Or lucky for you really. I'd spend all my money on rides on things and there would be none left for Christmas presents. I'm afraid you would have to do without."

Marguerite said, "I'm making my mummy her Christmas present, she says she likes that better."

Liz joined the conversation, feeling an intruder, wishing she could enter into it without noticing herself. "What are you making for her?"

"It's a secret," she said shocked. "You might tell her."

"I would not."

"Well, I've never met you before so how can I be sure?"

Ian laughed. "Fair enough. But if you come here I'll whisper to you what I'm getting for Liz." The two of them scuttled up the row, Marguerite climbed into his lap, knowing him better than Harriet did. The two heads were close to his, Ian's arm was round Harriet, pulling her closer. Suddenly they both pulled back a bit, their eyes glowing, and giggling with delight.

"If you're coming to our house for Christmas," said Harriet, "will I see it?" And Marguerite looked cast down with the unfairness of the thought.

"Yes, you will," said Ian, "I'll tell you what. I'll ask Nancy, I'll ask your mother, if I can bring it round the night before and you can look after it for me." And turning to Marguerite he added, "And we'll come and show it to you too, I promise."

Something special and thrilling, to them at least and probably to Ian too if he had thought to tell them about it. She could not imagine what he might give her that would excite the children so: not furniture, or books or clothes. She suddenly felt quite child-like, as she had tried and failed to feel all evening; a fluttering sense of anticipation tempered with the fear that it might not be worth it, lightened with the conviction that this time it surely would be.

As the lights went down again, Harriet said, "Not last Christmas but the one before Mummy and Daddy gave me Hughie for my present."

"What's that?" asked Marguerite.

"My baby brother, silly. Shush, here come the elephants."

Please Father Christmas, please. If you love me at all. A baby for Christmas. But here come the elephants.

She practically had to shake Harriet awake to get her off the tube, when they arrived at the right stop. Ian and Marguerite had got out two stops earlier. Liz had not been able to ignore the palpable relief of the other passengers when they were given an excuse for realising that the two little girls were not one family. She was glad they had gone no further than vague talk from

Ian, in adopting an Asian child. She was ashamed of herself for being glad, ashamed for even noticing the curious glances they got with two different coloured children in tow; but she knew she was more at ease shaking Harriet into pink wakefulness.

The night air shocked them both back into life. It was cold. Harriet bubbled home, excited, giggling, going over the events of the evening, preparing them for her parents. She kept wanting to check details and confirm impressions with Liz, they were close to each other. But the minute the door opened and Edward hugged Harriet, exclaiming, "Poppet, you're frozen. Why didn't you wind your scarf round and round?" Liz felt excluded, inadequate. She had forgotten the scarf, she had let the child get cold, she could not even look after one child properly for one evening. She was the kindly maiden aunt who comes once a year to visit. The children like her because she comes bearing gifts, but she does not really count. Edward's invitation to come in, have a drink, thank you so much, glad you're coming for Christmas, did not dispel her sense of redundancy. Sure, Harriet had enjoyed herself: she would have enjoyed herself whoever had taken her to the circus and bought her popcorn and too many ice-creams, but that did not matter. Mummy and Daddy were important, telling them what had happened, being back with them when it was over, having an experience all her very own to share with them: that was more important than the expedition itself. She was excluded from that closeness and all the treats in the world would not buy her that importance in the mind of a kid she liked.

Damn, she thought, damn and hell. But it had been a good evening. Why did everything have to lead back to that void?

The flat was empty. Ian had obviously stayed, accepted the invitation and would be smoking dope with Bob, or going down to the pub with him. She could easily have gone in, helped get Harriet ready for bed, sat in Nancy's warm kitchen, suffusing her circus images with a warm afterglow, competing with Harriet over the shape and flavour of the performance, sharing the memories with Harriet and giving them to Nancy and Edward as a gift. If she couldn't be mother, she could at least be child: she and Harriet united by something shared, against the grown-ups who had not shared it. She could have enjoyed the faintest whiff of envy from Nancy because she was free to decide to go to the circus with a child whose sick she would not have to mop up in the night; whose over-tired whines she would not have to cope with in the morning. No worry about baby-sitters, no domestic traps. She might feel excluded from sharing the responsibility of Harriet, but Edward and Nancy often longed to be so free. Nancy said she had a romantic view of motherhood—a shitty, unrewarding task in the reality of their society. But she was not deceived. She had seen the secrecy of Nancy's love. Wanting your sisters-in-the-movement to be more willing to baby-sit for you, wanting to be able to do your work and organise your own time, were only diversions, minor kinks in the road which really led straight to that glance of passionate tenderness, pride, even startled guilt, which she had watched Nancy cast over her children like a sweet spell, even as she berated her hard and thankless lot.

On Christmas morning she and Ian were both hung-over. Not even a fresh hang-over; but one derived from three days of hang-overs not recovered from. She woke herself as gently as possible, feeling the dryness of her mouth and the stiff, slightly painful sensation in her back. That was not the hang-over though, that must be where she had pulled her back moving furniture at the new house yesterday afternoon. Probably where she had got the chest-of-drawers stuck on the stairs and had heaved and grunted vainly for several minutes. She sensed that Ian was awake too and feeling as bad as she was. At last he said quietly, "At least there's no patter of tiny feet at half-past six in the morning, and piercing voices penetrating my own personal fog to yell, 'Look what Santa brought me, Daddy.' Dear God."

He looked over at her as though he was afraid of being found guilty of blasphemy. He really must be feeling rough, that was exactly the sort of remark he usually avoided studiously. But from the warmth and comfort of the bed she could not help but agree.

"Though of course, if we had the tiny feet to patter we would not have been whooping it up till after three in the morning."

"True. Well, happy Christmas."

"Happy Christmas."

"Thank God we're here and not at either of our respected families."

They giggled weakly, arms wrapped round each other, too tired and queasy to make the love that they both thought might be fun, trying to summon the energy they both dreaded that they might need.

Nancy's flat was hot and draped in Christmas decoration in two distinct styles. The trimmings that Harriet had made at school and in the secrecy of her own room: clumsy paper lanterns, cotton-wool snow-men, and looped, crushed paper-chains. And the decorations that Nancy had made or chosen, either alone or with Harriet, delicate filigree snow flakes, sprayed with silver glitter which covered the tree, and little candle holders made out of fir-cones and painted in shiny colours. The children were over-excited. Nancy looked slightly frayed at the edges. Alice was tired, and her baby, breathing in the change of routine and atmosphere was twitchy and unsettled in its carry-cot. Periodically Alice would scoop it up and try to feed it, but the kids wanted to see, the room was noisy and the baby could neither concentrate on feeding nor go to sleep. Liz tentatively suggested putting it in one of the other rooms where it would be quieter, but Alice clearly could not be bothered to make up her mind, and Nancy kept insisting that there was plenty of stimulation and it would not hurt Miranda to absorb the atmosphere and enjoy herself in her own way. Liz felt effectively put down for her ignorance.

After they started drinking, things got better. Ian and Edward settled into naked competition and showmanship with Harriet's huge new Lego set: Edward knew the potentials of the toy better, but Ian was cleverer with his hands and more open to new and original ideas. The women prepared the food; they did it with irony and resignation.

"The simplest thing to do," Alice said, but it was easier for her to be smug, not having a man to expose himself to her friends, "is to classify them, for the time being, as children. Thus they can stand acquitted, without us having to stand accused of acquitting them."

After a while Harriet broke up the men's game, to ask with urgent excitement, "Ian, when are you going to give Liz her You Know What?"

Ian shook himself—he had obviously clean forgotten—and said, "Why not now? Why don't you go and get it? Has it been okay?"

"Yes, I was terribly careful and did everything that you said."

"Liz!" The men both yelled for her and the three women came from the kitchen and stood in the living-room doorway.

Ian said, "Because of its peculiar nature I had to leave your present here overnight. I hope Harriet has taken good care of it."

Edward said, "You bet she has." How had these two men who really neither knew each other well, nor liked each other much, managed to form so swift an alliance, somehow between the eagerness of the children and the sensibleness of the women? They were so different, almost different generations, the ten years between them ought to have been an insuperable barrier, but there they were together, joined in a close, tight, exclusive silliness that allowed no penetration by the women. Harriet came back in carrying a large cardboard box with a concentration and carefulness that made her tongue stick out of the corner of her mouth. She put it tenderly in the middle of the floor.

"Can she open it now?" she asked Ian, almost out of control with her excitement.

"Do you think she's been good enough?"

Harriet giggled and said she thought so, with an attempt at solemn dignity.

Liz looked at Ian. She walked across the room almost frightened that after so much drama it would be something boring,
something she would not be able to conjure up an adequate response to. She knelt down and opened the box: at the bottom,
sitting up and looking at her was a terrier puppy. His huge head
and heavy forehead, his diminutive body looked suddenly so ab-
surdly like Alice's baby that she giggled. She reached in and
scooped her out, her soft under-belly round and quivering in
Liz's hand. She held the puppy up to her face, enchanted. She
looked Liz right in the eye, and sneezed. Liz laughed. "Oh Ian."

Then, looking up, she did not see Ian's face almost shy with
pleasure, or Harriet's enchanted one, or even Hughie giggling.
What she saw was a tender kindliness in the glance that Alice
and Nancy exchanged. More compassionate than the glance that
mothers use when their child has done something cute, but with
the same kindly superiority in it. Satisfaction that their poor
friend should be given such pleasure, satisfaction that they
needed no such substitutes. She saw herself nursing the puppy
on her own flat chest; and saw Alice's rich breasts, designed to
nurse a real child. She hated them. She hated Ian for exposing
her to this savage onslaught of pity. She hated the puppy. She
was going to cry.

The rest of the grown-ups were aware that something had
gone wrong, but they could not know what. Ian was cast down,
thought she did not want his present. None of them could even
guess at her naked anger that she should be pitied by her
friends. "Poor old Liz," they had said as she left the hospital
ward. Poor old Liz needs something to love; a bit old for a teddy-
bear and not quite mature enough for a real baby.

But Harriet was oblivious, thrilled. "Please Liz, can we take
her into the garden? Please? She hasn't been out yet, 'cause it
was after night-time when Ian brought her. Please."

"Sure, come on." The best thing, bless Harriet, a graceful
way out of that hot room. They went through the kitchen and
into the garden, Liz still carrying the puppy. She put her down
and watched Harriet crouch down beside her, trying to encour-

age her to scamper out on to the shabby lawn. Liz was so moved by her smallness, her furriness, her cuteness, damn it. That was what she had been to her father, a substitute puppy: cute until it chews on its own master's slippers, and then it has to be beaten. Other people's slippers may be gnawed with impunity, because that is amusing, but respect must be shown for the owner.

Harriet was not watching her so she let her face relax for a moment and was shaken by the rage that it assumed. She would not cry, she would not pity herself, she would not enter into that mildewed contempt that Nancy and Alice held for her. She did not need her biology to prove herself on, she would not accept those definitions. She did not need her friends. She would not accept their love if it came with these sugared-sorrow wraps on.

She watched the damp garden and Harriet and the puppy, beginning to venture outwards now into this new environment, sniffling and taking little experimental bounces. The little thing was so defenceless, so unable to care for itself. Whatever she felt she would have to take care of it. Her mind turned to the practicalities, she hoped Ian had had the sense to buy in enough of whatever it was that the animal was meant to eat. Today, Boxing Day, maybe Tuesday as well all the shops would be shut. Today was Sunday. Today was Sunday. Jesus Christ.

"Harri," she called, "I have to go to the loo. Don't let her get in the long grass or she'll be soaking wet, and may catch a cold."

"I'll be careful, Liz."

"I'll be right back."

The loo was just inside the back door, thank God she did not have to go back into the living-room. She sat on the edge of the bath, and pulled down her jeans and knickers. They were clean. She counted weeks again, she must have got it wrong, she must have got it wrong. She knew she had not.

Eight or ten hours. Only eight or ten hours. That was nonsense, she was being silly. Ten hours, supposing you went to a doctor and said your period was ten hours late. He'd laugh at you. Laugh. It was the string of late nights, her body confused by wrong bed-times and changes in rhythm. It hadn't happened last Christmas. It was the strain on her back moving the furniture yesterday. That was better. Why was she so frightened? Didn't she want to have a baby? Ten hours. She refused even to think about it. She pulled up her clothes, rebuckled her belt. What could she say, "Ian, I've got a Christmas present for you." She had not. She did not know. She was not going to put that down his throat, she was not going to have him watching her every minute for the next week, watching, hoping, trying to pretend he wasn't. She had strained her back trying to move a chest-of-drawers up the stairs. That could easily affect it. Couldn't it? Yes, it could. She would not say a word, to anyone. Was she pleased? No, she was frightened. She went back out to the garden.

"Harri, I think you had better bring her in now. She'll catch cold." She gathered the puppy into her arms and felt its quivering vitality. She wanted only to hold her against her heart and warm her. She was angry with herself now, not with her friends. Angry with her body for this new trick. She did not trust it anymore. Eight hours was nothing anyway. A joke.

Nancy called them for the great dinner. She fed the puppy with some slop that Ian had sensibly laid in. Then she put it tenderly back in its box. She could not help noticing that Alice was going through exactly the same motions with Miranda. She refused to care. She refused to let herself go to the loo again. She sat down between Hugh and Edward and concentrated on getting drunk. Eight hours, no more now. Nothing to count. She should not have tried getting that chest upstairs all on her own, what a silly thing to do. It was not true to say her period had never been late before: she remembered one time while she was still an undergraduate. She had spent from breakfast to mid-afternoon worrying that she might be pregnant, wondering which day she had not taken her pill, wondering who might be the father, wondering what she would do about it. Knowing that you cannot rush, panicking to your friends for a few hours. It was her regularity that was freaky, not this matter of some hours.

She went to the loo again.

They walk home through the quiet dark streets. Ian holds a carrier bag full of their presents and the puppy's food, and Liz holds the puppy tucked in under her jacket. They don't make a lot of noise in their rubber-soled sneakers. Ian is drunk, Liz only slightly less so. The cold cuts into the drunkenness and it is a long walk. At first they are both silent; Liz feels the puppy scrabbling inside her clothes, warm against her breasts. She refuses to be moved to tenderness. She thinks only that she must not tell Ian, that it would be cruel to entangle him in so frail a hope, that there is nothing to tell him anyway, except that she strained her back yesterday and must have strained her internal organs as well.

After a while Ian says, "I don't understand what happened there."

"Where?"

"When I gave you the puppy you were happy, then you weren't. You went out in the garden with Harri, and when you came in again something had changed. I bungled it, I'm sorry."

"You bungled what?" She is stalling.

"The puppy. You didn't want it."

"No. No."

"It was an impulse really. I was walking up that path behind Kensington Church Street. There's a dog shop there. There were these beagle puppies in the window. They were extremely endearing." She knows he is being careful, because he is drunk and because this is important to him. She knows he deliberately avoided saying "very sweet." "Extremely endearing" comes over emotionally cautious, drunkenly precise. She cannot tell yet which is uppermost. "You know how everyone looks at puppies in shop windows, I just looked. Then a little kid comes past, about eight or ten I suppose, you can't tell. I mean I can't tell. He looked at those puppies. He pressed his nose right up hard against the window and just looked in delight. After a moment he went into the shop. I knew he had gone to buy one, I even wondered what his mother was going to say when he arrived home with it. A minute later he came out and he was crying. I thought that kid was me." Emotional caution is thrown to the winds now: the raw child with no puppy who knows he does not belong and does not know why. "It was for me really that I bought the puppy. Not the one in the window. The kid was crying because they cost over £90. I gave her to you, but I bought her for me."

The puppy is warm and sleepy, she can feel its nuzzling breath against her right nipple. She did not know Ian when he was a child, she knows only the man he has become because of the child she did not know. After a little bit he says, "I'm sorry."

"No," she says. "It's not so simple. I've wanted one always: just . . . you giving it was fine. It was the others. Not the kids, not Harri—she thought it was wonderful, the best present in the world, the thing every kid wants for Christmas, even if they don't know it. You could see her writhing with delight. I liked that. I'm the kid too, the one who always wanted a puppy of my own. But"—she is nearly overcome with grief, which she does not want Ian to know, and with suppressing her excitement which may make the grief irrelevant and foolish—"it was Nancy and Alice, so kindly from their security. Ian, I just don't want to be that sort of grown-up. You know, surrounded by dogs and moonstruck over roses in the garden sparkling with raindrops. Yearning in corners, you know, and finding crack-pot consolations. And the wave of tenderness, of delight that the puppy gave me—then I knew that that was where I really might be heading."

They walk on. "It's Christmas sentimentality gone awry through drink," he says as bravely as he can. They know that is not true.

"Why are you so sad?" she asks him, because suddenly the hope is beginning to course through her blood. She cannot tell him but she would like him to know that there may not be any need for so much grief.

After a long pause he says, "Because it is the last Christmas we will ever be alone together like this."

She does not answer. She does not even dare to shape a question. He does not wait: "By next Christmas," he says, "we will either have a baby or you will have left me."

"No."

"Yes."

There is a long pause, the puppy is asleep, there are no cars on the road, only behind tightly drawn curtains there are families finishing their Christmas tea, and there are lonely people pretending to have Christmas tea all on their own. She cannot counter his immense despair with her own frail hope. They walk in a silence that his anger shatters.

"Damn you. You know it's true. I've come a long way; I no longer think that you love me because of the baby, or that you blame me because of the baby, but you have identified me with the baby, with life that includes the baby. That you think you have failed me. When you can't bear that failure any longer you will leave. And I will probably be glad by then, because I cannot stand your guilt, your hope, your mourning. I cannot cope with that. But it will be you who does the leaving and that will be your right. I know that. Oh bloody damn."

With the bags in his hands and the cold and the puppy in her arms he cannot even hug her or hit her or cry himself; they just have to go walking through the emptiness of the London street, he with his misery and she with her minute ray of hope. She is frightened. She thinks she will tell him, but she knows that will only make it worse. He is in no mood to be calmed by twelve hours. He will smash her hope, kill it for her as well as for himself. He cannot even afford the luxury of it anymore, because of what might happen if he embraced it and found it false.

"And what do they say, you know what they say, they say 'You will come to terms with sterility, with childlessness, it's not the end of the world.' Of course it's not, that's the trouble, if it were the end of the world that would be all right. It's not the end of the world. And there are no terms, there are no terms."

Her father had a good friend who was an Anglican nun. She sometimes came to dinner with them on her day off. She was older than Liz's parents, but not old. One evening as her parents were trying to hurry Liz to bed and she was stalling skilfully—asking for a Bible story, knowing that with Sister Gabriel there they would not be able to deny so apparently holy a request—she climbed into her father's lap and curled there triumphant. Sister Gabriel had suddenly said, "Do you know that I am guilty of the sin of envy?"

Even her mother stopped what she was doing and stood poised, watching the nun with something like shock, and her father had said, holding Liz tighter on his lap, "Dear sister, I'm sure there are the most glorious compensations."

Liz did not know what they were talking about, but she could feel her father's love for her coming out hard through his vest, his shirt and warming his tweed jacket as it slid through to her pyjama-ed flesh. But the nun had been angry.

"Don't be so stained-glass sentimental. Of course there are no compensations. There are good things in my life, and I love it, but they are never compensations for that. You have to grow up and grow strong and grow loving with a great big hole in the centre of you. There aren't any so-called compensations, you just have to lug this great big void round with you for the whole of your life, while your flesh grows flabby and useless."

"Liz," said her mother, unusually firmly, "go to bed now. I'll come and read to you there."

And she had gone at once, slipping off her father's lap and leaving the room as fast as she could; but she was hardly through the door when she heard the nun's voice sobbing, "You are a stupid man. Compensations. What do you think I am? A habit hung on a clothes-hanger? And you offer me bloody compensations." Liz had been shocked to hear a nun use that wicked word, she had been shocked to hear Sister Gabriel cry. She had been frightened, had buried under the blankets and had told her mother when she came that she did not want a story now; they had promised her one before and they had broken their promise and she did not want any bloody story. Her mother had not even said, "Don't say that." She had kissed her and gone back downstairs.

And now Liz says, the words squeezed out painfully but at least meeting Ian's mood, "Okay. There are no compensations."

He says, "I cannot be your baby."

"I never tried to make you."

"What I hate, what I hate most, apart from your apologetic face when you wake up every four weeks and are bleeding, what I hate most is that the more I examine our motives the worse they seem to be. . . . I cannot think of one single reason why I want this child now which does not arise out of my own weakness and inadequacy. I look at the fathers I know, and I'm sure there are good, healthy loving reasons for having a baby. I know when we first planned it, it was a strong thing, a thing to build, something tough and good. But now I just want to prove to the world that I am a man; I want it because I know my childhood was battered and deprived of that simple love, because my father did not love me, and I want to fill that hole by being a father myself. Because I despair of the present and want to lay a claim upon the future. Because I want to own the love of someone and a child is the only love that I can ever own, demand as a right."

"Ian."

"Now I meet gay guys, or even coming home from the pub I pass some notable hang-out and I think that is easier, that is easier, I can go back there, I don't want this demanding grown-up love. I watch you and I think I'm not so sexy as some of the men she's been with, I'm just a fucked-up queer and she can't really love me. I want to batter a baby into you. I want to be fucked and humiliated by shits who don't care. I don't want to have to endure the fact that you love me, when all I can do is fail you."

"Ian."

"I fail you. I don't believe the crap that that doctor tries to sell you. I know you are a woman, and I know that women are on the other side, and you scare the shit out of me with your great big love, and your needs and your willingness to love and protect me. And I want to divert all that energy into a baby so that I can be free of it. Then I think of how I was before I met you and I cannot bear it and I don't want you to have a baby at all, I want you never to leave me and I don't know how to hold you and sometimes I wonder if it is me, not you, who kills those sperm in my prick so that I can be your only baby, so that you will hold me and keep me safe in your arms, and shelter me under your wings. And already I'm jealous of that damn puppy."

"Ian, for Christ's sake." Doesn't he know there has been a stay of execution, doesn't he know that right now all this is out of place, doesn't he know that at that very minute there may be a baby lurking, hardly visible, but very much alive. In his anger and desolation she feels the same pounding rhythm as of Tony making love to her on the office floor; tides of passion rising out of control, spilling into something dangerous and deadly. Ian must not be like that: out of his gentleness will come fruitfulness. She demands it.

"Ian," she says, and now it is true although she is angry and hates him, "Ian, I love you." And into the silence that follows this profession she says, "We are going to have a baby." She does not dare to believe it, but she believes it.

He does not understand her to have said what she will hardly admit she has said. But it is a statement of fact, as potentially true as his fury that they will not have a baby. It sobers him. They both withdraw abruptly from the painful closeness; they both put back on their protective clothing; they are both unsure whether they protect themselves or the beloved other. She contemplates her body and knows that still she is not bleeding. He changes the bags round so that both are inconveniently in one hand. He reaches out the spare hand and puts it firmly round the back of her neck. He laughs a little shakily and says, "I could strangle you now if I wanted. But I won't."

Perhaps it was her sudden relaxation which affected the sleep-

ing puppy; it pees hard down the front of her jersey and the inside of her jacket, warm and wet.

"Oh bugger," she says, "this bloody puppy has weed on me."

He giggles and says, "Who says there are no compensations:
dribbly milk and wee and shit and sick. Yuck."

They are almost back where they started. She does not think
she can bear this new hope through the next few days. A week.
I will not hope until after a week, but she knows she will not be
able to stop. Despair she thinks would be a fine and glorious
thing, compared to this pointless and painful hope. Why can't
they just say, "We will never have a child" and accept the consequences? Why is she afflicted with this ghastly disease of optimism, of believing that this time, this month, this chance? The
more reasonable the grounds for hope, the more painful it is. Ian
is walking silently beside her. Hope binds them painfully together; flickers in the darkness when they are honest enough to
try and stamp it out; crops up again whatever means she tries to
kill it with.

It is over twelve hours now. She hopes.

She is tired after the childbirth. Very tired. The pelvic ring is
smaller than the baby's head; the biological facts remain even
after their meaning is destroyed. The immaculate flesh is flesh
still. She had not prepared herself for that, foolishly imagining
assent alone to be sufficient. She has unified herself, going out
through the dichotomies and dualisms of body, soul, mind; of
heart and tongue. But now all that this means is that she is tired
throughout the whole of her being.

She looks at Joseph. He has never seen a childbirth before:
indeed, but for the inconveniences of over-full lodgings and long
journeys he would not have seen this one. He sees different
things from her in this birth. He sees the blood, the exhaustion,
the damp head plunging out into the world from between her
legs; he sees the eagerness of the scarlet child to reach his
mother's breast. He sees here an end to the strange, the miraculous, the different. When he looks at the softness of down on

the baby's head, sees the tiny pulse of breath lifting and lowering the minute bundle, he is reassured; here after nine months there is a return to normality.

He has wrapped the child in swaddling bands and laid him in the manger, there being no room for them in the inn. He is not sure what to make of the sudden influx of shepherds except that they are disturbing his woman. She, however, is proud of the baby; still held up by the high tide that swept him out of her womb and into these rather squalid quarters. She rallies herself to show the young men the infant, glowing again despite the tiredness. With a town so full of strangers certain irregularities are bound to occur: young men get drunk, prophesy, see visions, dream dreams. Joseph is a little concerned at the slovenliness of leaving sheep alone, unguarded on the pale hillside, but he is proud of his baby. Not of his begetting, but of his house, his wife; his in the ways that count.

She is glad that he is happy, although she does not know that it is the very ordinariness of things that pleases him. But she herself is not perfectly content. There is a longing in her for that same ordinariness, which is part of his life and his self: the way he handles planks of wood, and the knowledge of them is transferred from his hands to his head along perceptible channels. She envies him the way he can ask his God for a favour without having to be frightened that it will be granted, promptly and inescapably.

She looks again at the baby and realises that the beginning is now. In the glorious moment of her assent, in the rich song of praise that flowed from her in the arms of her cousin Elizabeth, in that moment she had thought to end it all. Had thought the moment would be total. She had brought all things to an end; even death had been destroyed in her flesh; she had riven the barriers between the begetting and the begotten; she had torn the veil between flesh and soul. Once was enough. No more pleasures of the flesh; no more needing and wanting in the body. It was done: the circle was completed.

But the spiral was started: she was returned to where she had begun. Virginal, alone, complete, she was now bound inextricably to the product of that perfection—and on what strange routes would this boy child drag her? With what sword would he pierce her heart?

She had thought in the conception to have ended all things. She had only begun them. The conception meant the birth and the birth meant the death and in between was the important thing. The oneness of her and the child, drawing the milk of her flesh into his blood of his: that cord she could not cut, ever. She had started what she could not control; what she could not name or finish. The carrying him in simplicity had seemed like enough. It was not enough. She was tired already. She would be tired for a long time. Conceiving meant only a child; freedom meant only a new bondage. She had born again the root on which she grew. She could not understand, she only knew that there was more to come. Her body had thought the conception a beginning, the birth an ending. It was not an ending, just another beginning.

When the baby cried softly, Joseph lifted him from the manger and gave him to her. The tiredness in her thighs and hips flowed upwards into her breasts. She fed her baby, without fear, with love. This was the beginning of the end.